AUCTIONED TO HER DAD'S MAFIA ENEMIES

A MAFIA AGE-GAP ROMANCE

STEPHANIE BROTHER

AUCTIONED TO HER DAD'S MAFIA ENEMIES Copyright © 2025 STEPHANIE BROTHER

All Rights Reserved. This book or any portion thereof may not be reproduced or used in any manner whatsoever without the express permission of the publisher except for the use of brief quotations in a book review.

This book is a work of fiction. Any resemblance to persons, living or dead, or places, events or locations is purely coincidental. The characters are all productions of the author's imagination.

Please note that this work is intended only for adults over the age of 18 and all characters represented as 18 or over.

ISBN: 9798316843909

ITALIAN TRANSLATIONS

Gattina – kitten
Signora – Mrs.
Idiota – idiot
traditore - traitor
Stronzo - shit
Sfigati - losers
Doppio - double
Triplo – triple
Bella – pretty/beautiful
Mio bello – my dear
Posto stupido – stupid place
Il pettegolezzo – gossip
Grazie – thank you
Chiaccherone – chatterbox
Pignolata di Miele – a type of Sicilian sweet
Goomar – mistress
Piccolina – little one
Ma che vuoi – what do you want?
Dolcezza – sweetheart
Uoma di merda – shitty man
Va fan culo – fuck off
Cogllione – idiot
Il Coltello – the blade
Amuri miu – my love
Amore mio – my love
Si amore – yes love
Mi amore – my love
Ti amo – I love you

CHAPTER 1

AEMELIA

MY FIRST MISTAKE

Tonight, I serve wine and champagne to mafia devils and pretend the air is scented with roses and jasmine, not blood and death, the real perfume this life is built upon.

I keep my expression neutral as I survey the sprawling estate, but my fingers tighten around the silver tray I'm balancing, knuckles whitening under the weight of both glass and expectation.

Marble pillars rise to meet a high vaulted ceiling, their sheer enormity designed to impress. Chandeliers spill light like liquid gold, setting the room aglow, and a string quartet plays a melody so sweet it makes my chest ache.

It's a world of power, indulgence, and ruthlessness, and I don't belong.

I shift my shoulders, adjusting the thin black straps of my waitress uniform as they dig into my skin. The dress code is supposed to make us blend in—simple, black, professional—but in a room of haute couture gowns and tuxedos tailored with lethal precision, I might as well be wearing a neon sign that says, *Less Than.*

My heart races as I weave through the crowd. Guests lounge around circular tables draped in ivory linens and festooned with flowers, their laughter too loud, their gestures exaggerated, and their conversations laced with an effortless arrogance.

"Table five, girl. Move it," barks my supervisor, a wiry man with a permanent scowl.

"Yes, sir," I mutter, my cheeks heating as I hoist the tray higher, the weight of my low-paying gig settling over me like a lead blanket.

Smile. Serve. Disappear. That's the unspoken rule. And yet, in a room full of power players, I feel the weight of too many eyes, some indifferent, some appraising.

And one pair, weightier than the rest, watches too closely.

This is the wedding reception of Rosita Venturi, the beloved daughter of one of the city's most powerful mafia families. It's a spectacle of wealth, of power, of untouchable luxury, a demonstration of prowess.

The bride glows in custom lace, laughter spilling from her lips as she twirls with her handsome groom. We played together when I was five and she was six, but she won't remember me. My father was wrapped up in this world before he disappeared, and we moved away. A shiver skitters over my skin, raising the hair on my arms. Are the memories of the past rising to the surface like oil on water, or is it fear?

There used to be four Venturi brothers. Now there are three, and they seem to be everywhere. Tall, imposing, sinfully handsome, with power emanating from them like a drugging scent.

One twirls his mother around the dance floor, his dark curls tumbling over his forehead, hazel eyes animated, and full lips smiling like it's what they were created for. He's discarded his jacket and tie and rolled the cuffs of his white shirt, revealing brightly colored flame tattoos that lick up his ropey forearms: the youngest, Alexis.

Another prowls the room's edges, his steel gray eyes suspiciously trailing over everyone, talking to brutish men stationed around the perimeter like sentries. His dark hair is cropped shorter, practical, and his black suit and shirt fit his muscular, looming frame like a second skin. He moves with panther-like grace and a fixed, almost mean stare: the middle brother, Antonio.

But only one has noticed me.

Luca Venturi. The current boss of this family. His presence commands attention like a silent storm, powerful and dark. Well over six feet and broad-shouldered, he's a man built for war but draped in the elegance of a black suit so precisely tailored it looks like it was made to worship his body. The crisp fabric contrasts with the pale of his shirt, the sharp angles of his jaw, and the dark gleam of his slicked-back hair.

But it's not just his appearance that unsettles me.

It's his vivid blue, cold, piercing, unrelenting eyes that strip away pretense and hold a weight I don't understand but can feel pressing through my flesh and into my bones.

Tonight, they're locked on me.

Does he recognize me? I don't think so. The last time he saw me, I had chubby cheeks and was wearing a party dress that was so pink and fluffy that it resembled cotton candy. I'd fallen in the sprawling Venturi gardens, cutting my chin, and he'd scooped me up and pressed his shirt to my face to stem the bleeding. I was crying, but his unemotional demeanor quieted my childish sorrow. I still remember how it felt to be carried high against his chest, the sharp, clean smell of his shirt, and the command in his voice as he told me I'd be okay, like he could make it so just with his words.

A slow, deliberate awareness prickles down my spine. I try to ignore it, brush it off like an itch I refuse to scratch, but each time I pass his table, his stare lingers. Heavy. Intrusive. As if he owns me and is keeping track of his possession.

I shouldn't look at him.

I do, anyway.

For the fifth time that evening, our gazes collide and the air between us shifts and thickens. My pulse jumps, betraying me, and I force myself to look away, shoving the feeling down. Luca's a guest at a wedding—more than that, the host—and I'm a waitress. He's a mafia prince turned boss, a man who's nearly double my age, and I'm nothing but a glorified kid with baggage I can barely carry. Our worlds don't touch.

But my skin still burns from his gaze.

I shouldn't have come. It was a reckless, impulsive decision. When Mama asked me about tonight's job, I lied. I told her it was a wedding, but not whose, knowing she'd warn me against stepping too close to the fire again. She'd remind me that this dark underworld has already burned us once with its glittering surface excess and shady, ruthless players.

But the pull was too strong. After what happened before we left home, the need to see these people, the ghosts of my past, the remnants of a life that once belonged to me, was impossible to resist. Even from the fringes, watching from the outside, I felt something I haven't in years: a tether to something real.

The life I've lived for over a decade has never fit quite right. It's like wearing a borrowed coat, too big in some places, too tight in others, and constantly uncomfortable, no matter how much I try to adjust. But here, even in the shadows, I feel less like an imposter. Less like a woman pretending to be someone else.

Here, I remember who I was.

Aemelia Lambretti. Mafia princess. Daughter of a powerful man with enough wealth and power to keep us comfortable.

Nothing like the girl I am now.

And even though Luca's gaze is as heavy as his palm on

my skin, it's nothing compared to the fear I felt back in Maryland when I was being watched.

I exhale a shaky breath, pushing away those memories and shifting my focus to the guests. A polished woman in her forties gestures sharply at her empty flute, her red lipstick smeared just enough to make her look like she's baring her teeth. I lower my tray so she can grab a fresh glass, her bony fingers flashing with rings.

I reach for the empty glass, my hands trembling as I place it on the tray, desperately trying not to overturn the whole thing. I keep my face neutral, but inside, I think: *Seriously? I'm doing my best here. It's not like your glass is going to die of thirst.*

And yet, even as I move away, the heat of Luca's stare never wavers.

I don't have to look to know he's watching me. I feel a slow burn spreading across my skin like fingers tracing my flesh. Three Venturi brothers exist in this world, each one striking in their own right. But Luca? He stands apart in his intensity.

The scar bisecting his cheek is legendary; a sharp, deliberate cut that slices through his left brow and traces a line down his face, just above his jawline. It should make him ugly. It doesn't. He wears it like women wear diamonds. Not a flaw, but an enhancement. A badge of deadly intent. A mark of survival.

I force myself to move, ignoring how he makes me feel like a moon caught in his gravitational pull. I have bills to pay. Responsibilities. A life that has nothing to do with Luca Venturi or the shadows that follow his family.

Yet my traitorous body betrays me once more because when our eyes meet again—when that sharp, unreadable stare pins me in place—my stomach flips.

I look away.

I keep serving.

I tell myself it means nothing.

He doesn't recognize me. It's impossible. And if he did,

he'd remember the silly little girl whose pigtails he used to pull and whose snotty nose he once wiped with his pristine white monogrammed handkerchief. Nothing more.

It's hard to determine if the awareness I'm feeling is fear or arousal. My responses to both are the same. I know fear well, but arousal, not so much.

My pulse quickens as I hurry back to the kitchen. The clatter of pans and the chefs' sharp voices offer a strange relief, grounding me in the grind and chaos of my everyday world. I lean against the counter to catch my breath.

"You look like you've seen a ghost," Tania, one of the other waitresses, says. She's scraping the remnants of a chocolate soufflé into the trash, her sharp eyes missing nothing.

"I think a ghost would be less intimidating," I mutter, trying to laugh it off.

Tania raises an eyebrow. "Let me guess. Tall, dark, and broody? There's a Roman legion of them out there, so you'll have to narrow it down."

"It doesn't matter," I say quickly, feeling my cheeks heat.

Tania smirked. "Suit yourself. But if one of those Venturi guys has his sights set on you, I'd run. Or... don't." She winks and saunters off, leaving me flustered. Before I'm shouted at again, I refill my tray and head back into the ballroom.

Distracted by my thoughts, I don't notice the napkin on the floor, which disturbs my balance. A champagne flute teeters on my tray, the golden liquid sloshing dangerously close to the edge. My breath catches. No, no, no—

The glass falls.

It shatters against the marble floor, the sound too loud, too sharp, drawing too much attention.

A ripple of silence spreads through the nearest tables. Murmurs. Gasps. My stomach turns to stone.

"Careful, darling," comes a sharp voice. Table five again. The woman's tone is dripping with condescension, her lips curling with barely contained amusement. "That flute cost more than your rent."

Heat rushes up my neck, humiliation licking my skin. I drop to my knees, hands shaking as I reach for the broken shards.

And then—

"Apologize."

The word isn't loud. It isn't sharp.

It's a command that brooks no argument.

The air shifts thickens and cracks like a storm waiting to break.

Slowly, I look up.

Luca stands a few feet away, his gaze locked on the woman, his expression unreadable. But the ice in his voice? The weight of it? That is unmistakable.

The woman stiffens. "I—"

"Apologize." His tone doesn't waver.

Her lips part, outrage flickering in her expression, but she knows who he is and what he's capable of. She swallows. Her spine stiffens.

"I'm sorry," she mutters.

My breath hitches.

Luca Venturi made a woman who could buy my entire existence apologize to me.

He turns to me next, and something unreadable flickers across his face.

"Leave it," he says, nodding to the mess. "Someone else will take care of it."

"I—I can't just—"

"You can," he interrupts smoothly, extending a hand.

I hesitate.

But then, against all better judgment, I take it.

His fingers curl around mine, warm, strong, steady. When he pulls me to my feet, a strange sense of security washes over me, like I'm back in his father's garden, wrapped up in his protective embrace.

Safe.

"Thank you," I whisper, unsure why my voice barely

makes a sound.

His lips curve, the faintest ghost of a smile, then he glances down at where we're still joined, at my wrist, which is turned up to face him, my heart birthmark on display, and that ghost of a smile is replaced by the darkest expression I've ever seen.

CHAPTER 2

LUCA

WALKING THROUGH MY MIND

The moment I see it, I know.

The heart-shaped birthmark on her wrist is small and faint but unmistakable. The scar on her chin, from an accident in my father's garden. The way she's been walking through my mind all night like the ghost of a memory. It clicks into place like the final move in a long-anticipated chess game.

Aemelia Lambretti.

The daughter of the man who laughed and joked with my brother then conspired in his death without a second thought.

Does she know who I am—who we are? Does she remember playing and dancing with Rosita all those years ago while we talked business over red wine from our vineyard in Sicily, and her father grinned like a shark?

My stomach tightens, and so does my grip on her small hand. It's her. It's really her.

When my gaze flicks to hers, she's wide-eyed, and for a moment, I can't tell if it's fear or guilt.

She's so beautiful that it makes a long, dead place in my chest ache, like a lonely echo in a cave cut deep into the cold earth.

I'm on my feet in seconds, moving through the room with purpose, dragging her behind me. She doesn't resist; she just keeps pace with me in her cheap shoes, her breath coming in gasps that trigger my suspicions.

"Where—"

"Just walk," I growl, low and commanding.

"But I—I'm working—"

"Not anymore."

I steer her through the crowd, and she tugs against my grasp.

"Don't make a scene," I warn my voice like iron. "Unless you want every pair of eyes in this room on you and more than a few guns pointed."

That stops her.

She glances around, but no one's noticed us. The band is playing, the champagne is flowing, and the guests are too busy basking in their importance to care about a waitress being disciplined for spilling a drink.

I guide her through the back entrance and into a side room—a private study filled with dark wood and low-burning lamps. As soon as I close the door, I let her go, and she whirls on me, her chest rising and falling in rapid breaths.

"What the hell's wrong with you?"

I ignore her, already pulling out my phone. I send a quick message to my brothers.

Found something interesting. Dad's study. Now.

She takes a step back. "Look, if this is about the broken glass, I swear I'll pay for it—"

I lift my gaze to hers, freezing her with my icy stare, and she stops talking.

"You think this is about a broken glass? Try again,

Aemelia."

She opens her mouth to speak but hesitates, blinking rapidly. "What's it about then, *Luca?*"

My name on her lips is like a breathy sigh, and in normal circumstances, it would have made me half-hard with interest. Aemelia Lambretti is everything I look for in a woman. Hair as dark as a raven's wing, soulful melted chocolate eyes kissed with a dark liner that gives her a feline appearance, red lips that are pouty even under my scrutiny, and a tight little body that I'd punish and relish if the circumstances were different; if I didn't remember the feel of her body in my arms; if her youth didn't make me feel like a man on the other side of a wall, too mature, too weathered, too tarnished to match her perfection.

I take my time, watching her, looking for panic, but she seems curious, and when she folds her arms across her chest, squeezing her pretty tits together, a little put out at my sudden accosting, my dick twitches.

A knock at the door makes Aemelia jump.

Antonio enters first, followed by Alexis. My brothers loom tall and broad, filling the small space, and Aemelia glances at them, her breathing growing more ragged.

Antonio crosses his arms, and Alexis leans against the wall, his mouth smiling but his eyes burning with suspicion.

"Will someone tell me what's going on?" she asks, her voice uneven.

"I think I'll leave that part to you. What are you doing at my sister's wedding, Aemelia Lambretti?"

Alexis and Antonio don't react to her name, maintaining their cool, uninterested demeanor, but now they understand why I've dragged them away from the celebration.

"Waitressing," she says. "Look, I know it's a little weird. When they told me about the gig, I considered turning it down. I didn't want to make your sister uncomfortable." She smooths her hands over her dress, highlighting her current status as a server rather than a guest. "I just... I need the money, okay?"

"Aemelia Lambretti needs waitressing money?" Alexis asks, his hazel eyes drifting over her. I can read my brother like a book. He's thinking about her ass and what it would look like pink with his handprints.

"You don't have to keep saying my full name, you know. Aemelia is fine. And yeah, I need the money."

"What happened to Daddy's fortune?" I ask.

"I don't know. You should ask him if you can find him. I haven't seen him in over a decade."

I lean against the desk and cross one leg over the other, feigning relaxation. "Convenient."

"Not really," she sneers. "He left us penniless, and it broke my mom. It's not easy to get by on my measly salary. Now, my aunt is dying, and we had to come back from Maryland. I'd rather be anywhere but here."

I share a look with my brothers. Without a word, I can tell that Alexis doesn't believe her, and Antonio is reserving judgment.

Alexis steps forward, and she tips her head to look up at him but stands her ground. "You expect us to believe that you just happened to end up working here at our sister's wedding?"

"I need the money. That's all. My mom… she's… and my brother… All he does is get into trouble. If I don't finish my shift, I won't get paid, and we—"

Her throat bobs, but she raises her face further, elongating her slender, elegant neck until her chin is high. She looks like a ballet dancer, poised before a graceful movement, eyes determined, posture straight.

For a long moment, no one speaks.

I glance at Antonio, then Alexis. They're watching her the same way I am—measuring, assessing. Liars have tells. And Aemelia has none.

She's telling the truth.

I exhale through my nose. "Give me your phone."

She hesitates before pulling it from the pocket of her dress. I take it, flipping to her banking app. She doesn't protest when I ask her to open it so I can check her recent transfers, and the address listed on her account. She has less than a hundred dollars to her name, and her banking address is in Maryland.

I hand it back, and she clutches it like a lifeline.

Standing, I turn to the dark window, running a hand down my face over the scar that's still rough after all these years.

If she's telling the truth—and I'm sure she is—then this isn't a threat. Aemelia's no villain or assassin. She walked into this wedding like prey into a hunter's snare.

She's not a danger. She's an opportunity.

But...

I turn to Alexis. "Check her."

Alexis raises a brow, then grins like I've just handed him a gift. "With pleasure."

Aemelia tenses as he approaches, her spine going rigid, but to her credit, she doesn't back away. His hands are quick but clinical, patting her sides, under her arms, along her calves. When he reaches the hem of her dress, he crouches, sweeping his palms up the inside of each thigh until she gasps and jerks.

"Relax," he murmurs, not unkindly. "I'm just making sure you're not hiding a wire or a blade between these sweet little legs."

Her eyes narrow, but she says nothing, breathing shallow as he finishes and stands. He holds up his empty hands. "Clean. No weapons. No wire. Not even a lipstick knife. Disappointing."

"Write down your address in the city," I say, sliding a sheet of paper to her. She strides forward quickly, her cheeks flushed, scribbling in an elegant cursive that perfectly matches her refined features, giving the vital information with an innocence I don't understand. When she's done, she slides it back, and I catch a glimpse of the heart birthmark that was her tell. The last time I saw her, she told me in her sweet little voice that an angel had kissed her wrist, and the heart meant she'd find true love. I wanted to tell her that true love doesn't exist, but I didn't. I may be a heartless son of a bitch, but even I wouldn't go as far as to crush a little girl's romantic dreams. I scribble my phone number, tear it from the top corner, and hand it to her.

"If you have trouble while you're in town."

She nods, accepting the scrap and folding it neatly.

"You can go," I say finally.

She blinks. "I—what?"

I nod toward the door. "Go back to work."

Relief softens her expression. She's thinking about the money. "Thank you," she whispers, pushing past Antonio and Alexis in her haste to leave.

We don't stop her.

At the door, she turns. "Tell Rosita I said congratulations, okay?"

I wait until the door clicks shut before turning to my brothers.

"She's not lying," I say before they can question me. They don't. I lick my lips, giving myself time to sort my thoughts. "But that doesn't mean she's useless."

Antonio raises a brow. "What are you thinking?"

I lift and drop one shoulder. "She's Lambretti blood. That makes her valuable."

"Yes," Alexis says darkly.

I stride to the door and push it open, walking the short distance back to the ballroom.

Aemelia is there, clearing plates, dodging drunk guests, trying to disappear into the crowd again, but I keep watching, and eventually, so do my brothers, flanking me on either side. I tug my sleeve and finger the cufflinks Mario bought me for my eighteenth birthday.

Alexis rubs his jaw. "Aemelia Lambretti, huh?"

"All grown up," Antonio says.

Alexis snorts. "She looks like her mama did twenty years ago. I always said Carlo was punching above his weight, but mothers tell their daughters to avoid the most handsome men because they'll stray. Pick an ugly man, and he'll stay loyal." Alexis pushes his hands into his dark jeans. I love my brother, but he never dresses like a Venturi should, not even on an occasion like tonight.

"Is that why we're all still single?" Antonio asks dryly.

"I fuck more than every married man in here." Alexis cracks his neck, and I grit my teeth.

Antonio shakes his head. "She shouldn't have come back."

"I held her when she was a child," I say, more to myself than anyone else.

Alexis raises a dark eyebrow, his hazel eyes dancing. "Your dick doesn't need to feel guilty."

"Not yet," Antonio says, walking away.

***

Long after the wedding ends, when the music fades and the guests leave, I stand in the shadows, watching Aemelia shrug on a tattered coat and hug it close against the cold. I watch as she pulls out a phone and has a brief conversation with her mom, which is mostly reassurance that she'll be home soon and that she made some tips, so they'll be okay. I watch as she disappears into the night like a ghost.

I exhale a long breath, the weight of old memories pressing down, and pull a cigarette from the packet, lighting it and inhaling deeply. Smoke swirls around me like Medusa's snakes, and I exchange the darkness of the night for the darkness behind my eyelids.

Aemelia Lambretti. A mafia princess turned Cinderella.

Mario should have been here tonight. He was the oldest of us, and walking Rosita down the aisle was his job, not mine. All day, his shadow has trailed me, and his ghost has lingered in the cavern of emptiness in my chest.

He should have been at this wedding, not Carlo's spawn.

Aemelia Lambretti.

I toss the cigarette and crush it with my polished leather

shoe.

>She has no idea what she's worth.
>But she'll find out soon enough.

CHAPTER 3

ALEXIS

THE PRICE OF REVENGE

The city penthouse apartment is dimly lit, the amber glow from the liquor cabinet casting long shadows across the sleek leather furniture. Luca stands by the window with his hands clasped behind his back as he stares over the city. The balcony door is open, and the faint tang of smoke, car exhaust, and the distant blooms from rooftop gardens scents the air. The skyline sprawls before him, stars blinking in the darkness like diamonds spilled over black velvet. He's lost in thought, and I understand why.

Antonio sits in the corner of the couch, a glass of whiskey dangling between his fingers, his expression thoughtful. "She just fell into our laps," he mutters, breaking the silence. "Like a lamb to the slaughter."

Luca finally turns, determination making his jaw tight. "This isn't luck. It's fate."

I pace the length of the room, fire already burning in my chest at the thought of Carlo's daughter. Her *traditore* father's betrayal burns my soul. "So we use her. We drag her father out of hiding and make him answer for what he did to Mario." My voice is rough-edged with anger that never fades.

Antonio swirls his drink, watching the liquid catch the light. "Mario's in the ground, and that bastard has been walking free for too long."

"We searched under every stone, every rotten piece of wood for that cock sucker," I remind him. "He became air. His family, too."

Luca exhales slowly, controlled. "Not anymore."

The weight of Mario's death sits heavy between us. No blood has been spilled to avenge him. But now? Now we have our bait.

A sharp knock on the door breaks the moment.

Vito, one of Antonio's soldiers, steps inside, his face grim, eyes flicking to Luca before settling on Antonio. "Boss, I'm sorry to interrupt."

Luca straightens, and Antonio sets his drink aside. "Spit it out."

"One of my informants on the southside called something in. Something I thought you'd want to know." He waits for Antonio's nod to continue. "There's an auction tonight. Girls. The usual, except tonight, they have something special on the menu."

My blood cools. Antonio sits forward, his expression blank. Luca doesn't move, but the air shifts, heavy with menace.

"Who?" Luca demands, voice lethal.

The soldier swallows hard. "Aemelia Lambretti. From what I heard, Carmine Nero's out of pocket to her father. He's looking to close the debt, and she'll fetch a good price. She's a bonafide virgin, confirmed by some doctor in Carmine's pocket." He lets the information hang for dramatic effect. Vito always loves a little theatre. "Plenty of men who'd like to work out their frustrations against Carlo on his pretty daughter's unsullied body."

Silence. A heartbeat, then another. In my veins, my blood is lava, my fury explosive, but I hold myself tight because that's what's expected.

Antonio stands slowly, his body stiff, but his movements are controlled. He lifts one arm to sweep Vito out the door. In the hallway, they discuss further in hushed tones before he returns. My eyes are on Luca, not because I think he will explode. He rarely shows any kind of reaction, so searching for tiny flickers in his expression is the only way I can gauge what he's thinking.

Antonio lingers by the door. "I know when and where."

Tension vibrates through the open plan space. The ceilings in this place are too high, and the furniture too low. It always makes me feel uncomfortable as if there's not enough gravity. I flex my fingers, rolling my neck. "Looks like this might cost us more than we thought."

"It'll be worth it." Luca nods and turns back to the sky.

***

The scent of cheap cologne and sweat fills the warehouse packed with men, predators circling for fresh meat. This isn't our business. Our father forbade the Venturi name to be linked to prostitution. Three generations back, an ancestor fell on hard times. Her pain and redemption continue to shape our business. In all honesty, I'm grateful for it. I don't have the stomach for the sad faces and the broken dreams.

I can barely hear myself think over the dull roar of conversation and the occasional burst of laughter, which overlays the whimpering and weeping of the girls on stage.

Luca stands to my left, rigid as a steel blade, his cool gaze sweeping over the scene. To my right, Antonio wears his cold, deadly expression like a mask, but I know him well enough to see beyond. His fingers flex at his sides, betraying the storm brewing beneath.

Then, the bastard hosting this auction calls the next lot,

and the air changes. If the previous lots were fast food, Aemelia Lambretti, the untouched mafia princess fallen to the gutter, is wagyu beef. And these men are famished.

The moment her name is spoken, a hush falls over the room. My pulse slams into my ribs as a spotlight slices through the gloom, illuminating the stage. And there she is, nothing like the girl we reunited with at Rosita's wedding. This Aemelia is a fragile, trembling thing, shackled at the wrists and barely clothed in a white lace nightgown. Her porcelain skin glows under the harsh light, and her hair, dark as spilled ink, cascades in waves down her back. Her eyes dart around, wide and fearful, blinking against the bright lights, and still, she forces her chin high.

Antonio is motionless beside me, and Luca clenches his fists so tight that the leather of his gloves groans.

This is the daughter of the man who cost us more than a brother. Mario was the heart of our family—the head. We are but lesser imitations of the man he was, and nothing has been the same since he was killed. The rage that coils in my gut is instant, searing. Not because I want to save her. Not because I give a damn about the tremor in her hands or the silent plea in her gaze. No, my fury is for the men in this room who think they can take what should belong to us.

Nero wants his money, but we crave more. Blood. Pain. Revenge. Satisfaction.

Aemelia Lambretti is ours, whether she likes it or not.

We could take her from this place with violence, but it's not worth starting a war. Nero will pay for the money he takes from us through this auction. Luca will make sure of it.

The bidding begins, and the first number thrown out is pathetic. Insulting. Some *stronzo* in the front row leans forward, his watery eyes gleaming as he ups the bid. Another man, younger and cocky, offers more. The numbers climb, but it's a game they don't know they've already lost.

I chuckle darkly. "These *sfigati* actually think they have a chance."

Luca doesn't respond. His jaw is locked so tight it might shatter. Me? I'm burning alive.

I raise my hand lazily, throwing out a number that makes the crowd murmur. We don't have a strategy, but it doesn't matter. Money is nothing.

The host's lips part in shock before he covers it with a slimy smile. "Ah, a generous offer from Mr. Venturi."

The old man counters.

"*Doppio*," I say firmly. Double

The young bastard grits his teeth and hesitates before throwing in another number.

"*Triplo*." My voice carries, and the host nearly chokes.

"That's quite the bid—" He clears his throat. "Any more?" He scans the crowd, his beady eyes searching for hunger. Joey Costa turns in his seat, his hair slick, his expression oily, eyeing me and my brothers. He's not friends with Nero but always looks to grease his palms. "Double again," he says. I don't even think he wants the girl. He wants to inflate the price for Nero so he can call in a favor later.

"Five times the current bid," Luca states, his voice so low and sharp it's like ice cracking over a frozen lake.

The room echoes with a shared gasp. Luca bid himself, and enough to make it clear he's not backing down. The air vibrates as Aemelia shifts, her chest rising and falling more quickly. The dark shadow of her nipples and the hair on her cunt shows through the lace, and my dick notices.

Nobody moves.

The host stares at us, the gavel hovering. The idiot thinks he's Judge Judy, for fuck's sake. "Once. Twice…"

Silence. The other bidders shrink back, knowing better than to challenge Don Venturi. It could be their butchered body parts being sold at the dog food auction next.

"Sold."

Aemelia flinches at the final word, and her head drops, her hair covering her expression. She doesn't know yet. She doesn't understand.

We didn't just buy her.
We *claimed* her.
And we never let go of what's ours.

CHAPTER 4

AEMELIA

LITTLE KITTEN

The car ride is silent except for the engine's hum and the low music playing. My wrists ache where the zip ties dug into my skin, phantom pain lingering long after they cut them off. The men flanking me are strangers—dangerous shadows with unreadable expressions. The one driving, Vito, is built like a brick wall, his thick fingers gripping the steering wheel like he could snap it in half if he wanted to. He has a sharp jawline, peppered with dark stubble, and an old scar that bisects his neck. His partner, Andre, is leaner with a narrow face like a rat but is just as intimidating, his eyes a sharp, calculating green beneath a mop of tousled dark hair. They haven't spoken much, but their presence alone tells me everything I need to know. I'm not safe.

I haven't been safe since I was bundled into a car after Rosita Venturi's wedding by two terrifying men and held in a warehouse basement with seventeen other wretches. Blindfolded and gagged, I soiled my clothes, fear stealing my dignity. Before the auction, I was forced to shower in cold water and pull on a cheap white night dress like some hooker bride. No bra, no panties.

My chest hitches as fear grips me. I keep my hands twisted together so they won't tremble. If these men see I'm frightened, it will make it worse. Men like this are parasites who live off the fear-spiked adrenaline of those weaker than them. Even though I haven't eaten for over twenty-four hours, my stomach roils, and I swallow convulsively.

The city lights blur as we speed through the streets, and my anxiety rises with every mile that takes me further from the hell I just escaped. Did I escape? Or am I simply on the knife edge of falling into another trap? Someone bought me, that's all I know—bought my body, my virginity. I press my legs tightly together reflexively as the thought of what's coming floods me with dread.

In the auction, the lights shining on me blinded me to the faces of the audience. Panic was a serpent winding around my windpipe, stealing my breath and hope. It's like I'm trapped inside the kind of dream you wake from in a sweat, only half convinced it's not real.

We arrive at a towering glass building, the type that houses men in suits with bloodstained hands. The Venturi name glows in sleek silver letters above the entrance. My stomach knots. The Venturis. If they paid my price, does that mean they saved me?

Last night, they questioned me like a spy, but I thought they believed me when they let me go. I know nothing about my father and his business. I might carry his name but do it with bitterness and resentment. If he's even still alive, Carlo Lambretti is my father by blood only. I will never forget the violence he rained down on my family or the hateful words he spoke to us. My mother still carries the scars of his jealousy and fury. She was too beautiful for him, and he never trusted her motivation to marry him. I'll never know if the rumors that followed her were true or just driven by envy. All I know is that my father should stay away because

I'm not the terrified little kid I once was, and if he comes for us again, if he lays his brutal hands on me like he used to or tries to lacerate me with his insults, I'll kill him myself.

The Venturis have a legitimate grudge against him. I was young, but I had ears. I know why we fled to Maryland and hid with distant family. It makes me question: Am I free or just a different kind of prisoner now?

The night is cold, and it cuts through my skin even though I'm wearing Andre's jacket over my slut dress. As I climb from the car, I catch him looking at the place the lace dips above my thighs, revealing the shadow of my pussy, and I turn away in disgust.

Men are animals if they can think about sex with a woman who's vulnerable and captive.

Their base desires repulse me.

I pull the jacket closer around me, revolted by the cloying scent of his cheap cologne, catching sight of a white van slowing down across the street and the shadow of a man staring through the window in my direction.

Vito grabs my arm, and they escort me through to a private elevator, up, up, up until the doors slide open. The penthouse seems empty. It's pitch black, and our footsteps echo like we're walking through a deserted showroom. By the light of the moon, the space is sleek and modern, with marble floors and floor-to-ceiling windows that look out over the glittering city. The furniture is low and Italian-designer chic. Precisely the kind of thing I imagine the Venturi's choosing. Masculine and expensive but soulless like them. It's eerily quiet, as if the walls are joining me in holding their breath.

"This is where you'll be staying," Andre says, his voice a low rasp. He nods toward a door down the hall.

I don't move. "What do you mean? What is this place?"

Vito sighs, his patience thinning. "You belong to the Venturis now. That means you do as you're told. Now, go."

I want to argue, to demand answers, but these men are just paid goons. They probably know less than me. My legs feel weak as I hand the jacket back to Andre and walk the plank toward the distant doorway he indicated. When I open the door, I'm greeted by more of the same decor: a huge low bed in the center dressed in crisp white linens, mirrored nightstands topped with tall lamps, and a substantial white vanity with a mirror above it that touches the vast ceiling. I enter the room, noticing a door to an equally stark marble-filled bathroom. The door clicks shut behind me, and then, the sound of a lock sliding into place. Panic surges through me.

I spin, instinct pressing to pound on the door. "Wait! You can't just lock me in here! Let me out!"

Silence.

My breath comes in ragged gasps as I whirl around, scanning the room. It's more luxurious than I've seen since I was a young girl, but cold and impersonal—a gilded cage.

I pace, fists clenched at my sides, but exhaustion creeps in fast, and defeat forces me into a curled heap on the bed. My body betrays me, dragging me down into restless, uneasy sleep.

***

When I wake, my eyes fly open, half believing I'm in the small, cramped room at my aunt's house that smells of mothballs, cigarettes, and stale marinara sauce. In front of me, a tall white lamp stands on a nightstand that almost disappears beneath the weight of the room's dark reflections. The sight of it brings me to full consciousness of my situation. The air in the room feels different. Charged.

I blink, my vision adjusting to the dim light. My breath catches in my throat when the shadowy form sitting in a chair by the door comes into focus.

A man, his presence a dark, looming force, sits with wide-spread legs, hands resting casually on his thighs. The low glow of the city skyline from the window behind the bed casts sharp shadows over his face—high cheekbones, a strong jaw, lips pulled into a slash across his handsome face. But it's his eyes that hold me captive. A deep, endless gray, as liquid and reflective as mercury. They watch me with quiet, deadly focus as if he's already decided my fate.

"You're awake," he murmurs.

I swallow hard, pushing myself upright. "Antonio?"

His smirk deepens. "You remember me?"

I do, even after all these years.

He was captivating, even to a five-year-old; so tall I felt like I had to tip my head to the top of a mountain to see his intense beauty. My father would laugh when I talked about marrying him, a charming prince who would sweep me off my feet years into the future.

What a twisted joke!

"Why am I here?"

"Why do you think?"

I draw the white comforter, as soft as a cloud, closer around me, trying to hold my voice steady. "You bought me?"

"We did."

"Why?"

"Why do you think, *gattina*?

Little kitten. No one's ever called me something like that before, and as sweet as the pet name is, it fills me with dread. I could guess why this man and his brothers crossed the city to pay an exorbitant price for me, and I don't believe it's out of the goodness of their hearts.

I was young when I left this life, but my mama told me all the stories. I know more about the inside of this filthy world than most girls who are still connected to it. Women aren't brought into confidence unless they're married or have women in their family with loose lips. The loose lips only come with foolishness or a separation from the threat. My mama's tongue spilled secrets from a mixture of both.

But I remember this man myself. I remember getting lost in the Venturi house, opening the door to a room, and seeing him kissing a woman passionately against the wall.

His trousers were around his ass, and the woman was making funny noises I didn't understand the significance of at the time. He'd turned at the sound of the door rasping over the thick cream carpet and stared at me as I cowered and then ran.

It wasn't until years later that I realized what I had stumbled across.

"I don't think it was out of the goodness of your heart," I say. "Men always expect a return on their investment." I leave out the 'like you' part because I don't want to make this personal, even though it is. Poking the bear too hard is a risk I'm not ready to take. If there's even a slight chance he's playing with me and about to take me home, I need to leave the door open.

"A return." He rubs his chin, the stubble rasping against his rough fingertips, then he makes his fingers into a gun and pulls the trigger. "Bingo." His deadly expression steals the air from my lungs. "Your father," he continues, his voice a smooth, lethal purr. "Where is he?"

I shake my head, heart pounding. "I told you, I haven't seen him in years."

"That doesn't mean you don't know where he is."

"I don't. He left and didn't look back."

"Pity." Antonio leans forward slightly, elbows resting on his knees, the upper part of his face disappearing into the shadows. "If we can't extract blood through him, we'll have to take it from you instead."

A chill spreads through my veins. "I don't know anything," I whisper, my grip on the comforter increasing until my hands shake with the effort. "If I did, I'd tell you. I owe my father no loyalty. He's done nothing for me."

I don't tell him that I suspect my father is responsible for the death of Mario, the oldest Venturi brother. Or that I suspect the reason for his betrayal. I don't tell him that our family wears the emotional and physical scars Carlo doled out so easily before he disappeared.

"Ah, *gattina*. Family is everything. Loyalty is everything.

Blood is everything."

The blood rushing through my veins chills. "Even when blood betrays you?"

Antonio narrows his eyes, holding me captive through nothing but a narrow slit of icy steel. Tears burn my throat and dangle at the edges of my eyes, but I refuse to let them fall. I grit my teeth, fists clenching the sheets. Begging won't save me. Mercy is not something men like Antonio Venturi understand.

He stands and strides forward so quickly that it makes me scramble back. From the end of the bed, he towers over me, as heartbreakingly beautiful as Lucifer and just as deadly. His presence is as thick as incense in the air, as mesmerizing as a violin solo, hair dark and short as velvet, revealing the angles of his sharp jawline. His black sweater, most likely cashmere, looks more expensive than every outfit in my wardrobe, and he pushes at the sleeves restlessly.

He's a vicious weapon in a stunning shell. I bite the inside of my lips, holding tightly to my desperate instincts to beg for my freedom.

I want to go home. I need to see my mama. My aunt has little time left, and everyone must be worried sick about me. Have my family reported me missing yet? Are the police out looking for me?

Antonio kneels on the bed, his thighs stretching his crisply pressed dark pants as he moves closer, so predator-like, I quiver like prey. His hand, whip-fast, grips my jaw, and he tilts my chin until I have no choice but to look at him. His eyes are almost colorless in the low light, ethereal and unnatural, his breathtaking angular face set with dark determination. His hand is so strong that my bones creak. "Understand this," he says through gritted teeth. "From this moment on, you're ours. You belong to us. You're Venturi property. Not Aemelia. Not *Lambretti*." He sneers at my name. "You are *gattina*. No past, no future. You. Are. Bait. You understand."

Little kitten. Bought to secure retribution for a lost brother.

Little kitten. Owned by three ruthless mafiosi who want my father's head.

Little kitten. Captive and under Venturi control

I don't flinch. I don't move. But inside, I'm screaming.

CHAPTER 5

ANTONIO

THE COST OF DEFIANCE

I lean against the cold, exposed stone wall of the hallway, my jaw tight. The girl should have begged. She should have pleaded to be released. She should have wept for her own safety and fought against her captivity. All those are normal reactions. Instead, she looked at me with cool control in her beautiful, rich, dark eyes, twisting my insides with her resilience.

I'm a lot of things. Cold. Brutal. Unforgiving. Deadly. I'm the weapon of this family, the messenger of fate and death. My knuckles are scared from years of violence; my conscience deadened from my part in too many deaths.

So why did my body revolt at her quiet acceptance? Why did I crave the fight, the clawing, the screaming, the bitter hatred?

I'm fucked in the head. A monster. A man incapable of anything except executing Luca's will.

I rub a rough hand over my face, breathing hard.

The stronger her will, the harder I will have to push to break her. It is easier to respond to violence with violence, easier to fight to control someone who's lost the grip on their restraint. But Aemelia's holding herself so tightly, she vibrates with it.

Luca's talking on the phone, and the deep sound of his voice echoes in the dimly lit corridor. The penthouse is vast and luxurious, a stark contrast to the brutal reality unfolding within its walls. Everything's too smooth and shiny, casting sharp reflections that seem to mock me.

I push away from the wall, satisfied that Aemelia isn't going to wreck the room she's confined to. In the open-plan living area, the floor-to-ceiling windows showcase the glittering city skyline, indifferent to the darkness brewing inside these walls.

Luca adjusts the cuffs of his crisp white shirt. His sharp features remain unreadable, ice-cold beneath the ambient glow. The phone now rests on the arm of the sleek white leather sofa. "Antonio?"

"She understands."

He nods, his blue eyes, our mother's eyes, flicking to where Alexis is sprawled.

"She's defiant," I say.

"Really?" He shakes his head.

We all remember her mother. She was weak and emotional, always losing her shit with Carlo in ways that embarrassed everyone around her. Her daughter is nothing like her.

"Keeping her here will become a liability," I warn.

Alexis scoffs, running a hand through his wavy dark hair, his lean form relaxed. "Breaking her is the easy part. We just have to push the right buttons, right?" His eyes glint with something I'm not entirely comfortable with, something hungry.

I exhale sharply, shaking my head. "She's not a mafia hood, Alexis. She's just a girl who claims to know nothing. Luca said she wasn't lying about that."

Alexis smirks, amused. "No one's asking you to like it. But unless you've got a better idea, we do what's necessary."

That's easy for him to say. He's not the one who usually has to do the doing, although he's not averse. I prefer to keep my little brother's hands as clean as I can. No point in both of us dripping with blood and sin. My hands are too thick with it to be cleansed. He at least has a chance at repentance.

Luca nods. "We need Carlo to believe it. If he thinks we're being lenient because she's a girl, he won't take the bait. He needs to see her suffer—believe she's in real danger."

I clench my fists, the weight of it all pressing against my chest. I've done things, terrible things, in the name of family and power. But this doesn't feel the same.

Luca continues, ever the strategist. "We need to reach her mother. If she wants her daughter to return to her in one piece, she'll stay out of it. If she involves the police, there will be consequences."

Alexis grins, pleased. "We'll make sure she understands what's at stake."

"You think she'll hold it together?" If my memory of Carmella Lambretti is correct, I can imagine her falling apart over this.

"She must."

As always, Luca thinks he can will the world into the shape of his desires, but I know people. They're unpredictable and dangerous, especially the weak ones.

I let out a slow breath. "Fine. But we don't take it too far."

Alexis only shrugs as if to say, 'We'll see.'

"Bring her out," Luca says, rising from the couch. "We'll start now."

Start?

It's such a meaningless word, but in my experience, the beginning of anything is always the hardest part.

I walk back to Aemelia's room, twist open the lock, and

stride inside. She's lying in bed on her side, with the comforter clutched high around her neck, even though the room is warm.

"Get up," I order.

She scrambles to sit, pressing her spine against the plush white velvet headboard.

"Come with me."

Her eyes are so bright in the low light of the room that they glitter like stars. I reach out to hurry her along, but she evades my hand, slides from the bed, and walks out of the room with me trailing like a devoted puppy. The cheap lace get-up Nero's goons dressed her in is infuriating and alluring. Aemelia isn't a five-dollar hooker. She's regal and upright, her hips swaying as she walks, drawing my eyes to her ass. Her perfect, delicious ass. I shake my head. What am I thinking?

When she comes face to face with my brothers, her strides falter, and I regain my senses.

"Get on your knees for your boss," I growl from behind her.

She turns startled, her eyes searching over my impassive expression and finding no hint of weakness. She twists to Alexis, then Luca, and they both fix her with determined gazes. Like a flower wilting in the hot sun, she slowly lowers herself to her knees, resting her hands on the expensive rug beside her.

"Here's the thing," Luca says, looming over her, tugging at his cuffs again. "If your father comes forward quickly, it will be better for you. If you make him understand how vital it is for him to come back, it will be better for you. If you listen to us and do as you're told, it will be better for you. Many things happen to us in life that we don't like, but it's how we approach them and how we get through them that's important. You understand?"

She nods, and her dark, cascading hair slips over her shoulders, but I don't believe she has any idea of the reality behind Luca's words.

Even like this, she's stunning. Especially, like this. My body betrays me, heat coiling low in my stomach at the sight of her submission and helplessness.

"Kiss my feet," Luca orders. "Show me you understand."

Aemelia turns her head to look at me again as though I'm the one with the power here. Doesn't she know that hierarchy is everything in this business? Deference to authority is how everything functions.

The tension in the room crackles like a live wire. "Go to hell," she spits.

"Wrong answer," I hiss, reaching for the back of her neck.

Her fingers curl into fists, her whole body shaking as I push her face to the ground. When her lips barely brush against his skin, Luca nods. "Good girl. Now, the other one."

I release my grip so my hand rests against her back, and still, she hesitates, her breath quick and shallow, until she eventually obeys. Like this, with her ass in the air, the lace of her dress stretches thin, and the shadow of her cunt is revealed. My mouth fills with saliva, as weak as a slathering dog over a steak.

"Good girl," Alexis murmurs, though the satisfaction in his voice is laced with something darker. He likes women to be compliant. He enjoys being the puppet master. He's not usually brutal, as far as I know, just entitled.

Luca watches, detached, clinical. "Enough. Get up."

Aemelia does, but just as she straightens, Luca grabs her arm, spinning her toward the long mahogany dining table. The rich wood gleams under the warm light, and she flinches at the moment she realizes she isn't done paying for her defiance.

"Bend over."

She struggles, but she's tiny compared to my brother and weak in his grasp. Luca forces her down, his hand between her shoulder blades, pressing her cheek to the gleaming wood. I remain still, restraining myself as Luca delivers a precise strike to her backside.

Slap.

She gasps, her eyes widening with shock and pain.

Slap.

"You gotta big mouth on you, *gattina*. A big mouth and no respect."

Her lips and eyes press tight, hiding her emotion.

Slap. Slap. Slap.

By the fifth spank, she gasps, her resistance chipped away. My stomach tightens, my pulse pounding, the urge to intervene becomes a raging battle within me. My dick is rock hard, and I turn away, disgusted at my body's response. She whimpers when he's done, her cheek still mashed to the wood, leaking eyes staring ahead in shock or disbelief. Luca's big hand clasps the flesh he brutalized, then strokes over and over.

"There's something you need to understand if you have an ounce of common sense in your pretty little skull. Don't test me, Aemelia." The ice in his tone, or maybe the gentleness in his touch, makes her shiver and goosebumps break out over her slender arms. "Do as you're told, and we'll get along just fine." His palm leaves the cheek he slapped, brushing over the center of her ass where she's spread and exposed. His posture stiffens, and his tongue darts out to lick the center of his bottom lip. He leans over her body so his mouth is almost touching the shell of her ear. "Be a good girl for me," he whispers, "and we'll get along fine. And if you're not… Well, we don't want that now, do we?" He waits, but Aemelia remains still. "DO WE?" he yells.

"No."

"No, what?"

"No, Luca."

He smiles at the rushed sound of his name, and then he releases her. "Now, go to bed."

Aemelia rises slowly and turns without a word, her face

pale, her eyes dark as midnight but glittering with unshed tears. She walks away with her head held high, though I can see how much effort it takes.

I follow her, my footsteps heavy. When she reaches her door, she turns, glaring at me. "You're enjoying this, aren't you?" she whispers, venom laced in her voice.

I exhale. "No." I step closer, my voice low. "But every time you fight us, there will be consequences."

Her chin lifts defiantly. "Then you'd better be ready for war."

I swallow against the strange feeling in my chest as I lock the door behind her.

This is only the beginning.

CHAPTER 6

LUCA

TAMING THE KITTEN

"Send Rafa to Signora Lambretti." I say her name with a sneer and shake my head, the memory of her outbursts toward Carlo coming back to me. This whole business is the last thing I want to deal with, but my hand is forced.

Rafa Bianchi is the best choice. He's a huge brute of a man, built like a tank with a face like a battered slab of meat. In his youth, he was a bare-knuckle fighter, and now he wears every impact like a badge of brutality and strength. When he walks the streets, people flinch away from him, so he's the perfect person to make Aemelia's mother understand what's at stake for her daughter if she turns informant.

We have enough of the senior police in our pockets to make major problems disappear. Even if she wanted to raise hell to find her daughter, she'd be met with nothing but cool indifference from the men who live like kings off my generous donations.

"It's done," Antonio says, already dialing.

I look down at my bare feet, still tingling from the touch of Aemelia's lips. She kissed me and hated every minute of it, but she understood her place and that's what's important. My hand still stings from the impact against her ripe ass. It's still coated with her wetness, too.

She's like an angel but breaking her will take a devil's will.

"How did it feel?" Alexis asks.

"How did what feel?"

"Taking your hand to that sweet ass."

"I didn't do it for enjoyment," I say, fixing my youngest brother with a cool stare.

"But you did... enjoy it?" He grins, sly and filthy.

He thinks he knows what I feel but he has no idea. What kind of man gets turned on by the daughter of his old friend, now worst enemy? "She's a *bambina*," I say. "Half my age."

"She's a woman," he says. "A beautiful, pure, strong, vibrant, sexy woman."

"She was a sweet little girl. She loved Rosita. They were like sisters."

"That was a long time ago."

He's right of course. Aemelia isn't anything like the little girl I carried in my arms. She's all grown up, and ripe for the picking, but still my mind rejects the idea. There are lines for a reason. And too much sweetness can become bitter when temptation is too strong.

"She's Lambretti filth," Alexis drawls. "Her worthless father deserted her. What does that make her?"

"A pawn in a game she never chose to play," I remind him.

"Unfortunate."

Yes. He's right. All of this is unfortunate. "I'm going to bed."

"Vito and Andre are stationed outside."

I nod, already leaving him behind. If there's one thing I don't have to worry about, it's security. This building is a shiny fortress of my design, riddled with secret passages.

Anyone foolish enough to think they can break through its defenses will find themselves drowning in disappointment.

As I pass Aemelia's room, the soft sound of her crying carries through the locked door. I pause, remembering her whimpers and tears from so many years ago, and the way it broke my heart to witness her childish pain. And now? Now, her tears are salt water in the wound her father created. But still they snag at my cold, dead heart.

Women. They wield power they don't realize they have. Power that they don't deserve.

I walk away.

***

Morning brings with it fresh resolve.

Before I take a shower, Antonio confirms that Carmella Lambretti is clear on the status of her daughter's safety. She begged and pleaded with Rafa, dropping to her knees to clasp at his ankles, wailing like a banshee.

"She says she doesn't know where Carlo is?"

"Did Rafa believe her?"

"Yes. He says she'd have done anything to get her daughter back. She's not hiding her husband."

I nod. It's what I thought, but it's good to have confirmation.

"So, we do what we need to do."

Antonio nods, already crisply dressed in his dark uniform of expensive black sweater and dress pants. On his wrist glints the Rolex my father gave him for his eighteenth birthday, an expensive reminder of the family we've lost to this life.

"I'll be ten minutes," I say. "Make breakfast and get Aemelia up."

"Okay."

"Is her delivery here?"

"Andriana dropped it off in the night."

"Good."

He leaves me to shower and dress, and by the time I emerge, smelling of Parisian cologne, Aemelia is sitting at the dining table, her hair ratty with sleep, a piece of bread poised in her elegant hand.

Antonio has fixed an easy breakfast that reminds me of Sicily—bread, cheese, olives, fruit, cured meat, olive oil, tomatoes, cucumber, and a pot of black coffee. I sit opposite Aemelia and begin to gather my meal.

She watches me as I dip bread in olive oil and cover it with thin prosciutto.

"Eat," I tell her.

She takes a tentative bite of the bread and chews it like it's cardboard. In reality, it's soft and delicious, flavored with sesame.

Alexis strolls from his room, dressed in dark jeans and a polo shirt like he's ready for a day at the mall. His feet are bare, and his floppy, wavy hair is still dripping from the shower. If I had the energy, I'd lecture him like my father used to about discipline and people's judgement, but not in front of Aemelia. I won't waste my breath. He is what he is and there's no changing him.

He sits next to her, and she braces herself, her delicate arms pressing tight to her chest. Alexis reaches out to touch her unbound hair, letting a section run through his fingers. "Breakfast and a beautiful woman. I hit the jackpot this morning."

Aemelia's eyes meet mine, dark brown and haunting, and I hold the stare, waiting for her to break away first. When she does, she lowers the bread to her plate.

"Eat," I say again, this time louder. No one is fading away under my roof. She will leave this place physically strong if nothing else. If Carlo sees sense.

Antonio, who's still standing at the counter, watches everything. He'll be in control today. We need footage of Aemelia to pass to her father's last known contacts—footage that will draw him out of his rats nest.

"I'm famished," Alexis says, popping an olive into his

mouth. "I slept like a dog."

"Log," Aemelia says.

We all stop what we're doing to stare at her. Did she just correct Alexis?

She did.

I glance at Antonio who tips his head as if to say, I told you she was going to be trouble. Alexis laughs, his initial shock forgotten. "No, *gattina*. Like a big, lazy fucking dog. But I do have some nice thick wood if you'd like to see it."

She chews on a piece of mozzarella, seemingly unphased by everything going on around her.

"And you?" I ask her. "How did you sleep?"

"Like a cuckoo," she says softly. "In the wrong fucking nest."

I bite the inside of my lip, surprise almost making me smile. Alexis, showing zero restraint, barks with laughter. "This fucking girl." He slaps the table, making everything jump.

"You know who else is in the wrong fucking nest," I hiss. "My brother. He's been resting in the fucking ground in your father's place."

"Which is nothing to do with me." She leans forward, jaw set, mouth pressed into a grim line.

I fight a smile. "Oh, *gattina*. You're going to find out just how much it has become your problem after you eat your expensive prosciutto and drink your expensive coffee and dress in the expensive clothes we have ordered for you."

She looks down at herself. The room is warm but still her nipples are dark and tight beneath the lace. "You mean, you don't like this beautiful outfit. I thought you'd love it."

"Why?" I ask.

"Because it's cheap and nasty."

I narrow my eyes and slowly dab my mouth with a white napkin. When I'm done, I lower it to the table. "She's done with her breakfast. Antonio, take her to her room."

This fucking girl.

He's across the room like a shot, his hand around her

upper arm, half dragging her as she struggles to keep up with him. He gave her the warning last night. A warning she hasn't heeded. Although her rudeness isn't his fault directly, he'll take responsibility for it because that's the kind of man he is.

When the door has closed and he's locked her inside again, Alexis whistles. "She's going to be so much fun to break."

Although nothing comes between me and food, the bread has become paste in my mouth.

When I first stepped up to take a place in the family business, my father had given me a man to interrogate. Filled with the confidence of youth and ignorance, I'd thought it would be easy to extract information from him, after all, I was the one with the power and he was bound and defenseless. But he wouldn't tell me what I needed to know, no matter how much I beat and humiliated him. After two hours, he was dead, and I learned a valuable lesson, one I've never forgotten. Not everyone can be broken and those who can't be broken shatter a piece of you in the process.

***

Aemelia is dressed in white to remind her father of what is at stake. The new dress is satin, expensive, and cut close to her body to hint at what's beneath. The fabric catches the light, clinging to every curve, a vision of purity tainted by the weight of our intentions. I stare at her, my mouth dry, my dick half-hard. Aemelia Lambretti could wear a plastic bag and look like fire, but in this dress, she's a dream I don't deserve to have.

Andriana must have supplied her with makeup because her face is decorated with black winged eyeliner and her trademark scarlet lipstick—war paint to make her look powerful and put together. But I know better. I see the slight tremble in her hands, the way her pulse flickers at the base of her throat. For all of my denial to my brother, seeing her like this makes me want to tear the dress from her body and find all sorts of terrible, pleasurable ways to smear that lipstick from her pouty lips.

Is this the look that will bring Carlo running into the arms of death? Will he even care?

It's one thing to leave your family to protect yourself, knowing they're going to be safe. It's another to abandon your daughter to your enemies, letting the world watch as she suffers in your place. The Lambretti name is already mud in my eyes, but there are different kinds of mud. Getting someone from outside your blood killed is one thing. Allowing your blood to die out of fear for your own skin? Shameful. Unforgivable.

Maybe this whole thing is foolish. Maybe all we'll do is humiliate this girl and breed hatred into another Lambretti.

And what will we do with her if Carlo doesn't return? Antonio would do anything I asked, even snuff out her life, but I don't want that. She's a butterfly, a creature of beauty and fragility, not a rodent like her father. Flanked by my brothers, she looks smaller and more vulnerable, but I have to remind myself that she has a nasty bite.

"On your knees, *gattina*," I hiss.

Aemelia grits her teeth as she drops to the floor, and my dick jerks against my expensive pants.

"Tie her hands."

Antonio reaches into his pocket and pulls out a zip tie. He secures her wrists behind her back, and she winces as he runs his finger beneath, ensuring there's enough space for blood flow.

"Come here."

Alexis is filming, keeping my face out of the frame. Aemelia hesitates then begins to shuffle on her knees. It's ungraceful, jerky, humiliating. When she's close enough, I grab her hair, the silky strands filling my rough fist, and yank her until her face is tipped to me.

"Beg," I say. "Beg your fucking weasel of a father to come for you. Beg him to save you before we destroy everything innocent and precious about you."

Her eyes flick from me to Alexis, the camera rolling as she turns over her decision in her pretty head. Will she comply or will she rebel. I know where her heart is. She wants to spit at me, to tell me to go fuck myself. If I put my dick in her mouth, she'd bite it clean off. But she's deciding if her father is worth experiencing more pain for. Or maybe she's considering whether I'm worthy of her surrender.

"Fuck you," she spits, and I grip harder. "I won't beg at your feet, Luca Venturi."

I wave at Alexis to stop filming. He deletes what he has as I lean over the girl on her knees. Her skin is like porcelain, her eyes intense with fury and defiance, and as pissed as I am that she's not playing along, I'm turned on by her fire.

Your dick doesn't need to feel guilty.

That's what Alexis said at the wedding, and he's right. She's a grown woman now, one I paid a lot of money for. There were always two ways this situation could play out, and she is picking the hard way. My dick has always enjoyed the hard way the best. Nothing good ever comes easy. I've spent my whole life taking what should be mine, holding onto what my father built, forcing my way into new profitable areas and between the most converted legs.

I'm used to the brutality that's required to get what I want. I get off on wielding power.

Curving over her, still gripping her mane of hair, I run my hand down her cheek and neck, letting my fingertips play over the swell of her breast. Everything about her is young and fresh, her unblemished skin, the firmness of her ripe body. The dress isn't especially low cut, but it's low enough that when I let my fingers drift, the very tip brushes her nipple within the lace cup of her bra. She gasps, and I smile. "See. You might pretend to hate me, but your nipples tell a different story." I take one between my thumb and forefinger and twist, not to hurt but to arouse. To make a point that she is mine, and I can do whatever the fuck I want to her at any time.

"Stop," she says, but her voice is breathy.

"You don't want me to stop. Not really. Look at your eyes." I twist her head so Alexis can see how wide her pupils are blown. "You look like you're strung out on molly."

"Fuck you," she spits again.

I pull my hand from her dress and lick my index finger while she watches me with wide eyes. I crouch in front of her, still gripping the silky strands of her hair. Her shoulders strain as she tugs at the restraints on her wrists.

"Maybe, *gattina*, I should fuck *you*."

She gasps as I push my hand between her legs, finding the fabric of her panties damp. I smile; the knowledge that she's turned on a confirmation of what I already knew. Those moments at the wedding where our eyes kept meeting weren't just about recognition. There was lust in her eyes. The kind of lust that's laced with dark fear and even darker curiosity. Yesterday, after I spanked her, she was wet enough to soak through her dress.

I don't push inside her, but I rest my finger at the unbreeched entrance to her body, my smile widening when her pussy contracts against my touch, her sweet little hole fluttering. Her hips shift, like she's seeking more pressure and blood floods my dick.

"Should I fuck you? Break this little pussy open. Make you a woman with my thick cock?"

"No," she grits out through a rigid jaw. She's fighting with herself as much as she wants to fight me. Her body is talking to me, whispering secret fantasies and sweetness of the kind I haven't thought to taste in a long time.

I press a little harder against her, so that the pad of my index finger slips inside her a little. She moans so softly, I'm the only one close enough to hear. My dick is iron, imagining breaking through her innocence so that she cries out in pain before pleasure. "Are you sure? I know how to make it hurt so good."

"NO."

I hold my finger in place as her body tightens around it.

An invader. An intruder. Unwelcome but desired. She was wet, but she's getting wetter. "So, *gattina*, how are you going to make up for me not getting inside your sweet little dripping cunt? What are you going to do for me to spare you?"

"I'll do it," she says, her body trembling, fluttering around my finger. "I'll do the video."

"Yes?" I reluctantly pull my hand away, my wet finger cooling where my lust still blazes out of control.

I stand and she relaxes into my touch, no longer fighting the grip in her hair.

Alexis starts the recording again and Aemelia focuses on the camera.

"Please, Papa. Please. Don't let them hurt me. Don't let them break me. Pleeaaase, Papa. Please come back before they…"

I jerk her head again, and she gasps.

"Enough."

Alexis stops filming, his grin wide and pleased. "An Oscar-winning performance."

I don't let go of our little spitfire. "See, that wasn't so hard, was it?"

The hatred in her eyes turns the warm coffee depths to midnight black. "I hate my father," she says. "But you…"

"Ah, princess." I press my hand over my heart. "What have I done to make you hate me?"

"Touched me."

"You liked it."

She grimaces. "Made me kiss your filthy feet."

"There is nothing filthy about me, except my mind."

"You made me kneel."

"Why would you hate that? Is it so hard to submit to the will of another? Have I not cared for you? Fed you? Put a roof over your head? Clothes on your back? Are you not warm?"

Her eyes are murderous. "I don't want any of it."

"I could kill you now," I hiss. "Snap your pretty neck

like a chicken bone. Let your father come back for the pieces of your body, but I'm not a cruel man, at least not to those who don't deserve it."

She lowers her eyes like looking at me is too hard. I bring my index finger to my mouth and savor her flavor, the heady scent and taste filling my mind with desperate urges, then I swipe my thumb over her bottom lip, smearing the red lipstick. I bring it to my mouth and taste that too, watching her.

"Pussy and cherries?"

Her face twists. She has no idea how sweet she is.

"What do you want from me?" Her voice is a whisper. Alexis and Antonio wait, as still as the statues that once decorated the Colosseum.

"Obedience," I say. "Understand. You do what I say when I say it. Don't make this hard on yourself."

I turn to my brothers. "Take her back to her room."

They approach, eating up the distance between us with long strides. They take an arm each, lifting Aemelia to her feet and frog-marching her away.

I watch her go and ask fate to make Carlo Lambretti see sense quickly, because the longer Aemelia is in this penthouse, the less likely I am to resist doing to her all the things she fears the most.

CHAPTER 7

AEMELIA

MONSTERS AND MEN

I don't know how much time has passed since they took the video. Minutes? Hours? Time feels strange here suspended between terror and exhaustion, blurred by the dull ache in my arms from being tied up too long. My wrists burn from the zip tie, my shoulders stiff from the forced stillness.

They sent my face out like a calling card. Aemelia Lambretti, bound and helpless. A message to a ghost—a father who vanished without a trace, leaving nothing behind but a last name and a target on my back.

I should be furious. I should be screaming. But I just feel hollow.

Eventually, I have to call out. I can't use the bathroom like this, and I've held out for so long, I'm in danger of peeing myself. Alexis is the one who turns the lock and appears by my bed, his hazel eyes hungry and amused as he stares down at me.

"Can you remove the zip ties? I need to pee."

"No, *gattina*. You didn't do what you were told."

"I did." My voice is a whine that makes me wince. I sound desperate, pathetic, like a teenager asking for more money to go out with her friends.

"Not until you were forced, right? Not until my brother made you."

"So you want me to piss all over this expensive bed?"

"No." He takes me by the elbow, his fingers punishing. "Come with me."

I'm half-dragged to the bathroom which leads from my room. It's spacious and marble with a double vanity and a walk-in shower with a rainfall head that must feel like heaven. It's a joke how much nicer this place is than my actual home. There's no mold in this bathroom, no cracked tiles or broken flush. And yet, I'd do anything to get out of here.

Anything.

The word taunts me. What would I do? Let Luca touch me, fuck me? What about his brothers? Would they want that, too? I've seen the way they look at me like they're imagining my naked body and all the filthy, corrupt things they want to do to me. How far would I go for my safety and freedom?

I don't know. I really don't know. And that's what scares me.

Alexis nudges me back towards the toilet with his colorful inked arms, the flames raging dangerously across his body, then he shoves his hand beneath my skirt and begins to tug my panties down.

"No," I say, but he doesn't listen.

"Do you want to pee through your panties?" he asks instead, shaking his head. "This fucking girl."

I flush hot with mortification when my panties drop around my ankles. Alexis pulls up the back of my dress and pushes me until I'm sitting. My cheeks burn as the pee drops out of me with urgency and Alexis watches with amusement lighting up his devastatingly handsome face. His eyes focus on my panties and my embarrassment increases a hundredfold because I know they're damp. When Luca touched me, my body reacted like a traitor.

What kind of sick person am I that his finger forced between my legs turned me on?

I close my eyes, wishing that the blackness between my eyelids could swallow me whole. I wish I could disappear into it, like the ocean at night, and escape this captivity.

The sound of the toilet paper roll unfurling makes my heart stop. I can't wipe myself with my hands behind my back. Is he going to do it for me?

"Spread your legs." Alexis crouches in front of me, so we're eye to eye. The dress is covering my bare pussy but for how long. I ease my legs open, watching him watch me. With his eyes downcast, his eyelashes seem impossibly long, his nose, which is slightly crooked, refined, his mouth which seems to carry sly happiness at its corners at all times, twitching. He's enjoying this and I hate him for it. I close my eyes when he dips his hand between my legs, and shudder as he draws the paper over my sex. A distressed whimper leaves my lips and his smile broadens. He thinks I like this.

Jesus, help me. This man is sick.

He releases the paper and stands, helping me to my feet, then he drops to his haunches again and begins to drag the stupid panties up my legs. It's not easy. Whoever shopped for me only bought white lace thongs that stick to my skin and twist around themselves. He works slowly, pushing under the fabric of my skirt but he struggles.

"Fuck this," he mutters, yanking the skirt higher so he can see what he's doing. I want to die as this stranger looks at my most private place, fumbling with my underwear.

I keep my gaze fixed to the corner of the room, where the marble tile meets the brilliant white of the ceiling, as Alexis Venturi, youngest of the ruthless mafia brothers, settles the edges of my panties over my hips and then reaches behind to position the string correctly between the cheeks of my ass. His fingers aren't sensual or soft, but it doesn't matter because I'm a woman with a very warped mind, it seems, and every touch sends heat pooling between my legs. He lingers a few seconds longer than is necessary, and when I look down, I catch him inhaling.

Motherfucker. Is he trying to smell me?

When he stands, he seems unsteady on his feet. And without any shame, he adjusts his pants, hefting a very thick, very erect cock to the side to ease his discomfort.

I gulp as the size of him makes my pussy clench inexplicably.

"You're seriously turned on by watching me pee?"

He laughs and it's a little manic sounding. "You say it like you're surprised." He heads to the vanity to wash his hands and when he returns, he pushes a lock of my hair behind my ear.

"You're a very beautiful woman, my little cat. And beautiful women turn men on with just a flick of their head or the sound of their laugh."

"And piss?"

He shrugs. "Some men like piss. Some men like worse. Me, I just like power."

"Men are weak," I say, and he grins.

"Yes, we are. For all the pleasures in life."

"Can you take me back to the bedroom?"

His hand on my elbow is warm. "You're not enjoying our conversation."

"If you keep me tied up, I'll enjoy nothing."

"Oh, *gattina*. I beg to differ."

But even with ominous words hanging between us, he waits while I settle onto my side on the bed, and leaves, locking the door behind him.

***

It's Antonio who removes the zip tie from my wrists when it's time to eat. I don't get to join them in the dining room.

Instead, he brings me a bowl of pasta and some grapes and sits in a chair to watch me eat. The pasta is really good. Spaghetti coated in a delicious garlicky tangy tomato sauce infused with basil and a little lemon., topped with pungently strong parmesan, just the way I like it. I wolf it down with little finesse, even though my shoulders are screaming, and my hands barely work.

"Slowly," Antionio says. "I know it's good, but I don't want you to choke."

"Who made it?" I lick my lips like a wolf. "Maybe I should ask for the recipe."

"I did," he says.

I stare at the brute of a man who makes the normal sized chair he's sitting in look like something from a kid's playhouse. His hands are scarred, his expression always dark like he's loaded up with a weight of sin too heavy for any one man to carry. He's the Venturi enforcer. The one who handles the problems with only one option left. My mother told me the stories of these brothers. How Mario was the lover, Luca the ruler, Alexis the joker and Antonio the assassin.

Except he doesn't seem like an assassin. He's too big to be stealthy, too stoic to be cunning. It's stupid to believe that a man who can create such delicious food shouldn't be able to destroy life like it's nothing, but I was never top of my class. Too distracted by my life to concentrate.

"Do you share your recipes?" I ask.

"No one has ever asked me to."

"Well, maybe, when you let me go, you can write it down for me. Every time I make it, I'll think of you."

His face remains impassive but his cold steel eyes flicker, and I look away, my heart making a painful thud in my chest. Maybe they won't ever let me go. If my father fails to respond to my begging plea, they won't just release me. Everything is riding on my father, a man who didn't have a reliable bone in his body and who hated a defenseless child. I lower my fork and drop it in the bowl, my appetite lost.

I push away the tray and curl on my side in the bed, burying my face in the pillow. Tears scorch a trail of fire in my throat, but I don't let them win. I swallow them down and wait.

"Aemelia," Antonio says in a voice that's soft, coaxing.

"I thought I wasn't Aemelia anymore. I thought I was nameless. A kitten. Stupid *gattina*. Nothing else."

"I'll give you my mother's recipe," he says as he lifts the tray from the bed. When he leaves the room, I let the tears flood out of me until I'm wrung out and I slip into a fitful sleep.

***

I wake with a gasp, heart hammering, the nightmare still clinging to me like cobwebs. Fire, the sound of screaming, of gunfire, of my mother crying out my name—

I bolt upright, breath coming fast and ragged, fingers clutching the comforter like it's the only thing keeping me grounded. My throat is tight, and my skin is damp with sweat.

And then I realize I'm not alone.

Antonio is sitting at the edge of the bed, watching me.

For a second, I can't move. He's too close, the shadows cloaking him in unreadable darkness. His hands rest on his knees, broad and strong, fingers curled loosely. He doesn't look surprised that I woke up.

"What—" My voice cracks. I swallow hard. "What are you doing here?"

His eyes flick over my face, and then, to my shock, he reaches out, fingertips brushing against my hair, smoothing it away from my damp forehead. It's such a small, unexpectedly gentle gesture that I freeze completely.

"I used to have nightmares," he says, his voice low, almost thoughtful. "When I was a kid. My mother used to sit with me until they passed."

I stare at him, still caught between fear and something

else, something softer.

Antonio's mother.

I remember her. When I knew her, she was a sweet woman who didn't say much but smiled a lot. She was proud of her sons and her daughter was the light of her life. I wonder what she'd think of them now, tying up a helpless woman and sending her pictures into the world like a maggot on a hook.

Would she be proud that they're set on avenging their brother? Would she respect the means they were taking?

Women in this underground world play mixed roles. Ambivalence is common. They ignore their husbands' criminal activities, sometimes even their infidelity. Sometimes, they're open in their support and vicious in their attitudes. I can't imagine marrying into this world. I think of the sweet all-American boys I grew up with, and how distant that life feels to me now. Even when I was there, living an ordinary life—trips to the mall with friends, going to the movies, bowling, working shitty low paid jobs—I felt like a fish out of water.

In the dim glow of the bedside lamp, Antonio doesn't look like a bad man. It's not that he's kind—none of them are. But he doesn't gloat, doesn't sneer, doesn't treat me like a problem to be solved or a prize to be bartered. He just *watches me*. He looks... human. And somehow, that unsettles me more than anything.

"What kind of nightmares?" I ask, my voice quieter now, afraid speaking too loudly will shatter this strange moment between us.

His fingers pause in my hair. He exhales slowly, as if debating whether to answer.

"Monsters," he finally says.

A humorless laugh escapes me. "And now you *are* one."

His gaze sharpens, but he doesn't deny it. "Maybe." A beat of silence, then: "But monsters don't comfort scared little girls in the dark."

I don't know why that sentence makes something ache

in my chest.

I turn my head slightly, just enough to see his face more clearly. There's a softness in his expression, a quiet understanding, like he knows what it's like to wake up drowning in fear. Like he recognizes something in me that he doesn't want to name, the same as I'm starting to with him. His eyes are so light grey that it gives him an otherworldly air that makes it harder for me to read him, but staring into them makes me lose myself just a little.

I should push his hand away. I should tell him I don't need his comfort, that I don't *want* it.

But instead, I let him stroke my hair, let the warmth of his palm against my temple lull me back down from the edge of panic.

He doesn't say anything else.

And somehow, it's enough.

CHAPTER 8

ALEXIS

FIND SOMEONE TO LOVE

"*Mio bello.*" Mama reaches out to embrace me, pulling me into her warm, soft arms. I stoop to wrap my arms around her, inhaling her familiar scent of jasmine and tomatoes.

"Mama." I kiss her cheek a little too hard, just how she likes it, and she cups my face with her rough hands, looking me over like she has the power to weigh the value of my soul. I don't know how she does it, but she always knows when something is wrong.

"Why have you and your brothers been staying at that *posto stupido?*"

She hates it when we use the city penthouse rather than staying at our estate. I guess she's lonely now Rosita's married and on her honeymoon. The last of her babies to fly the nest.

"We have business."

"You always have business." She pinches my cheek hard.

"Important business."

She turns to lead me to the kitchen. Food is always the priority in this house, and she won't be happy until she's fed me. "You can tell me," she tosses over her shoulder, "or I can find out from *il pettegolezzo.*"

The women's gossip grapevine reaches far but maybe not far enough to touch Aemelia Lambretti.

"I can't tell you, Mama. What's cooking?"

"Wait and see."

"I bought you some cannoli from that place you like."

"You did?" I hand her the bag, and she opens it to look inside. She can make great cannoli, but this place does something special with pistachio and rose that she can't seem to replicate.

"*Grazie.*" Her beaming face chases away some of the rage I've been feeling since the Lambretti issue rose to the surface. She sits me down at the table and assembles a huge plate of veal and pasta. I wolf it down while she watches from the adjacent chair with a satisfied smile. Nothing, literally nothing in this world, makes her as happy as feeding her kids.

"I spoke to your sister. She's enjoying her honeymoon."

I dab my mouth. "I don't think I want to know."

Her blue eyes narrow beneath a frown. "Don't be disgusting, Alexis. She's talking about the hotel and sightseeing."

I go back to eating.

"She told me that she thought she saw Aemelia Lambretti at the wedding." Mama arches a brow, and cups her hands over her stomach, smoothing her floral dress.

"Really? She wasn't on the guest list."

"That's what I said."

"Why did she think it was Aemelia?"

"She said there was a girl serving who looked just like Carmella Lambretti did when she was young."

"I didn't notice anyone like that." I don't meet her eyes because she's a hawk for lies.

Mama nods, offering me homemade bread from a bowl

to dip up the sauce left on my plate. "Carmella Lambretti was trouble," she says. "I don't know why she ended up with that man, Carlo. She was a beautiful girl who settled for the first man to look in her direction, then regretted her decision every day."

"She did?"

"She wanted your brother."

That's news to me. "Which one?"

She crosses herself, closing her eyes as she does it. "Mario."

I frown, dropping the bread to the plate. "Carmella Lambretti wanted Mario?"

"She looked at him like he was king of the world."

I used to look at him the same way. My older brother *was* my world. My protector. My champion. My greatest supporter. He was more like a father, filling the gap our actual father left in our lives, firstly because of the responsibilities of being a boss, and then when cancer stole him. Losing Mario carved out my heart and left a jagged wound behind that has never healed.

"I think he wanted her, too."

I lean back in my chair considering. "Well, Mario wasn't selective when it came to women."

"Not like that." Mama screws up her face. "Why is your mind always in the gutter?"

"He wanted to have an affair with her?"

Even though the fifties are a long time ago, that era is still alive and well in Sicilian households. Divorce isn't just frowned upon, it's forbidden in most circumstances. Mama shrugs. "He's gone so it doesn't matter."

The day we put my brother in the ground, I wanted to go with him. Living on with the pain, not just my own but my whole family's, felt impossible. It was Luca who held me up, cool and collected even under such terrible circumstances, even though he'd taken a bullet himself. I've never seen him cry, even when we went to identify Mario's corpse. Sometimes I wonder if he even has a heart in his chest but then I see him with Mama and Rosita and watch how seriously he works to keep everyone in our family safe and I know he has enough.

Chiaccherone, Luca's cat, winds its way around my feet and cries. It heard my voice and thought its master was home and now it's sad. The stupid animal doesn't like anyone except my brother. When we're home, it sits on Luca's lap, making him look like a Bond villain. He brings him treats in his pockets and kisses him like he's a baby. No wonder the cat loves him so much.

I nudge it aside with my foot.

"So, this business?"

I use the napkin to wipe my face one last time, my belly now perfectly full. "That was delicious, Mama. Thank you. Nobody cooks like you."

"Not even Antonio?"

I smirk. "He's a passable alternative."

"You all need wives to cook for you. Look at me. I'm old, and not a grandbaby between four children. At mass, they pray for me."

"Who prays?"

"Everyone."

"Rosita will come back pregnant."

Even though thinking about my sister that way makes me want to murder someone, I'd be relieved if it gets Mama off my back.

She repeats the sign of the cross. "Maybe, but you..." She wags her finger at me like I'm a toddler who's misbehaving. "Don't waste your time like your brothers. Thirty-two is a good age to start a family. I can help you find a good girl."

"What about Luca and Antonio?" I'm the youngest of her sons. Why the hell is the pressure to carry on the family name falling on my head?

"You think your brothers can mold around another person now? Luca is like marble, and Antonio is like steel. Don't leave it too long... I don't need another brick for a son."

"Mama." I stand and dip to kiss her warm soft cheek.

She grips my face between her palms again, assessing me with Luca's eyes. "This life has taken a lot from me, Alexis. My husband. My son. Don't let it steal the future of the Venturi name. It's time."

"I love you, Mama," is all I can think of to reply because although there's never a shortage of women in my bed, none has ever registered as a marriage prospect. What kind of woman can put up with this life; the risks, the dubious conscience we need to hold onto power when behind you there are even worse people looking to steal everything you have. It could only ever be a half measure of love. An expectation for someone to love the parts of me that are acceptable and look past everything else. A love like that isn't worth it.

I think of Aemelia and the disgusted way she looked at me as I crouched at her feet to wipe her. That disgust I can deal with. I prefer it because it's honest. The women who look at me like I'm an angel on the inside as well as the outside can never be anything but fake. Disgust turns me on because it's something I can push against. It's something that burns with heat like rage and shame.

Mama taps my cheek a little too hard for affection. "I'm going to be dead soon. Find someone else to love."

***

I call Antonio from the car on my way to meet my crew. "Anything from the rat?"

"Nothing."

"You think the message has got to him?"

"Who the fuck knows? He's at the bottom of a well. The coin has to sink."

"So we wait?"

"We wait."

I'm not a patient man. Neither are my brothers, and the

longer we have to wait, the longer pretty little Aemelia is going to be under our roof.

"How's the kitten?"

"She has claws."

I laugh at the idea that little Aemelia Lambretti might have hurt my huge, vicious brother.

"I like claws."

"So does Luca."

Our older brother always keeps his life private. If he has a woman, he meets her in secret, and keeps the relationship under lock and key. It's only through throw-away comments that I suspect the kind of sex he seeks out isn't vanilla.

"He wants to fuck her?"

"Yes." Antonio's tone carries a hint of disapproval, and I tap my fingers against the steering wheel, considering.

"And you? Do you want to fuck her?"

"She's practically half my age."

"And half your size."

He snorts. "The little girls always like the big boys."

Ain't that the truth. "What about the big boy, Antonio? You thought about what it would be like to declaw the cat."

"She's not a bad person," he says, his tone gentling. "If you were locked in a room, and forced to your knees, you'd have claws, too."

"Mmmmm... you like her."

"*Idiota.*"

"Hey. I know what I see with my own eyes."

"It sounds like *you* like her."

"And I'm not fucking denying it. If I could bend her over the table and fuck her until she screams, I would in a heartbeat, claws and all."

"So what's stopping you?"

He makes an interesting point. What's stopping me? "She's innocent," I say. "Her father will value her more this way. If we take that..." Why the hell am I talking myself out of this?

"How would he know?"

That's a very good point. "She'd lose the fire in her eyes, Antonio. You know the dead expression hookers have. You can't hide that. And anyway, what the fuck is your game?"

He laughs and sips a drink, making a slurping noise in my ear.

"Because listening to you get excited about pussy like a thirteen-year-old is brightening up my shitty day. That's why."

"Like you haven't thought about it, asshole. When she was wearing that lace dress that showed everything, you're telling me you didn't think about it?"

"I'm not dead."

So I was right. "You think Carlo will come?"

"There are still people who might lean on him if he's reluctant. His brother is still linked to the Mesinas. This won't look good for him."

"When I get my hands on him," I say, gripping the steering wheel like I'm throttling his stupid fucking neck.

"Join the queue. There won't be a piece of him left that's big enough to interest a rat."

"Would you do it? Come back to die?"

"For my nonexistent virgin daughter?"

"For Rosita."

"Don't even fucking joke about that, Alexis, you stupid fuck. I'd cut my own heart out of my chest for her. You know that."

"Me, too," I say. "Me, too."

When I hang up the phone, I consider what will happen if Carlo doesn't come back. How will Aemelia feel to know her own father wouldn't give up his life for hers? The thought of her having to face that sadness and humiliation makes me sick to my stomach.

What do we have in this life if we let go of our honor and our family?

CHAPTER 9

LUCA

HIGH STAKES

Our casino is a place of indulgence, with every detail designed to overwhelm the senses. It hums with temptation, vice, the electric charge of risk. The air is thick with the scent of expensive cigars, aged whiskey, and the faintest trace of desperation from those who don't know when to walk away. Neon lights flicker against polished ebony floors, the walls are lined with deep mahogany paneling, offset by decadent gold accents that gleam under the glow of recessed lighting. High above, a ceiling painted midnight blue stretches like an endless sky, tiny fiber-optic lights twinkling like stars.

The tables are sleek, their surfaces inlaid with mother-of-pearl, their edges gilded. The croupiers, masters of the house, move with practiced precision—women in slinky velvet dresses, men in sharply tailored suits that fit like armor. Their smiles are enigmatic, their hands quick and deft as they deal fate with the flick of a wrist.

A murmur of excitement fills the space, the low laughter

of high rollers, the quiet gasps of losers who bet too much, the rhythmic clink of chips stacking up in towers or scattering like lost hopes.

This is more than a casino. It's a battlefield where fortunes are made and broken in the span of a single hand. The house always wins, and tonight, as ever, we rake in more than we pay out.

I stand near the main bar, the scent of top-shelf whiskey and expensive perfume thick in the air, surveying our domain, the beating heart of the Venturi empire. Marco Venturi, my cousin and the casino's manager, steps up beside me, nursing a lowball glass of bourbon. He doesn't waste time with pleasantries.

"Enzo Lambretti's not happy about the video," he says, voice pitched low so only I can hear.

I lift my glass, swirling the amber liquid before taking a slow sip. "Do I look like I care?" He gulps from his glass. I add, "Is Enzo ever happy?"

Marco snorts, his sharp hazel eyes, the same as our fathers', and Alexis', sweep the room. "He's got reason to be pissed."

Good. Let him be pissed. He's not guilty of Carlo's crimes. They weren't even part of the same family, but he carries the same name. I tap my fingers against the side of my glass, calculating. If Enzo is reacting like this, it means our message landed. Now, we just need to see what shakes loose.

"I'll send Antonio to him," I say. "Tell him to see what Enzo knows. And make sure Enzo understands we're not fucking around. If he steps out of line—"

Marco nods, but before he can respond, a shift in the room's energy draws both our attention.

Alfonso Mesina strides into the casino, flanked by his brother, his cousin, and three members of his crew. The Mesinas move like they own the place with a swagger that grates my nerves.

"Trouble?" Marco murmurs.

"Maybe." I watch as they make their way to the VIP lounge.

Alfonso settles into a corner booth, his men fanning out around him, some ordering drinks from a server who quickly attends to them, others scanning the crowd like they're expecting an ambush. I don't like it. Not one fucking bit.

Time to find out why they're here.

I finish my drink and make my way toward them, adjusting the cuffs of my jacket as I go. When I reach their table, Alfonso leans back, draping an arm over the back of the leather booth like he's settling in for a long conversation.

"Luca Venturi," he drawls, flashing a too-white grin. "What a pleasure."

I offer a polite nod, keeping my expression neutral. "Alfonso. You should've told me you were coming. Drinks are on the house tonight."

His brother, Domenico, chuckles as he lifts a glass of whiskey. "Already making good on that offer, Venturi."

I smirk, waving a hand to the passing waitress. "Another round."

Alfonso studies me, his dark eyes glittering with something unreadable. "I heard you've been busy lately. Something about a certain girl."

I keep my posture relaxed, but every muscle in my body tenses, ready. "I've been busy with a lot of things."

He chuckles. "Right. But you know the girl I'm talking about. Lambretti's little bitch."

A muscle ticks in my jaw, but I don't let it show. Aemelia may be my captive, but hearing another man talk shit about her makes my blood boil. "And?"

Alfonso leans forward, steepling the fingers I want to shatter beneath my polished shoes. "Have you taken her cherry yet?"

Silence descends over the table. His men shift, watching me closely. Marco stiffens at my side, his hand casually resting on his belt, close enough to his gun to make a point.

I don't smile. I don't react. I simply tilt my head, regarding him with cold amusement. "A man should never ask about another man's personal affairs, Alfonso. You know that. Next, you'll be asking about the length of my cock."

His grin widens, but there's tension in it now. He's testing me, pushing to see where the cracks might be.

I straighten my jacket. "Enjoy the drinks. Play some hands, win some money. Or lose…" I wave my hand like I don't care either way.

Alfonso watches me for a beat longer, then lifts his glass. "*Salute*. Always a pleasure, Venturi."

I turn to Marco as we step away. "Keep an eye on them."

Marco's expression is grim. "I don't like this."

"Neither do I."

The Mesinas aren't here to gamble. They're here to see where we stand. And that means the friction that's been simmering just beneath the surface is one step closer to erupting.

CHAPTER 10

ANTONIO

THE TASTE OF INNOCENCE

Aemelia's hair is matted and filthy, her skin pale and greasy, and when I rest the tray of toasted bread and soft cheese in front of her, the scent of her unwashed body reaches my nose. She hasn't showered since she got here, despite having a private bathroom and all the cosmetics and toiletries she could possibly need. Since we forced her to make the video, she's retreated inside herself, and her descent from defiance to hopelessness fills me with dread. She pushes the tray away and turns from me.

I sit on the bed as worry becomes an unpleasant vibration in my skull. I can hear my mama's voice in my head. *'Eat'*. It's her favorite word to say to all of her family, as though she worries we'll face starvation tomorrow and need our body fat to survive. Food trauma passes from generation to generation, past experiences of food shortages lingering like a specter, but I don't say it to Aemelia. Not yet.

"You need to shower."

"Fuck you," she mutters.

Still with the mouth.

"You want to fester in your own filth?"

She scoffs. "If I stink, maybe your brother will think twice about touching me again."

This is a problem; this war that's being fought in her head where she thinks she can find a way to beat all the odds and win. I don't know how she hasn't worked out that her life is in danger and her compliance is necessary to survive.

I don't want to be the one to teach her, but Luca won't be as restrained if she tests him, and Alexis is already thinking about ruining her. If she needs to learn, I have to be the one to teach her.

"There's a lot you don't know about men," I say. "The smell of you now… it would only turn him on."

She swivels to look at me, her eyebrows high on her forehead.

"You think I'm lying." I lean closer and inhale, and the pheromones in her scent replace all the bad vibrations in my head with lust and desire.

"You're all disgusting."

"No, *gattina*. Just human. But it's not good to stay dirty."

"I'm not showering."

Her narrow-eyed determination thickens my cock. Jesus. This girl. Was she sent to Earth to defy us? To teach us some kind of lesson. Whatever the lesson, my skull is too thick to recognize it.

"Either you go of your own free will, or I'll take you. Do you understand?"

She grits her teeth and turns away again. Frustration surges, and before she has a chance to prepare, I throw off the comforter and scoop her into my arms. She writhes and twists, flailing her arms, but I pin her to me and haul her into the bathroom. Once inside, I lower her feet to the floor but keep her anchored against me, her back to my front, freeing a hand to flip on the shower. She fights, but she's so small and weak that it doesn't even register, which only seems to make her angrier.

"Get your fucking hands off me," she growls as her ass grinds into my dick. Even like this, feral and vicious, she's glorious enough to make me hard.

I wrap my free hand around her neck and press her head tightly against my chest. "Look in the mirror," I hiss in her ear. "Look at yourself."

She does, her eyes wide. Her hair has twisted into wild locks, making her appear as fierce and deadly as Medusa.

"Understand, *gattina*, that you will not win this fight. Any strategy you come up with in your pretty little head won't work. We hold all the cards, and you hold none."

She burns with resistance, her body vibrating against my hold. I walk forward to push her into the shower, but she fights me, trying to gain traction against the slick floor. She's wild and fearless, a force of nature, everything I thought I'd never want in a woman, but find I deeply respect. Even against all odds, she's trying.

I could shove her under the water, but I don't want to hurt her. If she slips, she could bust up her face or break something. Instead, I toe off my shoes and force us both beneath the streaming water. The shock makes her still and she whips her head to look at me. Water cascades down my face, flattening my short hair and soaking my sweater. She closes her eyes, tipping her face upward, arching her slender neck so her head rests just below my shoulder. She's breathing fast, like a rabbit that's been chased across the fields by a vicious fox, and I close my eyes, hating what we're doing to her. This isn't right. She doesn't deserve this. Every second she's under our roof will change her, and she'll never be the same. Sickness gathers beneath my diaphragm, driven by shame.

The end doesn't always justify the means. Just because this is the easiest way to get to Carlo fucking Lambretti, doesn't mean we should take it.

She swallows against my palm and shudders, and I move

my hand to wrap it around her chest instead. I curve my body over hers, wanting her to feel an embrace rather than restraint. "It's okay," I tell her, surprising myself but not enough to stop. "It's okay, Aemelia. It'll be okay."

Her body hitches, and I can sense her weeping before she makes a sound. I thought my heart was dead, but still, it seems to fracture and bleed for her.

I'm losing my fucking mind, but I can't help how I feel.

I loved Mario, and avenging his death isn't up for debate, but it doesn't have to involve torturing this poor girl.

Turning her in my arms, I press my hand to the side of her head, so her face rests over my heart. It beats rapid rhythm as I stroke her wet, tangled hair. The sound of her sorrow cuts my soul until I can't take it anymore. Grasping her face between my hands, I force her to look at me.

I swipe tears and shower water from beneath her eyes. Her eyelashes are coated with droplets like diamonds that glint in the bright light of the bathroom. Her nightgown clings to her form, almost transparent now that it's wet through, and my body sparks into an inferno.

"You don't have to be scared of me," I tell her. It's stupid. It goes against everything that Luca and Alexis want and expect from me. It goes against everything I've come to expect from myself, but this woman is an infestation that's crawled under my skin and changed me.

"You're holding me captive, Antonio. You've threatened me with violence."

"I do what I have to do," I say. "I do what's expected of me."

She blinks, her hands settling on my chest. She nods as though I've confessed something she understands. We don't know much about Aemelia except her family relies on her for money. She was a waitress, doing what she had to do, doing what's expected of her. Maybe, in some small way, she understands.

I let my thumb trace her lips, wiping away the water and her tears and she closes her eyes. Like this, with her armor washed away, she's transcendent.

It isn't fair that we've met like this, forced together to dance in the underworld. I think of the story of Hades and how he loved Persephone so desperately that he took her from the light and forced her to live with him in hell. Neither of us chose to be born into families with blood on their hands. We didn't choose this life, it chose us, and yet we have to suffer.

"Aemelia," I whisper.

"*Gattina*," she reminds me, staring into my eyes, this time with a soft challenge. Her fingers drift to my neck to trace the sharp tattoo there. All around us, the steam swirls until I forget we're in the penthouse, and I forget why we're standing together in the shower, fully clothed.

I want to kiss her like I've never wanted to kiss anyone before. It's a curse, a desire so thick, it's impossible to wade through. I shake with it down to the pit of my rotten soul, and I have to lower my eyes, afraid she'll notice my torment.

When her lips press against mine, I believe at first that this whole thing is just a dream. I can't move. I can't breathe. I'm a jagged block of granite being caressed by the cool Sicilian breeze. But then her lips move, soft and coaxing, and I'm molten lava, pressing into her, slowly backing her against the tiled wall, finding my way inside the heat of her mouth and dying slowly with every side of our tongues.

She's sweeter than *Pignolata di Miele*, more tantalizing than amphetamines. My consciousness dances like a prisoner freed after a life sentence. I slide my hands from her face, down her neck and lower, gipping her tiny waist, surging forward so there's no space between us. She moans into my mouth, her hands fisting my sweater like she's afraid I'll pull away.

But I can't. Threats from the devil himself couldn't drag me from her. I could drown in her and die a happy man.

My conscience prickles—this is wrong, so wrong. I'm almost twice her age, but I'm used to pushing aside any desire to be a good man. The last time I saw her she was a little girl. I shouldn't want her like this. But still, I kiss down her throat, across her collarbone, tasting her skin and the water coating us both, nipping her with my teeth, holding her still with the tight grip of my killer's hands.

Her hips flare wide, a woman's hips. Her mouth is sweet but desperate with a woman's desire. She moans softly; a woman's need.

The water washes us both, but it'll never rinse away the stain of my past. Hopelessness surges inside me, taking the strength from my knees.

What the fuck am I doing? This isn't me? This isn't who I am.

I drop down in front of Aemelia, pressing my face to her stomach, and wrapping my arms around her hips.

I have to stop this before it's too late, but I can't. Desire is a flood that's impossible to outrun.

I kiss her stomach through the sheer fabric of her nightgown, fever tearing at me with flaming hands. I'm a bad man, through and through, and this girl is so sweet and pure. Touching her isn't enough. I need to be inside her so her purity can wash me clean. But I won't do that. Not just because Luca would skin me alive but because Aemelia deserves more than I can ever give her.

She deserves a good man who loves her, a wedding filled with white doves and classical music and a honeymoon of romance and soft touches. She deserves pure memories that will last a lifetime and color her family with joy.

But maybe there's something else. Another way. I slide my hand from her knee to her thigh, pushing the soaked nightdress fabric higher. I wait for her to slap my hand away, but she doesn't. Higher still, my fingers touch the edge of her panties. Still no resistance. I look up and find her staring down at me, eyes bright, hands pressed to the tiled wall. I hook my fingers and pull just a little, our eyes still locked. She's breathing hard but there's no fear in her expression, just a calm acceptance.

"What do you want from me, Aemelia?" My throat is nothing but gravel. It would be easy to take, but I want her to give it to me.

"I don't know," she whispers. "I don't know."

"Tell me to stop."

She shakes her head, so I continue, using both hands to ease her panties down her smooth thighs. I press my face lower, still over the fabric of her night dress, breathing her in.

"Wash me," she whispers, but I shake my head, the scent of her driving me fucking crazy.

She's so natural, so perfect, exactly how a woman should be. Soft dark curls at the apex of her thighs, sweet musky scent that makes me want to rut like a fucking animal. I caress her over the seam of her sex, relishing the way her body shudders and her breath comes in soft pants, then I open her with my thumbs and press my lips to her clit.

I'm lost. Drunk. Stumbling in the dark. Wanting. Stealing. Craving.

Her knees tremble, and I wait, warming her flesh with my breath, letting her get accustomed to something she may not have ever done before, but mostly, I linger because I'm selfish. I want to burn this moment into my brain. I want my first taste of Aemelia's sweetness to hit me like a drug. I touch her clit with the tip of my tongue, and her hands leave the wall to grip my head. It feels like she doesn't know whether she wants to push me away or hold me against her. With slow teasing licks, I make her knees shake. I stare up at her over the perfect arc of her body, meeting her heavy-lidded eyes. As I lick her, I remember how she looked at the wedding, vibrant and beautiful, a rose among thorns. I recall the fire in her eyes, her chin held high, her regalness. She's so young but so strong.

Even in a room with three dangerous men, she could hold her own.

Maybe she'd be strong enough to return to the life that she grew up in before her father destroyed it all. A mafia princess instead of a Maryland waitress. Maybe she could be mine, but would I even want that for her?

If we let her go—when we let her go—she'll be free to return home. She could meet a kind man named Brad who'll take her for early-bird-specials and treat her kindly so that she can live out an ordinary, average, uneventful life. But even as I try to picture her there, I can't. I don't want to. I'm jealous of a fictional man I created with my own mind. Thinking about her with anyone else makes me sick, even though all I can give her is the darkness of the underworld.

"Antonio," she gasps as I rasp my tongue harder and faster over her slick flesh. I reach up, taking her tight little nipple between my thumb and forefinger and twist it just slightly. She groans, her grip in my short hair flaring painfully, then she spasms, her body collapsing with her orgasm until she slides down the wall into my lap.

I kiss her open mouth, tasting her whimpers and holding her to me like I'm drowning and she's the only chance of saving myself.

"Antonio," she whispers.

"It's okay," I tell her. "It's okay."

But even as I say the words, I know I'm a liar.

CHAPTER 11

AEMELIA

WASHED AWAY

Antonio Venturi, brutal killer, enforcer for his corrupt mafia family soaps my hair like my mother used to when I was a child. He washes me gently, touching my body in a tender methodical way that isn't meant to be erotic but feels that way anyway. Sitting on his soaked pants, his erection is obvious, but he doesn't push me to touch it. He doesn't even hint that he expects something from me in return for what he gave—pleasure so beautiful I now understand why the French call orgasms a tiny death. I watch him concentrate on soaping my feet, sliding his thick fingers between each of my toes like he doesn't want to leave even an inch of me unwashed, and I can't understand what's happening to me.

How is this man so different from my first assumptions?

He could force me to do anything, such is his strength, and I'd have no choice but to bend to his will, but instead, he pampers me, not like a captive but like a princess.

"I think I'm clean," I say.

He frowns. "There's one place I haven't washed."

He's right. He licked me there but left washing the place between my legs until last. The way his cheeks turn pink tells me he feels very different about this. "I'll leave you," he says, but I grip his arm.

"No," I whisper, holding my breath as I wait to see what he'll do next, letting my thigh's part enough for his hand. I tremble with anticipation, fascinated by his restraint as he goes still behind me. He hesitates; his breathing ragged. I close my eyes, waiting. His fingers are already soapy, so when they part my folds, skimming over my clit, it's smooth and easy, and I arch my back and hiss at the sensation.

Antonio is slow and tentative, touching me, washing me with reverent but thorough care, and my pussy clenches, craving more. He groans, the sound so pained, it makes me gasp, and then he eases me from his lap, pushing up quickly, his clothes so sodden they drop a rush of water. How is he going to get back to his room without drenching the place? I guess he isn't worried because he slicks his hand over his face and hair, grabs his shoes from the floor, and disappears through the bathroom door.

Confusion draws my brows together, and I shake my head. So, licking between my legs is okay, but washing me between them broke him? Antonio Venturi is a complex man, and it seems that I am a strange woman. Or mad. Only madness can explain my flip between rage and desire. Or maybe there's a closer relationship between the two emotions that I imagined.

I pull off my wet nightdress and wring it out before hanging it over the towel rail then I reach for a fluffy white towel. I wrap my hair and stare at myself in the mirror.

When Antonio forced me to look at myself, I hadn't recognized the woman he gripped by the throat, and now, my reflection is still unfamiliar. My cheeks are flushed, and my eyes are strangely bright. My body feels alive in a way it never has before.

One orgasm? Is that all it takes?

I see a ruthless killer worship at my feet, and I'm suddenly dragged into a deep thrall. His mouth was as soft as the down pillows in the bedroom, his tongue coaxing, searching out my pleasure like he held a map to the shortest path.

I shake my head and look away, following the wet trail he left with the floor mat hooked beneath my foot. The door isn't locked. It isn't even shut. Antonio dashed away so quickly that he forgot that he was supposed to secure his captive. In the hallway, everything is quiet. I glance to the left at the four black doors that hold other bedrooms inhabited by other men. I look right into the open-plan living area that seems empty. Where is everyone?

Fuck. Is this my chance to escape? I'm wearing a towel.

Just as I'm about to step back into my room, a rumbling, painful sound emanates from further down the corridor. At least, I think it sounds painful until I realize what else it might be. Antonio raced away with an erection that could obliterate the world. Did he...?

My face flushes hot at the mental image of him standing with his back against the door, dripping, while he palms his thick cock in rough strokes, thinking about what he just did to me. I shake away the picture, pick up the wet, wrinkled floor mat, and take it over to the hamper in the corner. I find clean panties and dress in a white lounge suit that's made of the softest luxury fabric, then I tiptoe out of the room. The sun is bright, even though the tall sliding doors to the balcony are tinted to prevent glare. I approach slowly, my damp bare feet sticking to the cool floor. I stare out at the expanse of the city where freedom resides.

I turn to find the front door and approach it slowly, craning my ear to listen. Voices carry from somewhere outside, probably Venturi soldiers. Escape was never anything but a fleeting hope. I'm a bird in a cage; one they do not want to release.

I test the handle for the balcony doors and find they slide

easily. Outside, the air is cool, but not unpleasant and I make my way to the edge, gripping onto the glass balustrade, staring down at the people below. Small as ants, they make their way past, oblivious to my plight. I'm Rapunzel without the hair to toss over the balcony or the prince waiting at the bottom to rescue me. I lean far over to try to work out where I am. The city isn't familiar to me, not after so many years. When I left, I was a child who didn't know much outside the walls of my own home.

Hands grasp my arms and haul me backward as I squeak in protest and whip my head around.

"What the fuck are you doing," Antonio growls. His face is twisted with anger. But he's panting like he's afraid. Did he think I was going to jump?

"What are you worried about, Antonio? Did you think I'd rather die than see you again?"

He holds me so close to his body that I can feel the rapid thud, thud, thud of his heart.

"Come inside."

He backs us up and closes the door, only releasing me when it's locked. His gray eyes are dark with gathered storm clouds, his mouth a grim line. He turns his attention to the kitchen, avoiding me. "You need to eat." He sounds just like my mother. What is it with Sicilians and their misplaced belief that food is a cure-all?

"Did my father come forward?" I ask.

He tuts and strides into the kitchen. I take it to mean no. No surprise there.

The sleek units stretch around a corner, revealing nothing of what's inside. He yanks open the door to a huge integrated refrigerator and stares inside. Just as he's about to reach for a tray of food, approaching voices make him pause. The front door flies open and serious Luca strides in, followed by a smiling Alexis, and the atmosphere immediately changes.

CHAPTER 12

LUCA

SHIFTED LOYALTIES

I stop in my tracks at the sight of Aemelia in the kitchen with Antonio. Something has shifted in the atmosphere in the penthouse. There's no tension. She leans toward him, her body language relaxed, and they seem comfortable together, like old friends passing the time rather than captor and captive. Aemelia's hair is damp, loose, and already beginning to curl at the ends, and Antonio's is also wet. My eyes narrow as I take in the details—his change of clothes, the way he stands closer than necessary, the way she glances at him before speaking.

"Why is she out here?" I ask, my tone sharp.

"To eat," Antonio replies simply, lifting the tray of food in his hands before placing it on the counter as if I'm an idiot for asking.

"She's not a guest," I remind him. "She's a—"

"Captive virgin?" Aemelia tips her head, her dark eyes sharp with challenge.

"Maybe," I say, my gaze sliding to my brother. "Or maybe not."

Antonio straightens. "Aemelia, go to your room," he orders. "I'll bring the food."

She opens her mouth to object, but at his raised brow and insistent glare, she reconsiders. Without another word, she turns and disappears down the hall, her clingy lounge suit hugging every curve like a second skin—a *masterpiece, still unsigned.*

When her door clicks shut, I approach my brother and lean in to speak in a hushed tone.

"I leave you for half a day."

"What?"

I inhale, catching the scent clinging to him—floral and sweet. Not his usual cologne. Aemelia's scent. My jaw ticks. "You smell like a whore's closet."

Antonio holds up his hands, his expression blank. "She wouldn't shower."

"So you took one with her?"

Alexis lets out a low whistle, shaking his head. "So I get the piss, and you get the shower. Nice."

I don't bother entertaining his jokes. "You fucked her?"

Antonio plants his scarred hands on the counter. "No."

I study him with my instincts tuned to every flicker of deception. He's telling the truth, but something isn't sitting right. "So, what? You washed her?"

He doesn't answer right away, his gaze fixed on the tray, the chicken and potatoes in the pan resting in bed together like husband and wife. "Yeah."

"And?"

His shoulders rise and fall, the movement tight. "*And* she tastes sweet."

Alexis whistles as the hair rises on the back of my neck. "You went down on her?"

Antonio scrubs a hand down his face, exhaling hard. "I lost my head."

"Damn right, you did. And what about you? What did

you make her do for you?"

"I didn't make her do anything. Fuck. She was crying, and then she wanted me to. And I handled myself."

Alexis folds his arms over his chest, eyes gleaming. "An unselfish lover. Good for you, Tonio. I didn't think there was a man in our world who would give pleasure to a woman without taking something for himself."

Antonio's nostrils flare. "It was a mistake."

I scoff, shaking my head. "The only mistake was letting yourself get attached."

Antonio turns his back on us, gripping the edge of the counter. "She's different."

I exchange a look with Alexis, and for once, my younger brother is as serious as I am. This is dangerous. Antonio never lets himself feel—not like this. He's a soldier, built for this life, trained to be cold and efficient. But now? Now he's looking at the girl like she's more than leverage.

Before I can say more, my phone buzzes. I glance at the screen and curse under my breath.

"What?" Alexis asks, already reading my expression instantly.

"Enzo," I say, shoving the phone into my pocket.

Antonio straightens, his entire posture shifting into his lethal stance. "Her uncle cares, but her father doesn't give a shit. Is he making a move?"

I shrug, pressing my lips into a serious line. "I doubt it, but maybe we should move her."

Alexis whistles low. "Where to?"

"A safe house. Small place on the outskirts of the city."

Antonio doesn't react right away. He looks past me, toward Aemelia's closed door. He knows what this means. Being a prisoner is easy here—luxury at her fingertips, space to breathe. The safe house will be different. Basic. Cramped. Mattresses on the floor, soldiers visible at the perimeter, no privacy. She'll be trapped with us in isolation.

Antonio's jaw flexes, but he nods. "It's an option. Let me talk to Enzo... see where his head is at."

"Okay, but take some of your crew. I've got a bad feeling about him."

I rub my jaw and head over to the liquor cabinet to pour myself some whiskey. We always knew this plan was going to bring rats out of their tunnels.

Aemelia cannot be our weakness. But as I watch Antonio turn away from me for the first time, I'm not entirely sure where his loyalties lie.

CHAPTER 13

ANTONIO

CUTS LIKE A KNIFE

When Luca needs something done, I am his go-to person. We need intel, and so I work my contacts, visiting places around the city where business is done.

At Emilio's Pork Store, the butcher's shop frequented by many families, the scent of raw meat mingles with the iron tang of blood. The saw hums as a man in a stained apron carves through bone with practiced ease. The place is dimly lit, a single overhead bulb flickering slightly, casting shadows that stretch unnaturally along the walls.

My men step inside, the bell jingling above the door to announce our arrival. Vito's first, with his fearsome face, followed by Andre who scopes the place, his hand on his weapon. Gabe Ferrano sticks close to me while they size up who's inside—only one elderly customer who's selecting two pork chops. Gabe's twin, Matteo, follows me, keeping watch for an ambush. We can't leave anything to chance. Outside, four of Alexis' men wait in cars, ready to step in if we need them.

Carlo's brother, Enzo, is waiting for me in the back, standing near a counter where fresh cuts are laid out like pagan offerings. He's older than Carlo, shorter, thicker in the waist maybe—who the fuck knows after all these years—but just as sharp-eyed. As a *made man* of the Mesina family, he's protected and wealthy enough that he doesn't need to take a hands-on role at the store his father founded, but he does because he enjoys carving up the dead. He wipes his hands on a rag, his mouth twisting into something like a smirk. His salt-and-pepper hair is slicked back, a deep scar cutting through one forearm which wasn't earned in the butcher's shop but on the streets. He doesn't look nervous, but I catch the way his fingers flex around the handle of his knife.

"Antonio Venturi," he says, his voice gravelly, thick with the weight of years in this business, smoking and drinking too much. "What brings you here? Buying or threatening?"

I lean against the counter, crossing my arms. The gun tucked in the back of my pants, hidden by my close-fitting black jacket, presses into my flesh. "That depends on what you have to say."

He chuckles, but there's no humor in it. "Ah, so you came for talk, not steak."

"Carlo's still hiding. The coward won't come out, even for his own daughter. I thought family meant something to you people."

Enzo shakes his head slowly, slicing through a thick cut of beef with a heavy knife. The blade glides through effortlessly, severing the muscle with a wet, slick sound. "You think Carlo doesn't value family?" His chuckle sets the hair rising on my arms. "You think you can click your fingers and everyone will come running?" Enzo sets the knife down, wiping his hands again, this time more slowly, as if savoring the moment before dropping a bomb. "Of course you do because that's how Venturis think. It's how you've always thought."

I frown, confused. We're a powerful family but Luca isn't an arrogant man. He doesn't throw his weight around. He treats every negotiation with respect for the other party. That doesn't mean to say that he doesn't enjoy the power he has, but Enzo is misrepresenting him. I'm about to disagree when he continues.

"There's a lot you don't know, Venturi. Carlo's wife wasn't faithful. She had a thing for your brother, even before she got married, and that one…" He waves his hand dismissively. "He never respected the sacred matrimonial vows. He always just took what he wanted."

"My brother?" A beat of silence stretches between us, thick and suffocating.

"Mario… it wasn't some one-night thing. It was a goddamn affair. He didn't even have the decency to hide it. He was arrogant, taking the one thing Carlo had achieved that was better than him. Carlo's prize. You think Carlo betrayed Mario, but it was the other way around."

My jaw tightens, my mind running fifty feet ahead while I struggle to pull it back. All of this is new news to me, and the implications—

"You're telling me Mario was having an affair with Carmella Lambretti?"

Enzo shrugs, the picture of innocence. "What does it matter now? That woman is old and ugly, and Carlo is gone. Your brother is dead. This is history."

"History you're resurrecting."

Could it be true, and if it is, I wonder what else we're in the dark about? Who knew and didn't say anything? Maybe our crew? They have their ears to the ground, but when Mario was murdered, telling us it wouldn't have been easy. I pull my arm from the counter, letting it hang by my side, schooling my body to remain unbothered by his words.

He lifts his hands, a picture of mock innocence. "There were rumors, Antonio. Rumors that Aemelia wasn't Carlo's child, you know, because Carmella wasn't faithful." He smiles a shark smile, and a wave of sickness rises up inside me like a tidal wave, obliterating my grip on control. I reach out to hold onto the glass cabinet, staring at row after row of bloody meat cuts. The scent that invades my nostrils only makes the nausea worse because he's trying to tell me there were rumors that Aemelia was Mario's daughter without saying the words.

He's wrong.

It can't be true.

There's no way. But even as I tell myself that Enzo is lying, I feel sick.

I think about Aemelia's dark brown eyes, exactly like Carlo's. As much as I despise it, I see him in her; the set of her jaw, something in her smile, and the shape of her hands.

He's lying about it all, twisting the knife in his hands without ever piercing my flesh.

Enzo watches me closely, measuring my reaction like a butcher deciding where to slice a fresh carcass. "So what now, Venturi?" He leans in slightly, his voice quieter, more dangerous. "You keeping her locked up, playing your little games? Doesn't look so good, does it? Buying her virginity at auction. Whether the rumors are true or not, you can't keep her."

I took Mario's death personally and carried the grief and rage for years, believing it was a power play from our enemies. But this—this would mean something far worse. It would mean a betrayal deeper than business. Deeper than money or power. It would mean Mario's transgressions were to blame for his assassination.

She can't be family. I know she can't be. But even so, my stomach roils.

I should never have touched her. She's innocent and sweet. She deserves so much more than me.

I meet his gaze, reading between the lines. He's not in a position to threaten me directly, not here, not yet, but his meaning is clear. If we hold onto Aemelia, this thing spirals out of our control. There will be talk. There will be questions. Whispers will turn to certainty. Who will believe us?

I push off the counter, my stomach tight with disgust, uncertainty, guilt. I think of Aemelia, of the way she looked at me with those dark eyes, trusting and defiant all at once. We've crossed a line we can't uncross.

Enzo tilts his head, his smirk widening. "You look rattled, Venturi. That's rare."

I don't respond. There's nothing to say. He doesn't know how far we've gone.

I turn on my heel and head for the door, my mind racing, flanked by Gabe and Matteo who heard everything. I need to get back to the house. I need to talk to my brothers and then approach the one person who might be able to clear this up.

Aemelia's mother.

Because if what Enzo is saying is true, that Aemelia isn't Carlo's daughter, then our plan to bring him out of hiding is useless.

Regardless, the shame I feel at taking from her what I never should have wanted has left me shaking.

She can't be Mario's.

Can she?

CHAPTER 14

LUCA

THE SICKNESS OF REVENGE

"What is it?" I hiss as Antonio storms into the penthouse, his steps uneven, his breathing ragged. He bends over the sink and spits, his body convulsing as though he's about to throw up. "Are you sick? Did you eat something bad?"

He wipes his mouth with the back of his hand, his chest rising and falling in erratic bursts. When he looks up at me, his gray eyes are wild, unfocused, and glazed.

"Tell me," I order, losing patience.

"I spoke to Enzo," he rasps, his voice stripped raw. "He says Carlo isn't coming."

My spine stiffens. "How does he know?"

Antonio swallows hard, his throat working, but he doesn't look at me. "He says Aemelia isn't Carlo's child. That he doesn't give a fuck about her. Never did."

I run both hands through my hair and turn, pacing a few steps away from my brother, needing some space from the suffocating weight of his words. My gut twists, instincts screaming at me that there's more. The stench of panic hangs around him like a deadly poisoned fog.

"And this made you want to throw up?" I turn to Antonio, narrowing my eyes.

"He said Mario had an affair with Carmella Lambretti." Antonio's voice cracks, his fingers digging into his temples as though he is trying to claw out the truth. "And Carlo killed him because of that. Mario was the one who betrayed Carlo, not the other way around."

"No." The word shoots from my mouth like a bullet, immediate and resolute. "That isn't true."

Alexis, who's been watching everything from the couch, stands and approaches. "I'd have agreed with you, except Mama hinted something about it the last time I was there."

"She did?" Antonio's voice is as strangled as it would be if I had my hands around his throat.

Could it be true? Mario had a wandering eye and an insatiable appetite for the carnal, but Carlo's wife? That would be another level of recklessness. Women come and go, but wives and family members, they're not to be trifled with. And yet, the weight in his eyes hints at something even worse.

And then it clicks.

A cold wave of realization slams into me, knocking the air from my lungs. "Carlo didn't believe Aemelia was his because..."

Antonio doesn't speak. He just shakes his head, staring at the ground like he wishes it would open into a grave and swallow him. My heart thuds unnaturally hard as I draw together the courage to ask what he cannot bring himself to volunteer.

"Who's child is she?"

"Carlo's," he says, wiping his mouth with the back of his hand. "She has to be. She looks like her mother, but she carries some of that cocksuckers traits. The eyes, her smile. But Enzo said that Carlo believed her to be Mario's daughter."

The silence stretches between us, thick and choking. The ground beneath me feels unsteady."

"We need to find out for sure," I say. "What Carlo believes and what is true could very different. She has nothing of Mario in her appearance. And there's no way Mario would have kept something like that from me. He wouldn't have left his child for Carlo to raise. He'd have claimed her while he was still alive."

"Exactly," Alexis says.

I straighten, forcing down the storm brewing in my chest. I'm the boss. It's my job to act, to keep a clear head when everyone else is unraveling.

"Get your keys," I tell him. "You and Antonio are going to Carmella Lambretti's house. You're going to get the truth from her, one way or another."

Antonio's expression hardens, a deadly edge creeping into his voice. "We'll make her talk."

"We need to know the truth."

They both nod. My eyes drift to Aemelia's room. "While you're gone, I'm going to call Dr. Rothberg. He'll be able to fast track a DNA test."

"So we know for sure."

"Exactly."

CHAPTER 15

ALEXIS

A MOTHERS TRUTH

I don't even have a chance to pull the belt across my body before Antonio accelerates from the parking garage, the dark Mercedes SUV leaving a cloud of dust and exhaust fumes in its wake.

"What the fuck?" I say, staring at my grim-faced brother. Antonio is usually serious, but today, he looks like he's facing the grim reaper.

"Don't make me talk about it, Alexis. Please."

The *please* guts me.

We're going to Carmella Lambretti's sister's apartment to ask her if what Enzo said is true. Did Carlo believe she was someone else's child? Who is Aemelia's father? Antonio barely ever says please. I didn't think it was within his vocabulary.

"Do you need me to drive?" I ask, worried his mind is elsewhere.

"No." He lets out a ragged-sounding breath. "I don't

want to think."

"Look," I say, smoothing my hands down my thighs. "What happened with Aemelia…"

I stop as he makes a desperate sound in his throat.

"We shouldn't…" He stops abruptly, the rest of the sentence becoming a gasp that he traps in his mouth. "Just put the damned radio on."

"If she was Mario's, we'd know," I say. "We'd see it in her. We'd recognize her."

He nods, but there's still a fraction of doubt in his mind and that's all it takes to drive him crazy.

We drive across town in silence. The gun cradled beneath my jacket is as warm as my body, ready for anything, but from the tension in the car, it'll be Antonio who leads this discussion. When we pull up outside the dilapidated apartment block, we both peer up. So this is where Aemelia was staying. This place is a shit hole no one should live in, but certainly not a woman like Aemelia. She deserves so much more; designer clothes, jewelry, cosmetics, the best that can be bought.

"Second floor," he says, throwing the door open without looking around. Nothing like my cautious, suspicious brother.

I follow with my hand under my jacket, ready because if Antonio isn't on his game, someone has to be.

We step into the building, the stench of mildew and cheap liquor clinging to the peeling walls. The hallway is dimly lit, a single flickering bulb casting long, eerie shadows. The elevator is out of service—no surprise—so we take the stairs, footsteps echoing with every step.

When we reach the second floor, Antonio raps his knuckles hard against a door marked with deep scratches, the number barely hanging onto the wood. A shuffle sounds from inside, followed by the slow, deliberate slide of a chain lock.

The door cracks open an inch, and a thin, gaunt face peers out. A woman—mid-forties, maybe older, but life has taken its toll. Carmella Lambretti.

Her eyes widen when she sees Antonio. "Venturi," she breathes, voice rough from years of smoking.

"Open the door, Carmella."

She hesitates, but the dark intensity in Antonio's expression and the roughness of his voice makes her obey. If she didn't, he'd have kicked it in without breaking a sweat. The door swings inward, revealing a cramped, rundown apartment. The place reeks of stale smoke, sweat, and desperation.

A man slouches on the stained couch, his shirt wrinkled and speckled with old food. Aemelia's brother? His glazed eyes flick toward us, then mist over. Strung out on something. Useless.

In the corner, an older woman sits in a recliner, wrapped in a blanket that looks as threadbare as she does. Her skin is gray, and her breath is wheezy. The smell of sickness clings to her like rot. Aemelia's aunt Christina—if she's even still alive.

Antonio looks around, scanning the terrible surroundings. If his heart isn't breaking for Aemelia, he doesn't have one anymore.

"What do you want?" Carmella says, her hand pressed to her throat. "Is Aemelia okay?"

"She's okay," I answer, giving Antonio a chance to formulate his scattered thoughts. He's still gray as old water, his hands fisted at his sides, not with violent intent but like he's braced to hold himself together.

"Then what?"

"Did you have an affair with Mario?"

The question slices through the room like a gunshot. Even I jolt, my spine snapping straight.

Carmella stiffens and coughs, clasping her thin hand over her mouth. "What kind of question—"

Antonio steps forward, his presence swallowing the tiny space, making her recoil. "Don't lie to me."

Her eyes dart toward Aemelia's brother, then back to

Antonio. She must decide that CJ will be no help against Antonio. I want to laugh that she even considered him an option. "I—"

"Carmella." Antonio's tone is ice and her name grounds out through gritted teeth. "Tell me the truth."

She swallows hard, her hands wringing together. She was a beautiful woman once. I remember thinking Carlo was a lucky man. She had all of Aemelia's beauty and a laugh that could have made angels jealous. I study what life has done to her. Fifteen years have taken the toll of thirty. This is what will happen to Aemelia unless...

"It was a long time ago."

A sharp exhale leaves Antonio's lips, but he presses on, voice even but laced with lethal intensity. "Is Aemelia Mario's child?"

Carmella flinches. Her silence stretches, long and weighted. She's considering her options, weighing what she can gain, what she can lose. If she says no, what will that mean for Aemelia? If she says yes, would we release her, or want to keep her?

What would that make her? Our niece? I shudder, thinking of all the filthy thoughts I've had about her. What my brothers have done. No wonder Antonio looks like he wants to tear out of his own skin.

Antonio leans in, his body vibrating with menace. "We're getting a DNA test," he warns, his voice sharp enough to cut. "If you lie, we'll know."

Carmella's gaze drops to the floor, and for a moment, she looks like she might crumble. She pulls her pink floral blouse closer to her throat and takes a step back, trying to put distance between her and my brother, but he only seems to expand into the space. But then she inhales, straightens her spine, and meets Antonio's glare with a deadened expression.

"No," she says. "Aemelia isn't Mario's child."

The breath I was holding rushes out of me, but the nausea still lingers. Antonio stays motionless for a long moment, his jaw flexing, his hands tightening into fists.

"What difference does it make?" Carmella asks, studying us both. Too many of our emotions rest plainly on our faces.

"If she's Mario's," I say, the words like shards of glass in my mouth, "then she's family."

Carmella's face twists, the yellow of her skin flushing pink across her cheekbones. "She's my family, and Carlo's, though he was always too stupid to realize it. He didn't deserve her. Didn't deserve CJ, either. Didn't deserve me."

Sadness rolls off her. One bad choice led to a hard life. I stare at her son and the waste of life he's become.

This isn't what I want for Aemelia. Letting her go to return to this family is not an option.

No matter how much Carlo wanted to believe otherwise, no matter how much damage his paranoia caused, Aemelia was never Mario's. But it doesn't change the fact that we took her. Or that Carlo Lambretti isn't going to play our game.

"Where is he?" I ask. "Where's your deadbeat husband?"

She shakes her head. "If I knew, I would have sold that information to you after Mario—" Her breath hitches and tears well in her yellow eyes. She fumbles in the pocket of her beige slacks and pulls out a packet of cigarettes. Her hands tremble too much to take one from the packet, so I reach out to help her.

"All we want is an eye for an eye," Antonio says.

The woman on the recliner laughs and wheezes. "An eye for an eye. You hoods reading the Bible these days? Don't you know it also says thou shalt not steal, thou shalt not kill, thou shalt not commit adultery?"

"Chrissy, don't." Carmella moves towards her sister, who coughs like two sentences were enough to permanently steal her breath.

"They need to hear it, and what do I care if they don't like it. What are they going to do? Kill me?" She laughs again, her watery eyes dancing. "Your brother was happy to stick his dick where he had no business, and Carlo wanted revenge for the disrespect. Now you want revenge for revenge. Where does it end?"

"We're talking about a cold-blooded assassination," Antonio says, although it sounds to me like he's trying to convince himself more than the two terrified women and half a man that are his audience.

"Look to your own heart, Antonio Venturi. Look at your own hands. Let he who is without sin, cast the first stone."

My brother steps back like he's been slapped. For all my mama's religious aspirations, we haven't been to church for years.

"Let my daughter go," Carmella says.

"You started this." Antonio's voice is nothing but a hiss. "You and Mario started this. There is only one way to end it."

"No." The word is barely a wheeze from the mouth of a dying woman. "There are many ways to fix a problem. You just never learned how to choose the right one."

"Come on," I tell him, wary that this will descend into a deeper argument. All I want to do is get back to the penthouse and tell Luca that he doesn't have to be sick over what he did with Aemelia.

And then, we have to figure out what the fuck we do next.

***

When we climb back into the SUV, Antonio starts the engine but remains stationary, his hands throttling the steering wheel.

"You okay?" I ask.

"I knew," he says. "I knew she wasn't but…" He hangs his head, and I feel his despair and relief deep in my bones.

"I know," I say.

"If she was…"

"Don't." What the fuck is the point of going over that sick scenario? We have better things to do like find a place to eat before my stomach devours my insides and tell our brother that Aemelia is Carlo's spawn who he doesn't give two flying fucks about.

"Do you think Luca will let her go?" he asks, turning to face me.

I rub my jaw, uncertain of a lot of things. Why does Antonio look like the thought of releasing Aemelia is going to rip his heart through his mouth? Will Luca want to push harder to get someone in that fucking Lambretti family to break about Carlo's location? How do I feel about Aemelia staying with us for longer, or leaving today?

I don't want her to leave.

"I don't know."

"You like her?" he asks, his breathing harsh. Would it be so hard for him to hear, yes? Does he have actual feelings for the girl outside a desire to get inside her and break open the thing we paid for?

"She's..." I pause to find the right word. Sexy. Gorgeous. Funny. Strong. Determined. Brave. "Intriguing."

"And Luca?"

"Who the fuck knows what Luca wants."

My words make his middle tighten, like I kicked him in the gut.

"We should let her go," he says. "We're no good for her. We're too old. Too fucked up. Too tangled up in this shit."

"And let her return to this? It's like the Addams Family in there. Fuck." I laugh, unable to hold it in, and Antonio snorts and then fixes his mouth into a grim line.

"It's bad," he says.

"So, we keep her?"

He shakes his head, but I can tell he wants to agree with me. He's torn between doing the right things and doing what he wants, and it's not a place either of us are that familiar with.

"For a while."

For a while.

***

We don't go back empty-handed. If we're keeping Aemelia, even for a little while, she should have some creature comforts. We stop at a local trattoria and load up—fresh bread, meats, cheeses, olives, and a selection of pastries, including a box of cannoli and some sweets and chocolates. The scents of roasted garlic and freshly baked focaccia cling to our clothes as we step back onto the street.

We pass a small boutique, and Antonio lingers in front of the display. "Stay here," he says.

I hang by the open door and watch as he picks up a thick, plush robe, running his fingers over the fabric like he's trying to convince himself she needs it. He doesn't say a word; he just pays in cash and walks out with the bag. I don't press him. His actions speak loud enough.

By the time we get back to the penthouse, the sun has dipped below the horizon, casting long shadows over the tall building. Luca is waiting for us on the balcony, his arms crossed, face unreadable. The cool night air is thick with the scent of the city, mixing with the faint aroma of espresso from inside the house.

"Well?" he asks the moment we step through the doors.

Antonio grips the bag in one hand, tension radiating from him where there should be relief. "She's not Mario's."

Luca exhales, long and slow. He nods once, absorbing the words. "The doctor will confirm for certain, but I knew Enzo was lying. And Carlo?"

"Doesn't give a shit, according to Carmella."

"Never did," Antonio adds. "Enzo was right about that."

Luca's lips press into a thin line. "They could both be lying. Think about it. Enzo plants the seed of doubt about her parentage. Carmella plants the doubt about Carlo's love. They're trying to make us think it's pointless to keep Aemelia. Pointless to try. The one person we haven't heard from is Carlo. He's the only one who knows the truth."

"You think that rat has any humanity in him? He gunned down Mario like a fucking dog."

Luca shrugs. "I don't know.

"We should give it time," Antonio says, like we agreed in the car, his voice low. "Make sure Enzo isn't bluffing about his brother. If Carlo isn't coming, we need to decide what we do next."

Luca nods slowly. "And Aemelia?"

A moment of silence stretches between us, heavy with unspoken desires.

"We don't let her go back to that," Antonio finally says, his tone firm, resolute. "Not yet."

Luca studies him, then me. "Not yet," he agrees.

CHAPTER 16

ANTONIO

ESCALATION

Aemelia is still sleeping, curled on her side in her massive bed. It's so white she almost looks like she's resting on a cloud. Her breathing is soft, her face relaxed in a way that it never is when she's awake. The tension that usually lingers in her dark eyes is gone, the fear of her nightmare in the past. I watch her from the doorway, my arms crossed as I exhale slowly. She's too trusting now. Too comfortable. That thought sits uneasily in my gut.

I head into the kitchen to make espresso, which will give me a welcome hit of caffeine. I hardly slept last night, my mind twisting over the panic I felt at the thought that Aemelia could be Mario's daughter, the sickness. I've done a lot of terrible, unforgivable things in my life, but that would have been the worst. And now we know she's Carlo's, I don't feel any better about what I did. The guilt hangs around me like a black cloud. My feelings of attraction toward her, lust for her, feel forbidden and sinful.

Luca's already up, studying something on his laptop. He likes to keep on top of the news and how world events or changes in government policy will affect our assets and interests.

"Where's Alexis," I ask.

"Sleeping."

"You want coffee."

"Sure."

He turns his attention back to his screen as I manhandle the coffee machine.

A knock on the penthouse door breaks the silence, and I turn sharply, my body instantly on edge. Luca looks up, questioning, as I move toward the door.

Vito is standing there when I pull it open, his large frame filling the doorway. But it's not him that makes my pulse spike. It's what he's holding.

A bouquet of flowers.

Blood red roses, delicate and fresh, wrapped in crisp white paper with a silky ribbon tied in a perfect bow. An expensive arrangement, no doubt, but the sight of it makes my stomach twist.

I don't move to take it. "Where did it come from?"

"Delivery," Vito says, his tone wary. He holds the flowers out, but his eyes flick between me and Luca, reading the tension radiating from both of us. "A guy downstairs handed them off. Said they were for Aemelia."

Luca stands slowly. "What guy?"

"Delivery guy." Vito shrugs and Luca's posture tightens.

"Did you get a look at a badge or uniform?"

Vito frowns, glancing down at the bouquet like he's just realized how fucked up the situation is. "I thought you ordered them for the girl." He tips his head in the direction of Aemelia's room.

"The van?"

"It was white with tinted windows. Unmarked."

I curse under my breath. "You didn't think to check before bringing them up here?"

Vito tenses, his face darkening. "We checked the flowers."

I grab the bouquet from him, my fingers closing around the delicate stems as I rip through the soft petals and glossy wrapping. Something small and metallic clinks against the marble floor.

Luca bends down, picking it up between two fingers and turning it toward the light.

A single bullet.

I lean closer, studying it. "Look at the side."

Luca flips it in his palm, and my blood turns to ice.

Aemelia.

Her name is carved into the brass casing, neat and precise, like it was made just for her.

"Fuck." I exhale, barely resisting the urge to crush the bouquet in my hands. My fingers dig into the ribbon still attached, something small and stiff tucked inside the folds of the bow. A card.

I pull it free and flip it open.

One letter.

C.

We stare at the initial in heavy silence.

Luca is the first to move, turning back to Vito with a look that could burn through steel. "Find out who delivered them. Check every florist in the city, Vito. Don't make me wait for an answer."

Vito straightens under Luca's glare, his jaw tight. He nods, but Luca isn't finished. His voice is low, lethal. "And find the guy who delivered them."

Vito turns on his heel and strides out, already pulling out his phone. I toss the shredded bouquet onto the kitchen counter, the soft petals spilling across the surface like blood.

"Her own father wants to kill her?" Luca mutters, his voice high with disbelief.

I grit my teeth, looking down at the bullet in Luca's palm. The message is clear. Someone wants her to be afraid. Or maybe for us to believe there's a threat.

"We don't know it's him," I say.

"It's him," he says. "I don't like any of this."

"We'll find out where they came from."

"Maybe." He returns to sit in front of his laptop. "Or maybe we need to move her now."

CHAPTER 17

ALEXIS

NOT THE PLAZA

This isn't the first time we've been confined to a safehouse, but it's the first time we've had a woman with us. As a rule, families—the women and children—are kept out of business. To break that rule would be the end of this world. Everything would burn. We have rules for a reason. Even chaos requires order to contain it. But with one bullet concealed inside a beautiful bouquet, Aemelia has become the focus of this vendetta, not the pawn. We left the penthouse via secret passages with only our most trusted men, Aemelia sheltered between us.

She doesn't fit into this basic environment. Not anymore. Not now that we've dressed her in designer clothes, adorned her like the mafia princess she is, even if she doesn't realize it yet.

Fuck.

She's exquisite, like a swan gliding through the filth of the world with her head held high.

She tastes sweet.

My brother's words ring through my head like a damn gong, over and over. And every time I remember, my mouth floods with saliva. How did he get her to open for him so easily, spreading those pretty legs like butter over warm toast? When I tried, she looked at me like she wanted to carve me up with a rusty blade. If looks could kill, she'd have liquified me in a fucking second.

I drag a hand through my hair, pushing the messy curls back as I follow her into the house, my eyes locked to her perfect ass. The place reeks of dust and stale air, motes spinning in the bright shafts of light that slip through the ratty curtains. This house is a relic, barely livable, a place we retreat to only when we need to disappear. It's in desperate need of a woman's touch—anyone's touch—to make it habitable.

Aemelia looks around, her chin high as always, her expression surprised, then she turns to me. "Here? This is where we're going to stay?"

"The Plaza was fully booked."

She rolls her eyes. "Is there a vacuum at least? I've never seen dust so thick."

"Are you offering to clean up for us?"

"I'm offering to help. We'll get allergies."

Luca and Antonio enter through the back door, carrying bags. They're followed by four men from Antonio's crew. The older two look unfazed, having been through this before. The younger ones? Much less excited to go to the mattresses.

Antonio seems unable to keep the grim expression from darkening his features, even though Luca encouraged us to keep things light. We don't want to scare Aemelia by telling her of this outside threat. She has enough to deal with worrying about the threat we pose to her.

She's still our prisoner, after all.

One thing is certain—Aemelia won't have her own room. I smile, already foreseeing her reaction and the chance it will give me to get closer to her.

"Let's see," I say, gesturing to the stairs. "Go up."

She moves past me, her hips swaying slightly. I'm not used to going this long without pussy, so my body is hungry. But that's not the only reason I'm fixated on her. Aemelia has the rare ability to surprise me, and I like it more than I should.

Upstairs, the situation isn't much better. The mattresses are old and bare and have seen better days. She wrinkles her nose. "We have sheets, right?"

"Of course."

I dump the bags on a mattress and toss my jacket on top. Aemelia drifts toward the window, but I block her way before she gets too close. "Stay away from the windows, *gattina*." Her eyes dart to me, then back to filthy glass. "You don't know who's out there."

She presses her hand to the hollow of her throat before dropping it. "We better get cleaning."

Downstairs, the house hums with activity. Antonio has his sleeves pushed up, ready to unpack the bags of food lined up on the counter. At least with him around, we won't starve while we're holed up in this dump. I start rummaging through cabinets for anything resembling cleaning supplies and discover an old dustpan and brush, a few ratty cloths, and a vacuum that looks like it belongs in a museum.

Aemelia, dressed in black leggings and a fitted sweater, glances down at her expensive attire. "I'd change if I had anything older and less expensive to wear."

"Don't worry. Clothes aren't an issue if money isn't an issue."

She nods, and I consider that this might be the first time she hasn't had to worry about where the next outfit or meal is coming from. A girl like Aemelia should never have to serve others.

She twists her long, glossy hair into a neat bun, securing it with a band from her wrist. Then she takes a cloth and starts cleaning. There isn't much furniture, but once she's wiped those surfaces down, she crouches to tackle the baseboards, and I catch every man in the place staring at her ass.

Luca, who's probably never lifted a finger for housework in his life, eyes the vacuum like it's a foreign object. "How do you get this thing working?"

I smirk. Has Aemelia Lambretti achieved the impossible and domesticated the boss of this family? Is that how much he wants to get in her cunt?

Man, this is fucked up. Antonio's already licked his way to half a claim on her body, but what does that matter? We're not proposing marriage here. Best-case scenario, Carlo comes back, and we set Aemelia free. She leaves, and we all go about our business. Worst case? We're forced to do something none of us wants to do.

Her virginity is still a bargaining chip. We cannot take it from her without losing leverage. But there are many other things we can take. Many places on her body to taste.

"Plug it in," I tell Luca, watching as he awkwardly fumbles with the cord. The vacuum roars to life, belching out a cloud of dust before revealing a clean streak on the floor beneath it. Luca nods, satisfied, and keeps going as I stifle my laughter.

I meet Antonio's confused eyes, and we both shake our heads. Thank fuck the men are outside, watching for threats instead of witnessing this circus.

I use the brush to sweep the stairs, and the scent of frying onion and garlic fills the air as Antonio makes something to satisfy our bellies. The first time we went into hiding was after pop died when Mario's grip on the family wasn't strong enough, and other families were circling like vultures. I remember him lying next to me, hands behind his head, telling me that going to the mattresses was a tradition. A chance for men to be men.

If he could see us now, he'd turn in his grave.

The ache of missing him never fades. The memory of his blank face staring up from the floor of Carlo's club, his blue eyes fixed to the ceiling, glassy and dead, will never leave me. The sound of Antonio's cry and Luca's wounded gasps for breath still come to me as fresh as if it happened yesterday. Worse, the pounding blood in my ears and my own harsh breaths as my heart felt like it had been skewered.

Aemelia follows behind me, wiping the fine layer of dust I leave behind. "I bet you never thought you'd be cleaning with the Venturis," I tease, flashing her a smirk.

"Why does that sound like a Netflix show?"

I laugh. "Would you watch it?"

"There's a lot of money to be made in shirtless cleaning," she says. "Just saying."

I chuckle and shake my head. "You're funny," I tell her, then, just to push her buttons a little, I add, "Since my brother made you come."

I expect her to blush, to get flustered, but she just seems amused, and my dick perks up in response. "He has a clever tongue, but not that clever. My humor is my own."

"You ready to come to bed with me?"

She frowns at my quick shift in the conversation, flushing a little at my bravado.

"To put sheets on those old mattresses."

Biting back another smile, she brushes past me on the stairs. "Now there's a proposition I can get behind."

***

Antonio takes food out to the men guarding the house, ensuring they take turns to eat. The cool night air blows in through the backdoor, but the men barely seem to notice, exchanging a few quiet words before he heads back inside, his hands shoved deep into his pockets, braced under the weight of the night's tension.

Inside, Luca washes the dust from his hands at the kitchen sink, his sharp blue eyes scanning the room. It's still a shithole, but it's as clean as we can make it. He even vacuumed the twenty-year-old couches, an effort that hasn't gone unnoticed.

Aemelia, who seems to have worked up an appetite from cleaning, doesn't hold back as she digs into her plate. "Oh my god. So good." she groans.

"He learned it all from our mama," I tell her. "She's old school."

"Shouldn't this have been passed to Rosita?" she asks.

"Our grandfather was a chef," Antonio explains. "Mama sees cooking as a life skill."

"So Luca and Alexis can cook like this, too?"

Antonio pauses serving the food to smirk. "They can cook, but not like this."

She licks her lips. "You promised me the recipe," she says.

Luca tuts, shaking his head in mock disappointment. "I didn't know Antonio was so easy with our family secrets. What else has he told you?"

His tone is teasing, but there's an underlying edge to it—smooth as silk but sharp enough to cut. He's watching her closely, his expression unreadable. He's worried. Worried that Aemelia is burrowing under Antonio's skin in a way none of us anticipated. Worried she'll find a weak spot and take advantage.

She tilts her head, cat-like, a knowing little smile curving her lips. "That's for me to know."

There's a beat of strained silence as Antonio and Luca exchange an intense look. The way Antonio squares his shoulders just slightly and Luca presses his lips together for the briefest second before taking another bite, tells a story.

In the end, Luca leans back in his chair, draping an arm over its back. "A recipe has to be earned, *gattina*. How do you propose to earn it?"

Her gaze flits between us, her fingers toying with the stem of her fork. Maybe Luca didn't realize how his words would sound, or maybe he did. He enjoys playing with people, leading them through a maze when a straight line would do. She arches a brow. "The cleaning wasn't enough."

He shakes his head slowly. "Cleaning's a good start, but maybe *you* should tell us some secrets."

She shrugs; an infuriatingly slow, elegant movement. "Any secrets I have about this life are for women's ears only."

"So, there are secrets?"

She tips her chin and smiles slowly. "Men think their indiscretions are private, but women have eyes everywhere."

Antonio leans forward, intrigued. "Who's being indiscreet?"

She rests her hands in her lap, her expression almost innocent. "Mesina has another family. Did you know that? An African American *goomar*."

"Alfonso?" I ask.

She nods, her eyes calculated.

Luca stills, his fork poised midair. "He does?"

"They have three kids."

Antonio barks out a laugh. "How did you hear about that?"

"My aunt is dying. People tell her things thinking she'll take them to the grave."

"Motherfucker." Luca wipes his mouth on a napkin and drops it onto the counter. "What else?" His voice is calm, but there's a tightness around his jaw that I wouldn't trust if I was Aemelia.

Oblivious, she smiles and picks up her fork again, taking a slow, deliberate bite. He watches her, waiting, expecting more. When she's done chewing, she smiles slyly. "What? You wanted me to earn the recipe. A secret for a secret."

"Quid pro quo," I laugh, enchanted.

She points at me with finger guns. "Exactly."

Luca exhales, dragging a hand down his face. "I think this girl wants my hand on her ass again." He raised his right hand, mimicking the kind of slap our mother used to give us when we misbehaved as kids.

Antonio, who usually looks somber at best and

miserable at worst, has a glint in his eye, a smirk playing on his lips. In this dilapidated house, we seem far from our world of power and threat. The bullet with Aemelia's name was left back at the penthouse, along with our restraint. Aemelia has a way of making me forget who I am, who she is, and why we're doing this dance. She makes me want to do another kind of dance, and my brothers are acting like they feel the same. I don't remember the last time my brothers were this lighthearted. It's like something that was rusted shut inside them has been forced open and greased.

Aemelia lifts her chin, a picture of defiance. "A spanking has to be earned, Luca Venturi."

The sparks between them are electric, the air charged, and my laugh is loud enough to wake the dead.

Going to the mattresses is supposed to be about men being men, but with Aemelia here, something very different seems to be happening.

CHAPTER 18

AEMELIA

PLAYING THE GAME

Secrets. They shimmer like rare gems, delicate and dangerous, meant to be hoarded and protected. I carry so many inside me, each one as fragile as a Fabergé egg, each one a risk waiting to crack.

And the Venturis? They have their own.

Something has shifted. It changed the moment Antonio's hands were on me, his mouth, his whispered confessions. It changed with my acceptance of my position and my choice to take a different approach. These men are used to violent resistance. They're not used to subtlety.

I stand beside Alexis at the sink, scrubbing the dishes as he dries, our movements easy and practiced. Across the room, Antonio and Luca converse in hushed tones in the dimly lit den, their words clipped and heavy sounding. Shadows stretch over them, and I listen without looking, focusing instead on the warmth of the water against my skin, considering what will happen to me as the days slip by. I need to be careful. Every moment here is borrowed time, and borrowed time runs out.

My father won't return for me of his own free will. I know it deep in my bones. The Venturis, for all their cruelty, still live by an honor code. Carlo Lambretti has no honor. He left us with nothing. Less than nothing. His betrayal turned our name to filth, and his absence made us prey. We clung to the foolish hope that time would erase his sins, but we were naive. He never cared when he left, and he won't risk his life for mine now.

And when he doesn't come back, the Venturis will have to decide. Kill me or let me go. My survival hinges on one thing: whether I can carve out enough empathy in their cold, dead hearts to make them hesitate—or make myself too valuable to lose.

"How did Rosita meet her husband?" I ask, aiming to keep the conversation light as I pass Alexis a plate.

He smirks, drying it with exaggerated flourishes. "He was introduced to her, like the old days."

"Seriously? Like an arranged marriage? I didn't know it still worked that way for some people these days."

"She could've said no, but when they met, it was like—bam!" He claps his hands together, making me jump.

I shake my head with a small laugh, amused at his performance and willingness to be open and funny with me. "She got hit with the thunderbolt?"

"Exactly." He grins, stacking the plate back into the cupboard.

"They make a good-looking couple. He's very handsome."

Alexis tilts his head, considering. I let my gaze sweep over him, soaking up the sharp line of his jaw and the perfection of his olive complexion. He really is a very handsome man himself.

"You think so? He looks preppy like he just walked out of a country club."

"Not like you, you mean?" I tease, drying my hands.

His eyes gleam with mischief, hazel darkening to a rich caramel. "Not everyone is as good-looking as me."

I snort, tossing the dishcloth to the counter. "Be careful, Alexis. If your head gets any bigger, it will blot out the sun and wipe out all life as we know it."

He throws up his hands. "It's not being big-headed if it's true."

"Looks aren't everything." I counter, knowing full well how much of his confidence is built on his appearance.

"If the book cover is ugly, no one picks it up."

"If it has a pretty cover but the story is boring, no one sticks around to finish it," I fire back.

He nods begrudgingly but with his trademark smile. "This is true."

"So, your story," I say. "What is it?"

He spreads his arms wide as if unveiling a masterpiece. "A tale of excitement, romance, drama, suspense."

"Romance?" I arch a skeptical brow.

"Well, maybe erotic passion," he corrects.

"The erotic passions of wiping your captive's privates?"

His grin widens shamelessly. "My dick was hard. That should tell you all you need to know about how erotic I found that experience."

"I get a feeling your dick is hard most of the day."

"Only when he's ignored."

I chuckle and bite my bottom lip. This, at least, is familiar—banter, teasing, something resembling normalcy in the midst of chaos. He likes me. This big mafioso with the flamboyant charm finds me amusing. And despite the fact I'm spending time with him under duress, I can't help liking him, too. But my mom was clear when we came back to nurse my aunt. Don't get involved with anyone in *the life*. They're snakes in sharp suits. They don't just have fangs to eat.

There's a balance here, and I need to play the game. Teasing is one thing, but I can tell it would be easy to take things too far with Alexis.

"I'm going to rest upstairs," I tell him, taking a step back. His eyes drift over the length of me, lingering on my breasts and hips. It's not an invitation for him to join me, but he wishes it was.

"Okay, *gattina*. We'll continue this conversation later."

As I make my way upstairs, I turn to find him watching me, with his trademark shark smile still in place. He'd eat me alive if I let him and spit me out like an olive stone.

"Careful," I whisper to myself as I reach the top and can finally breathe.

CHAPTER 19

ANTONIO

MAKE ME CRY

The sound of the TV hums through the walls, carrying up the stairs. Luca is watching some Italian American comedian—one of the few with the rare ability to make him laugh. Alexis is in the shower, washing away the filth of the day and probably jerking off. We have no privacy in this fucking place.

Aemelia sleeps beside me, her breath slow and steady, her hair a dark halo against the mattress. When I checked on her and found her like this, I couldn't leave. She has nightmares, and if she wakes up alone in this strange place, she might panic.

The sun has drained from the day, leaving behind the heavy weight of dusk pressing down on the house. There are only two rooms on the second floor, one for my crew to sleep in shifts and one for us. Four thin mattresses almost cover the floor in a tight arrangement, forcing proximity whether we like it or not.

Carlo knows we have her. The coin rests at the bottom of the well, but he's playing games instead of returning for her. What kind of piece of shit sends a bullet with his daughter's name engraved on the side? He wants to kill his own flesh and blood? It has to be a game. He's telling us to go ahead and kill her if we dare.

"The DNA test came back," Luca had said earlier.

I jerked my head back. "Well."

"Definitely not Mario's kid."

Even though I knew, the confirmation settled the last butterfly of anxiety in my stomach.

"The video wasn't enough to scare Carlo out of hiding," he continued. "They don't believe we'll kill an innocent woman."

It's our reputation that's complicating this situation. In a city ruled by powerful families, we're the only one that doesn't trade in sex. That alone makes our enemies think we're soft when it comes to women.

So we need to change that perception. We need Carlo and whoever is protecting him to understand that Aemelia will die if he stays in his rat hole. We have to show her suffering. If Carlo wants to play games, he needs to understand that we're going to win. The thought churns in my stomach like acid.

Beside me, Aemelia stirs, her lashes fluttering before her dark eyes open, still fogged with sleep. Her first conscious breath is sharp, a small gasp as she blinks against the dim light. She stiffens when she sees me, scrambling back so quickly that she nearly falls off the mattress.

"Antonio?"

"I'm sorry to scare you."

She exhales, shoulders slumping as recognition settles. "Is everything okay?"

"No, kitten." I hesitate. "Nothing's okay."

Her face falls. "What is it?"

"Your father…"

"He isn't coming." There's no question in her tone. Just

cold certainty. She already knows. Of course, she does.

"The video wasn't enough to drag him out."

She nods once as if she expected it. "So, you need more?"

Nausea rises in my throat at how easily she says it, how readily she accepts the cruelty of this world. "Yes."

"What?"

"We need to show you suffering. Enough to make him panic. Enough that he believes—" I can't finish the sentence. The words taste like poison.

"Okay." She doesn't hesitate. "I can play along. It'll be okay."

I swallow hard. Sweet Aemelia. So sweet since I stripped her resistance away with a shower and my tongue. And she stripped away some of the armor around my heart.

"It has to be real."

"I'm a good actress." Her lips curve slightly, but it's a sad smile. "I can make it real."

I search her face for any trace of fear or hesitation. Instead, I find only quiet determination.

"What do you have in mind?" I ask.

She shifts, sitting up with her arms wrapped around her knees. "You need to show them something brutal. Something they can't ignore."

"Something convincing," I murmur, running a hand through my hair.

She tilts her head, studying me. "How far are you willing to go?"

I don't answer right away because I don't know. When she looks at me, all I want to do is wrap her in my arms and go to sleep. Disappear into a world where I don't have to face what's coming next or remember what I've done in the past.

Aemelia takes a steadying breath. "You have to hit me."

"No." The response is instant and firm. What am I even saying?

She blinks, surprised. "It won't be real, Antonio. We can

fake it."

I shake my head. "There's a difference between faking pain and showing it in your eyes. If it doesn't look real, they won't believe it."

She considers this, chewing on the inside of her cheek. "Then we'll make it look real."

I exhale sharply. "Tell me."

She shifts closer, lowering her voice. "Choke me. Not hard, just enough for the red marks to show. Mess up my hair, drag me to the floor like you're punishing me. If we cut the right angles in the video, it will look worse than it is."

I don't realize my hands have curled into fists until she reaches out and uncurls my fingers, pressing her palm against mine. "I trust you."

Her words settle deep and tighten around my ribs like a constrictor. I don't deserve that trust. What have I done to earn it? Held her against her will. Threatened her family with death. Threatened her with the same. Cradled her body and tasted her sweetness. Not exactly the foundation for trust building, but I nod anyway.

I lift a hand to her throat, hesitating when she doesn't flinch. "Tell me to stop the second you feel uncomfortable."

She nods. "I will."

I press my fingers against the sides of her neck, enough to leave impressions without cutting off air. Her breath hitches, but she holds my gaze.

"Struggle," I murmur. "Make it look real."

She does. Her fingers wrap around my wrist, tugging weakly. Her lips part as if gasping for breath. She kicks once against the mattress.

I let go immediately, pulling my hands back like I've been burned. She blinks up at me, rubbing at the phantom sensation.

"Good?" I ask, my voice rough.

She nods. "Again. Mess up my hair."

I exhale through my nose, dragging a hand through her soft curls until they're tangled and wild. She runs her hands over her own face, smearing away the traces of sleep.

"Now, the final touch," she says. "Make me cry."

I hesitate. "Aemelia…"

She grips my hand again. "Say something cruel. Something that would break me."

I clench my jaw. "I don't—"

"You have to."

I close my eyes for a moment, then open them. My voice is quiet when I say, "You mean nothing to him. You mean nothing to anyone. You're alone in this world."

Her breath shudders. The pain in her eyes is so real before her tears spill over, slipping down her cheeks. What I said shouldn't have cut so deep. She has a mother, aunt, and brother who love her, doesn't she? Friends. Other family members. As do I. But my own connections don't fill the space inside me. What I said is the thing that would gut me the most.

I want to take it back. I want to wipe away the proof of her pain. But she tilts her chin up, ready.

"You should start recording."

"I'll tell my brothers."

Downstairs, Alexis is finished from his shower, rubbing a towel over his hair and laughing at the TV with Luca. I grab the remote and flick off the TV. Luca turns quickly, annoyed, but I put up my hand. "We have a plan."

"What plan?"

"Aemelia is going to fake her suffering for the next video."

"It has to be convincing, Antonio. She's no Oscar-winning actress." Luca stands, folding his arms across his chest. He's still wearing his suit pants and a white dress shirt, always formal despite our surroundings.

"She's willing to do whatever it takes," I say. "We'll stage it carefully. Bruising, distress, something that looks worse than it is."

Alexis tilts his head. "But you're not planning to actually hurt her?"

"No." My voice is firm. "But it has to be real enough to make Carlo believe it."

"I can do it."

We all turn to find Aemelia halfway down the stairs. She's clutching a towel around herself, her smooth, shapely legs bare, her white bra straps still in place over her shoulders. She's stripped off her clothes for the scene. My blood runs cold at her obedience. Already, she's changing. Already, she's losing her spirit. "You need to make me cry," she says. "Make it look like I'm going through hell."

Alexis whistles low. "Damn. This girl has more guts than half our men."

"You think you can handle what it will take?" Luca asks, his blue eyes sharp.

"I can." She fixes her jaw, but her knuckles are white as she's clutching the towel to her.

"We played it out," I say, more to reassure her than Luca. "She's good. Very convincing."

Luca studies me for a moment that drags on way too long, his assessing gaze looking for holes in my story. He's always been like this with others, but not usually with me. Before, we would have just done what we needed to. Hurting people isn't something any of us have shied away from. This is the life we live. There's no hiding from the brutality. But suddenly, we're all relieved to fake the violence and threat.

We're changing. All of us.

"Fine," he says eventually. "We do it now."

"Now," I repeat as dread moves through me like silt settling against the river floor.

The next moments are a blur of preparation. Luca adjusts the lighting to cast deep shadows. Alexis shifts the position of the furniture while I stand in front of Aemelia to mess up her hair, teasing it between my fingers until it looks as wild as it did before I washed it. "This—" I start, but I don't even know how to finish. What can I say to her with my brothers standing behind me? What choice does she have? It's this or—

I don't even want to think of an alternative.

She rubs at the skin of her throat, making it red. "Press your fingers here," she says. "Make a mark." I wrap my fingers around her slender neck and press, wincing when she shudders and pulls away.

Fuck.

I've killed men like this, throttled the life from them with my bare hands. It's never been easy, but it's also never been this hard. Aemelia shudders, but she doesn't pull away. The trust she has in me to let this happen floors me.

"Time for the real performance," Luca murmurs, holding up the phone. "Aemelia, are you ready?"

She nods, her breathing quick and uneven, dropping the towel.

My breath catches in my throat as she reveals herself in white lace underwear, the kind a bride might wear on her honeymoon. Her breasts are high and lush, her waist tiny, and her belly gently curved above the panties that barely cover what's beneath. My hands flex at my sides as I restrain a maelstrom of emotions. This isn't right. None of us should see her like this, almost naked, stripped of her dignity. I swallow against a fist-size lump wedged in my throat, desperate to pick up the towel and cover her, raging to tell Luca that avenging Mario this way is wrong.

The cost is too high.

But how can I go against my brothers for a woman I've just met? We're loyal to blood. We avenge blood. Nothing can come before that.

"Aemelia," I say, and she smiles tightly.

"Like this, he'll believe you're violating me. It's the best chance we have."

She says 'we' and can't look at her anymore. How easily she has allied herself with us against her own family. Either we're so terrifying, she's too fearful to remain defiant, or her father hurt her enough for her to be unfeeling about his life.

Her feet are bare, and I think about Luca forcing her to

kiss his feet, and I want to drop to my knees and plead for forgiveness. Of all the horrors I've committed in my life, hurting Aemelia has cut me the deepest.

She perches on the edge of the sofa, and I kneel beside her, dragging in a long breath. I have to pull myself together before either Alexis or Luca sees how wrecked I am. Gripping her shoulders, I meet her wide brown eyes. "Struggle," I whisper. "Make it real."

She thrashes against my grip, letting out a ragged sob. Her hands hit my face and chest, vicious slaps raining down on me. Tears spill down her cheeks, her expression one of raw, desperate fear as I push her back and overpower her. It guts me to see her like this, even if it's an act.

Aemelia chokes on a breath. "Please," she whimpers, voice breaking. "Papa, don't let them hurt me. Please. Please, I'll do anything."

I tighten my grip just a fraction, my jaw clenching. I need to sell this, even though every instinct in my body is screaming at me to stop. "You're running out of time, Lambretti," I growl. "If you care about your daughter at all, you'll come for her before it's too late."

Luca nods once, and the camera clicks off.

Alexis mutters a curse. Even he looks rattled.

The silence that follows is thick and suffocating.

Aemelia is crying for real now, her frame shaking. I release her immediately, hands hovering as if I could erase what just happened by letting her go. I want to pull her close to me, stroke her hair, kiss her sweet lips, and tell her everything will be okay, but I can't even look at her. I turn away, catching Luca exhaling a ragged breath, rubbing his hand down his face. Even Alexis is quiet, his usual cocky expression absent.

What do I do? What can I do to make this right?

I force myself to meet Aemelia's eyes. "I'm sorry."

She wipes her tears with trembling fingers, giving a watery laugh. "It's okay," she whispers. "That was the point, right?"

I nod, but the truth is, I feel wrecked. And by the look in Luca and Alexis's eyes, I suspect I'm not the only one.

CHAPTER 20

LUCA

PLANETARY SHIFTS

Something is shifting. Like a meteor knocking a planet off its axis, Aemelia Lambretti has come into our lives and changed our course.

After Antonio helps Aemelia cover herself, he leads her up the stairs. I exchange a look with Alexis, and through silent communication alone we decide to follow them.

The video is on my phone, and I should distribute it to Enzo immediately, but somehow, it doesn't seem as important.

In the bedroom, Antonio strips his sweater and gently pulls it over Aemelia's head. He encourages her to put her arms into the sleeves, gentle and patient as a father with a small child. The sweater is oversized on her, covering her thighs as she lets the towel fall. Her eyes are glossy and wet, her hair still in disarray. With tender hands I don't recognize as belonging to my brother, he begins to stroke the knots from her hair, and she closes her eyes and lets him try to undo the damage we did.

Will it ever be possible?

I recall the first time I saw my father kill a man. It was nothing like those stupid TV cop shows or the movies. The bullet left my father's gun and pierced Alberto's gut, and he bled like a stuck pig, groaning and writhing for what seemed like an eternity. I couldn't watch, so instead, I focused on my father. He was a tough man. Nobody becomes the boss of a family without being hard as nails, but he wasn't like that with his kids. Strict but fair, we grew up respecting him more than we feared him, but that day, I saw a different side of him. Cold. Hard. Ruthless. And once I saw it, I couldn't unsee it.

For the rest of his life, I viewed him through different eyes and faced a truth I wish I hadn't had to face about someone I loved. Men, when pushed, are capable of anything. It's a fact I learned about myself in time, the limits of my conscience easing outwards until I was no longer restricted by the boundaries I'd grown up with.

We've all done things our mama would be ashamed of but will always find a way to look past. I, too, look past horrors when it suits me but watching my brutal brother pet Aemelia Lambretti is a gear shift. Seeing him touch her with such tenderness is unsettling. In the garden of the Venturi estate, there's a low wall that we all used to walk along, balancing on the narrow stone. Right now, it feels like I've misstepped and am about to tumble off the edge.

Antonio finishes combing through Aemelia's hair and helps her lower herself onto the mattress where she curls up, hugging her knees close. Without a word, I leave the room, descending the stairs. In the kitchen, I uncork a bottle of red wine and pour it into four squat glasses that would be better suited for whiskey. If I had some whiskey, I'd have poured that. Aemelia needs this. Pretty sure Antonio needs this, too.

My head isn't on straight like it usually is. I gulp back a full glass of wine and pour more. The scar on my ribs, long healed, aches. It wasn't a life-threatening injury like Mario's, but it's a permanent reminder of the night that changed all our lives. The night that brought us here.

Emotions are a weakness. I gave up on feeling anything a long time ago. Those who were already in my circle of love and trust have remained there. Anyone new is kept out in the cold. The world could burn around me, and I'd usually keep my composure. Alexis calls me the eye of the storm. But tonight, I don't feel that way.

I take the glasses upstairs, clutched in my broad hands. The snake around my left wrist seems ready to pounce, ever the reminder that evil lives in the shadows, ready to strike at any time. Some people get tattoos to remember good things. I got mine so that I'd never forget how easy it was to trust a man who could have ended us all.

Back in the bedroom, Alexis is slumped on a mattress, his back pressed against the terrible pink wallpaper left by the family who used to live in this house. The room is dim, casting shadows that stretch across the walls. Antonio is sitting behind Aemelia, who's still curled into a ball.

"Luca," Alexis says as soon as he sees me. "You brought out the good stuff."

It is good. Wine from our own vineyard, carrying the warmth and the sweetness of the Sicilian summer in its depths. He reaches up to take a glass from my hand. I place my feet carefully between the mattresses, allowing Antonio to take two glasses. "Aemelia."

Like his voice is the only one that can rouse her, she sits suddenly at his call, and he passes her the glass. Her dark eyes find mine as she brings the glass to her lips.

"To good wine," I say softly, tipping my glass.

Silence stretches between us as I settle onto my mattress, the one nearest the door.

I rest my head against the cool plaster and close my eyes as I swallow the wine, allowing the rich flavor to warm me down to my stomach.

"Do you like it?" Alexis asks Aemelia.

"It's good," she says, licking the remnants from her top lip.

"Have you been to Sicily?"

She shakes her head. "No. I don't even have a passport. It must be beautiful."

"It is," I say. "Very beautiful. The sea glitters like a never-ending spill of sapphires, and the sun shines like it's found its favorite place and never wants to leave."

"And, if you hadn't already noticed, Luca missed his vocation as a poet."

I ignore Alexis teasing. There isn't much beauty in this life, so I will never regret seeing it or finding the best words to describe it. Then Aemelia speaks, stealing my breath. "Do you ever wonder what your lives would have been like if you weren't born into this?"

I glance at Antonio, finding his expression flat, then Alexis, who's considering an answer but doesn't share his thoughts. Finally, I sigh. "I don't know. Maybe easier. Maybe not. The world's cruel, no matter what side you're on."

"Can you imagine Luca with an ordinary job as a car salesman or a server in a restaurant?" Alexis says.

Aemelia shakes her head.

"What about me? Can you imagine me working in an office with a wife and three snotty brats at home?"

"Definitely not," she says.

"And Antonio? He'd make a great priest, don't you think? He has a fierce intensity about him, and he's a great listener."

Aemelia finishes her wine and rests her glass on the floor. "Antonio could have made a great priest."

Alexis grins in the dark, and I study Antonio, trying to imagine him wearing the black robes of a catholic priest. He might have had some of the traits required, but he couldn't have remained celibate, that's for sure.

"I'd be in prison by now," Alexis adds.

"Or dead."

Aemelia focuses on Antonio, maybe realizing from his tone that he's talking not just about himself but about all of us.

"And me?"

"You should have stayed in Maryland," I say. "You would have been safe."

She tenses but doesn't respond. She knows as well as I do, there's no changing the past.

"Will you go back there?" Antonio asks. "After this is over."

Her head swivels quickly to scan his expression, but he's looking directly at me when he says it. He's given her hope that her leaving us is an inevitability, a surety, so that she feels confident of her safety. We haven't discussed it, but Antonio has made his feelings clear. If Carlo doesn't come forward, our lust for revenge doesn't extend to his daughter.

The relief that spills through me makes no sense. Only revenge should give me this feeling. Only the tying up of loose strings. Not the idea that this beautiful woman will be allowed to fly free from our hands and return to her boring life of drudgery and self-sacrifice.

The room falls into silence again, but this time it's not tense. Something else has taken its place. Something like understanding. Like an easy kind of peace. In one sentence Antonio has brought Aemelia to our side.

Alexis yawns. "If you bastards snore, I swear to God…"

Aemelia lets out a quiet surprised laugh and for a moment, the weight pressing on all of us feels a little lighter.

***

Sleep has never come easy for me. My brothers seem to tumble into rest like kids rolling down a hill, effortless and unconscious, while my mind refuses to shut off. The room is dark but not so dark that I can't make out the shape of Aemelia beneath her blankets. Her breathing is steady and even, and I marvel at her ability to sleep between us, at the level of trust she must feel to do so.

Trust we don't deserve.

Or maybe it's just exhaustion.

I lay back against the pillows, hands behind my head, staring up at the cracked ceiling. We had never lived in a house like this—small, cozy, with walls too close together, forcing intimacy. I never shared a room with my brothers. My father's sense of pride in providing a house large enough for us each to have our own space eclipsed the childhood experience of growing up together in close quarters and the comfort that comes with it.

Solitude is something I was forced to grow comfortable with, not something that comes naturally. The need to have my brothers close is a secret I keep. Maybe they feel the same way. All I know is that no woman has ever come between us, and nothing in this business has ever challenged our unity.

But Antonio made a unilateral decision tonight, one he should have discussed with us before communicating, and for the first time, I can see how Aemelia might have already created a fissure in the foundation we've built.

But it's only a fissure if I disagree.

And I don't. Maybe the fissure comes from watching a woman, one who's barely been in our lives, change my brother. When I think of Antonio's gentle hands in her hair, I let out a ragged breath. That question Aemelia asked earlier about what we would have been like if we hadn't been born into this life still lingers in my mind.

There's no walking away so what's the point in thinking about it.

Aemelia stirs, then whimpers. It's not loud enough to wake my brothers, but it slides through me like a blade. She whimpers again, her hands gripping the sheets, her feet shifting under the blankets. She's having a nightmare. I push up to my knees and crawl from my mattress into the gap between her and Antonio.

Her hair is still tangled, despite his careful hands, and I

push it back from her face. "Aemelia," I whisper, my lips close to her ear. "You're dreaming. It's just a dream."

She moans, twisting, her eyelids fluttering frantically. "Aemelia," I say again, firmer this time. "Wake up."

Her eyes shoot open, wide, and unfocused before settling on me. "It's okay," I murmur. "You were dreaming."

I stroke her cheek gently, her skin impossibly soft beneath my calloused fingers. When her eyes brim with tears, my body reacts with instinct. I tug her against me, holding her close.

"It's okay," I tell her. "It's nothing. It's gone."

"Luca?" she whispers, small and unsure.

"Yeah, kitten. It's me." Even as I say it, I expect her to pull away. Instead, she burrows against my body, like she's seeking warmth and safety, her tears bleeding through my thin shirt. I hold her, trying not to think about how I might be part of the nightmare still haunting her.

I stroke her hair, adjusting so I'm lying on the edge of her mattress and she's pressed against me. She won't stop crying, and I don't know how to fix it. When I was a kid, my mama used to sing a lullaby, one I loved, so I sing *La Simizina* as softly as I can, like a whisper, the words brushing against the crown of her head, and she listens, and her breathing slows. She quiets in my arms.

When I'm finished, she whispers. "What does it mean?"

I think for a moment, then admit, "I never thought about the words much," I say. "My Italian is rusty."

"Mine, too," she murmurs, her voice small but steady.

"Are you okay now?"

"Yeah," she whispers. I expect her to pull away, but she doesn't. Instead, her grip on my shirt tightens, like she's anchoring herself to me. I duck to look at her more closely, and when our eyes meet, a frisson of electricity runs along the length of my spine. She's so tiny in my arms. Delicate. A beautiful rose on the brink of blooming. Awareness is a river of lava, burning everything in its path. I want this girl with a fierceness that could obliterate universes, but it's wrong. She's young enough to be my daughter, if I'd married when I was supposed to. Her father is my generation, a friend who turned into the worst kind of enemy. And yet, she's a woman in body and spirit. Strong and resilient with a soft vulnerability that makes me ache to be a better man. I want to kiss her soft lips, feel her lithe body against mine, and discover the sweetness Antiono described for myself. I want to chase away the green-eyed monster that squats in my stomach at the idea of this woman with my brother and not me.

"Aemelia." Her name drips from my lips like sweet wine, and she shivers in my arms. I draw the blanket over her, and as I pull her closer, her mouth presses to the corner of mine.

It's like I cease to exist in the real world and enter a celestial plane where soft music plays and only happiness and pleasure exist. I don't move because I don't want to destroy this precious moment and remind Aemelia where she is and who she's kissing. She's still half asleep.

She doesn't know what she's doing.

She can't because if she did, she'd never want to kiss a man like me. Her warm breath tickles my cheek as she lingers. I thread my fingers into her hair, holding her gently with just the pads against the warm skin of her scalp. I want to kiss her, touch her, wipe away all the misery of her life and leave only joy and ecstasy. I want to disappear into another life where money and power don't rule my mind and heart.

Her lips drift across mine like a ghost of a kiss and I close my eyes, waiting for more, but it never comes. Instead, she pulls away and snuggles against me.

And that's how I end up falling asleep next to Aemelia Lambretti—my captive, my prisoner, my possession, and the woman who is slowly, without effort, peeling away the layers of protection around my heart.

CHAPTER 21

AEMELIA

SMART ENOUGH TO SURVIVE

I wake first, needing to pee, and find myself smooshed against Luca, who is sleeping on my mattress. His body rests on top of my blankets while I'm warm and snuggled beneath. In sleep, with his face at peace, he loses all the sharpness. Even his scar, long and neat across his face, doesn't take away the ethereal beauty that he possesses. I take a few seconds to really study the man who made my whole body fizz with awareness with just a heated look across a wedding reception. The man who paid a high price for my virginity but hasn't taken it yet.

Time has changed him from the man who carried me when I was a hurt and helpless child. His brow and jaw are more defined, his stubble denser, his lips a little thinner. His dark hair is peppered with the odd fleck of white, but it only makes him more handsome. This man is old enough to be my father, but I could never see him that way. Even when I was a kid, I thought of him as handsome, like a fairytale prince who'd come back for me when I was grown. He's broad and muscular, fit in a thicker, more masculine way than men my age. And I kissed him.

What was I thinking?

I wasn't. That's the truth. I was scared from a dream that felt like reality, Cohen chasing me, hurting me, violating me, and Luca was a safe haven. I gulp at the realization that my mafia captor is the person I clung to when my stalker violated my dreams.

These men are my captors, but it's complicated. They're in the wrong for holding me against my will, but they're also my rescuers. If any of those other men had bought me at auction, I'd be deflowered by now. Maybe worse. Virginity can only be taken once, but men can make a fortune out of owning and selling what's between a woman's legs. I shudder at what could have happened to me if these men didn't see me as a method of revenge against a man I myself despise.

And if Cohen had caught up with me, he'd have destroyed me by now.

I pull away, careful not to disturb Luca, drawing Antonio's sweater around me and inhaling. The neck smells like his cologne, ocean breeze and alpine forest, and the subtle scent of his skin that inexplicably makes me feel safe. As I pad out of the room, Alexis stirs, rolling over, his hair flopping across his forehead. He's beautiful in sleep, too, like a Roman sculpture brought to the ground by time, created to be the very pinnacle of men's appearance.

I find my way to the bathroom and relieve myself, then wash my hands and face, staring into the cracked mirror before I look away from the disheveled, wide-eyed girl who stares back.

Downstairs, I search the refrigerator and cupboards, pulling together ingredients for breakfast. There's egg, sausage, tomatoes, and mushrooms, along with a loaf of rustic bread that will toast to a perfect golden brown. As I start to prepare the food, rich, savory scents fill the kitchen, drifting up the stairs, and sure enough, the first to be roused is Alexis. He's shirtless, his dark curls in disarray, and his eyes still heavy with sleep. I blush at the sight of all his smooth tanned skin, unable to prevent my gaze from sliding over his tight abs and nicely rounded pecs. The way his fire tats lick up his arms sends heat rushing through me like wildfire.

He flops onto a stool at the counter, rubbing his face with his hands before propping his elbows on the surface, this thick biceps bunching. "You look a lot nicer than the usual asshole who makes me breakfast," he mutters, voice rough with sleep, "although I think you might have the same dress sense."

I smirk, buttering the toast. "It's not the appearance of the chef that matters; it's what they do with the food." I nod toward the coffee pot. "You want coffee?"

"Definitely. Black with two sugars because I'm not sweet enough."

Behind him, Luca appears, looking fresh despite the uncomfortable way he slept last night. His hair is combed through, his face washed, and he moves with the kind of ease that says he's ready to face the day.

"This smells good," he says, sliding onto the next stool.

Finally, Antonio takes the remaining seat, still dressed in his undershirt, the muscles of his chest and shoulders stretching the white fabric to its limits. He wraps his fingers around the steaming mug of coffee that I hand to him and nods in gratitude.

"She's taken your place," Alexis teases, shooting Antonio a look over his cup.

"I'm grateful," Antonio replies, taking a sip. "Sometimes, feeding your hungry asses gets annoying."

"If Antonio wasn't born into this life, he'd have been a chef," Luca muses, raising a brow.

"Or some poor bastard's mama," Alexis laughs.

"Too much facial hair," Antonio says, running a hand over his stubbled jaw. The movement is casual, but my stomach tightens at the sheer masculinity on display.

I plate up the food and slide it across to them, pleased at their satisfied groans of appreciation as they dig in. My mother always said that learning to cook wasn't just a skill but an act of love. Food brings people together and creates warmth where there is cold.

She was right.

I stand at the counter to eat, but Alexis notices and quickly vacates his stool, dragging it around for me. "The chef should never stand."

I thank him, and my smile widens as I catch the glare his brothers shoot him as if annoyed that he's making them look bad. Despite the strange circumstances, this moment feels almost domestic. I shake my head at the thought. I'm the captive of three mafia brothers, being kept in a secret location. It's definitely not the setting for domestic bliss. And yet, when they think I'm not looking, they let their eyes linger on my face and body.

"So, we found Luca asleep on your mattress this morning," Alexis drawls, his smirk pure mischief. "Did he crawl over there by accident or…"

I arch a brow, matching his playful tone. "Was he tempted by my siren's call?"

Antonio snorts, shaking his head. "Luca doesn't get tempted by women. He decides he wants them, then takes them."

"She had a nightmare," Luca mutters, not looking up from his plate. I stare, fascinated. Luca Venturi—the ruthless, stone-faced boss—blushing because he spent the night in my bed, comforting me like some kind of reluctant protector.

"Another one?" Antonio lowers his fork, concern flickering across his usually impassive face.

Before I can answer, I decide to see how far I can push Luca. "He sang to me," I say, sweet as honey.

The fork in his hand stops scraping his plate. A muscle ticks in his jaw.

"Sang?" Alexis barks a laugh and smacks his brother on the shoulder. "This man? Luca Venturi? He sang?"

"Well," I amend, biting back my grin, "more like he whispered me a lullaby."

Antonio's expression shifts, something dark flickering in his gaze. Jealousy? I wouldn't have thought of him as the jealous type, especially not about me, but the way his jaw tenses tells me otherwise.

Luca exhales, setting his silverware down with precision. "I have a nice voice."

I blink, surprised. "You do?"

He nods, like this is a simple fact and he didn't just shock the entire room. "Yeah. Sometimes, in the shower, I forget myself."

"You shouldn't need to forget yourself to sing," I say.

"Do you sing, Aemelia?"

"Karaoke, back in Maryland."

Alexis hums "What do you sing?"

"Whatever feels right in the moment."

"I think Aemelia should sing for us today," Alexis suggests, his smirk widening.

I scoff. "You want breakfast and a performance. Your expectations are a little high."

"Our expectations stretch much further than that," Alexis says with a layer of innuendo, then just as smoothly, he adds, "For lunch, dinner, and a mid-afternoon snack."

"What are you? A toddler?" I laugh.

"Ignore my brother," Antonio mutters, stabbing a piece of sausage with his fork. "He can make himself useful today."

"You want to eat my cooking?" Alexis gestures to his plate. "Because I guarantee it won't be anything as good at this."

"Burned toast isn't on my menu today." Luca stirs his coffee, then lifts his mug to his lips. Our eyes meet across the table, and for a moment, everything else fades. The almost-kiss flickers between us, charged like a storm ready to break. It was reckless and stupid, but in the moment, it was real and beautiful. And I can't regret it.

Alexis pushes his empty plate forward with a satisfied sigh. "You know, Aemelia, for someone we bought and kind of kidnapped, you sure are spoiling us."

I raise an eyebrow. "Stockholm Syndrome can work both ways, you know."

Antonio smirks, but Luca only studies me, his expression unreadable. "You don't seem like someone who breaks easily."

I set my fork down, choosing my words carefully. "Maybe I'm just smart enough to know when to bend."

Silence lingers, thick with an unnamable tension. Then Alexis claps his hands together. "Well, in that case, I'm expecting lunch in exactly three hours."

Antonio rolls his eyes, Luca shakes his head, and I just laugh. But beneath it all, something unspoken simmers between us, something shifting, changing, pulling us toward a line none of us are ready to cross. Yet.

CHAPTER 22

ALEXIS

THE BEGGING TYPE

I stick around to wash the dishes, not because I like getting my hands wet because I don't, but because I want to catch a moment with Aemelia alone. Antonio disappears into the shower, and Luca heads outside to take breakfast to the men stationed there. The two currently passed out upstairs will be up in time for lunch, but for now, it's just the two of us.

She watches me soap the greasy pan, arms folded, head tilted, her dark eyes filled with amusement. "You know, I didn't think big bad mafioso like Alexis Venturi washed his own dishes."

"We don't." I pass her the rinsed dish, watching as she takes it from me, her fingers brushing mine for the briefest moment. I'm shirtless, and her eyes drift over my body like trailing fingers, lingering on the tattoos and scars that mark my skin like a history of sins. "Unless the circumstances demand it. A man has to be ready for anything—war, love, washing dishes."

She snorts, shaking her head. "That's an interesting combination of things to be ready for."

"And I'm ready for all of them."

Her lips twitch, but she fights a smile. "I can see it with the first and last, but love?"

I turn toward her and catch her biting her lip like she's enjoying herself a little more than she'd like. "You don't think I'm ready for love."

"Your reputation precedes you." Her eyes flick up to meet mine, dark and full of challenge. "I've heard about your body count, and I don't mean the corpse kind."

I smirk, drying my hands on a dishcloth, amused that even a girl from Maryland has somehow discovered my sexual prowess. "Sometimes they're like corpses after I've fucked their brains out."

She barks a laugh, shaking her head as she tucks a loose strand of hair behind her ear—a flirtatious move whether she's conscious of it or not.

"So, I wanted to ask you something."

She leans in a little closer, her scent wrapping around me, laced with something sweet and familiar. I let my gaze drop to her bare legs, exposed by the short hem of Antonio's sweater. It should bother me, the fact that she's wearing something of his, but strangely, it doesn't.

"What?"

"What does a guy have to do around here to get a kiss?"

She blinks her dark eyes, her lips parting slightly in surprise. "What do you mean?"

"Well, I know you had a little something with Antonio," I murmur, taking a slow step closer. "And last night, I saw you kiss Luca. And I'm over here feeling like a chump."

"A chump?" She laughs, turning away as color paints the sweet apples of her cheeks, a perfect contrast to the cool confidence she usually wears like armor.

"What the hell did Luca do to get you all soft and needy?"

"I'm not soft and needy."

"No?" I challenge, my smirk widening.

"Well..." She hesitates, then exhales. "Maybe sometimes." Her reluctance to admit it makes it obvious she doesn't like feeling that way.

"So..."

"I don't know what to tell you, Alexis." She tilts her head feigning innocence. "Maybe it's just a right place, right time thing."

I rake my hand through my messy hair, watching her carefully. Her gaze follows my actions, responsive and eager. "So good looks and a charming personality don't matter? Because I'd have been first in line if they did."

"I didn't realize there was a line," she teases, her lips curving.

"Oh, baby. There's a line." I step even closer, backing her against the counter. "And I want you to know I'm first in line right now."

She licks her lips—subconsciously inviting—and I track the movement, my blood running hot. "What have you done, Alexis Venturi, to deserve to be first in line?"

I tilt my head, letting my voice drop lower. This close, the scent of her mixed with my brother's cologne invades my scenes. We've never shared a woman before, but then, we've never lived with a woman as sexy and intriguing as Aemelia. "It's not what I've done," I murmur, reaching out, brushing my fingers along her wrist, feeling the way her pulse jumps. "It's what I could do that counts."

Her breath catches, the flush on her cheeks deepening as she leans in, close enough that her breath warms my ear. "I thought I was your captive, Alexis. Do captives get a choice?"

My cock, already half hard, thickens and strains against my pants. I lift a hand, tracing my thumb along her jaw, tilting her chin so she's looking right at me. "I've never fucked a woman who didn't beg me for it, Aemelia." My voice drops to a rough whisper. "And I mean, begged. On their knees, hands pressed together, pleading for my dick."

Her breathing stutters, but she doesn't pull away. Instead, her fingers curl around the counter behind her.

I grin, slow and wicked, loving how easy it is to turn her on. "Tell me, kitten. Are you the begging type?"

The back door opens, drawing Aemelia's attention away from me to Luca, who stands on the threshold, his jaw set and glacial eyes narrowed on us. I don't pull away from Aemelia immediately, though. Luca hasn't got a leg to stand on when it comes to keeping distance between us and our captive.

"Aemelia, you should shower," he says coolly. "I'm sure Antonio is done by now."

"If not, maybe you could join him like last time," I add, smiling as her cheeks flush at whatever memory she has of Antonio's tongue. Jealousy slides through me, not because I'm angry with my brother for getting a taste but because I want one for myself, with a fever and determination I haven't felt in a long time, maybe not ever. Why does the forbidden fruit always seem the sweetest?

Before she answers, something flickers in her expression—uncertainty, maybe realization. She inhales sharply, then steps back, slipping past me with a grace that's almost frustrating. "I should go upstairs," she says, her voice quieter now.

I let her go, watching her retreat with a smirk, knowing this isn't the end of it.

Luca steps inside just as she disappears up the stairs. "You're playing with fire."

I stretch my arms above my head before leaning back against the counter. "Is that your way of saying you don't want me touching her?"

Luca's jaw tenses. "I'm saying don't get too close."

I chuckle. "This coming from the guy who spent the night in her bed?"

His nostrils flare slightly. "That was different."

I push off the counter, moving toward him. "It was?"

"She was scared. She needed comfort."

I snort. "And if she needs comfort again? What, we take turns?"

Luca's glare sharpens. "This isn't a game, Alexis."

I smirk. "Who said it was? Look, I get it. You think she's some delicate thing who needs to be handled carefully. But let's not forget—we paid for her virginity. If she wants to experience what it's like to be with the Venturis, that's her choice."

Luca's lips press into a thin line. "That was never part of the plan."

"It wasn't?"

He lets his eyelids drop slowly, exhaling like this whole conversation is paining him. "She does it for the right reasons, or not at all."

I shrug. "We'll see."

He exhales sharply, shaking his head before changing the subject. "We need to talk about the video."

I nod. "Yeah. Carlo's still not taking the bait."

Luca crosses his arms. "We need to be ready. This could get messy."

I grin, my pulse thrumming with anticipation. "Messy is my favorite kind of fun, as Aemelia was about to find out."

Luca grinds his teeth. "We send the men out to gather intel. That should be the only thing we're interested in."

"When Carlo is a corpse, his daughter is ours," I say.

"If she wants to be," is my brother's pragmatic answer. It's the first time he's admitted that he wants her. The metaphorical line I was talking about is real, and I'm not remaining at the back of it until this vendetta is settled. There is nothing to do in this place except eat, watch TV and fuck, and only two of those options interest me.

CHAPTER 23

AEMELIA

NOT MY FATHER

Antonio left after breakfast with a lingering backward glance as though he was worried about leaving me in the house with four gnarled soldiers who barely speak, and his brothers. After showering one by one, the soldiers disappear to man the perimeter, and Luca spends most of his time pacing in the backyard on the phone, leaving me alone with Alexis.

His words won't stop echoing around in my mind like a drug, dissolving my composure and making me restless.

Are you the begging type?

I didn't think I was, but when he said it, my pussy tightened like a closing fist, and my knees softened like they were ready to bend for him. Heat pooled low in my belly, pulsing between my thighs. I remembered Luca ordering me to my knees, his fingers brushing against me, and instead of disgust, all I felt was rage and hunger.

Something happened to me during my captivity. These

men, who at first seemed like monsters, have become undeniably human in my eyes. The fear I once felt is no longer a scream in my mind. It's just a whisper now, an occasional shiver down my spine, something that lingers but does not command me.

So when Alexis drops onto the couch beside me to watch the only decent thing on TV—a quiz show—and starts shouting out answers, I should be frozen with fear. But I'm not. He sprawls out lazily, feet on the table, radiating confidence he hasn't earned.

"Which organ produces insulin?"

"Oh, I know this!" Alexis snaps his fingers. "The testicles!"

I choke out, "WHAT? No! It's the pancreas!"

"Listen," he argues, completely serious. "Guys get moody when they're hungry. That's gotta be hormonal. So logically... bam. Testicles."

I snort with surprised laughter. "Your logic is terrifying."

"The correct answer is the pancreas," the host confirms.

Alexis grumbles, shifting in his seat. "Whatever. Next question. I'll get the next one."

"Which Shakespearean play features the line, 'To be, or not to be'?"

Without missing a beat, Alexis smirks. "Fast & Furious 2."

I stare at him, horrified. "You cannot be serious."

"No, princess. That's John McEnroe. And Vin Diesel gets real deep sometimes."

I shove his shoulder, laughing uncontrollably. "I'm never watching a quiz show with you again."

Alexis grins, grabbing my wrist so I can't push him again, his face lit up with amusement. "Admit it, *piccolina*, you love it."

I do, but I don't admit it. Instead, I turn my attention back to the TV. I don't complain when he shifts closer until our bodies are pressed together from shoulder to knee. His warmth seeps through my thin yoga pants, his presence consuming and intoxicating.

From the corner of my eye, I catch him watching me, amusement playing on his lips. He's studying me, as intrigued as he is entertained as I answer more questions correctly than he does. Instead of pouting, he throws his arm around my shoulders and squeezes me like I just won the twenty-thousand-dollar jackpot. His body is solid and firm, and his scent—a mix of cedarwood, leather, and something sharp and clean like a storm on the horizon—wraps around me.

This man wants me. I know it in the way he looks at me, the hunger in his gaze carving invisible marks into my skin. It's a weight, pressing in, claiming me before he's even touched me. But it's more than that.

He likes me.

And I want him.

I want to laugh at his stupid jokes and observations. I want to know how far he'll push me, how much he'll make me beg. I think he'd enjoy making me wait, draw it out, teasing until I was trembling, dripping, desperate. He'd relish my total submission and his complete dominance. Could I give him that?

I'm getting under the skin of all the Venturi brothers. I can feel it. Antonio, despite his discipline, can't hide the way his eyes darken when I'm nearby. He touches me like I'm something precious, something more than a bargaining chip or an object within his control.

Luca, the coldest of them all, cradled me last night like I was someone he needed to protect, a woman on the edge of breaking apart. When I kissed him, his body shuddered as though he was about to come undone.

And Alexis? He's the youngest and wears his hunger openly, reckless and untamed. He doesn't pretend. He doesn't hold back. And right now, he's looking at me like he's thinking of all the ways he could break me apart and put me back together.

Desire is power. If these men want me, if I can be

something irreplaceable in their lives, maybe the threats they've made to entice my father to come forward will fall away. Maybe it's my best chance of survival. Yet, even as I think it, I can't imagine them hurting me unless it was in a way that I'd enjoy. Luca's sharp spanks across my ass proved that much. He stopped at five before it got too much for me to bear.

The intensity of my desire is terrifying. The boys back home were just that—boys. Immature. Uncertain. Or psychos like my stupid stalker. The Venturis are men. Strong, dangerous men. And the age gap? That only makes them hotter. There's something intoxicating about the way they move, hands talking as much as their mouths, the way they look at me with burning intensity, the way they speak in low, commanding voices that demand obedience.

I hear my mama's words in my head, warning me about my daddy issues, telling me to be careful of my subconscious need to replace the man who was only ever a shadow in my life.

But is it so wrong to want a man who will take care of me?

Or even... three?

Three men who would kill to avenge their dead brother. If they have so much loyalty for a dead sibling, what would they do for a woman they love? What would they do for me?

Alexis shifts beside me, his fingers tracing lazy circles against my shoulder. "You're quiet, *gattina*. Thinking about something?"

I turn to face him, my breath hitching as I meet his eyes—deep gold, flecked with green, brimming with amusement. And heat.

"No," I lie.

"Tell me," he murmurs, his voice low and coaxing.

"It's nothing."

His grin turns wicked and predatory like he can scent the arousal threading through my veins. His fingertip skims up the exposed side of my neck, lingering where my pulse beats erratically, his gaze following the path of his touch. A shiver rolls down my spine, my skin pebbling with goosebumps. "That so?" His hand trails lower, down my forearm, the pads of his fingers barely ghosting over my skin. "Why don't I believe you?"

Before I can second-guess myself, before logic can pull me back, Alexis cups my jaw and crushes his lips to mine. The kiss is demanding, unapologetic, his tongue teasing my lower lip until I let him in. Heat flares through me as he explores my mouth, a wildfire consuming everything rational, pooling low in my belly. My fingers clutch his shirt, fisting the fabric, anchoring myself to him as his other hand grips my hip, possessive and firm.

He pulls back just enough for his breath to ghost against my lips, "On your knees."

A shudder wracks my body, but I obey without hesitation, sinking between his legs as though my body was created for his command. My breath stutters, memories of Luca staring down at me with his piercing gaze flashing through my mind. Alexis leans forward, threading his fingers through my hair, his grip firm—not painful but in control.

"You know what you have to do for me to cross the line, *gattina*." His words hiss through his lips as though he's barely holding onto his own restraint, silk, and steel, seductive and dangerous. "If that's what you want."

He waits, staring down at me, knowing the desires that linger in me better than I do. "Now, beg."

My lips part, but no sound escapes. My throat is dry, my pulse has a frantic drumbeat. The weight of his command settles over me, intoxicating, dizzying.

"Don't make me wait."

"Please," I whisper.

His eyes glitter like gems, his lips drawing into a smile that could corrupt the purest heart. His fingers graze my lips, tracing the shape of my mouth. "Suck," he orders, pressing two fingers past my lips.

I obey, hollowing my cheeks around him, tasting the salt of his skin. His breath hitches, and his grip tightens in my hair. He pushes further, past the back of my tongue into my throat, testing me, and I open it for him the way I'd need to accommodate this long, thick cock. The dark pleasure in his gaze makes my stomach clench and heat coil tighter between my legs. I squeeze my thighs together in rhythmic pulses, seeking friction, anything to alleviate the throbbing ache.

And then—

"What the fuck is this?"

Alexis jerks back as if burned. I release his fingers with a wet pop, spinning toward the voice, my stomach knotting with dread. Antonio stands in the doorway, his face pale, his eyes a storm of fury and devastation. His jaw clenches so tight, I swear his teeth grind.

The air in the room shifts, thick with something far more dangerous than lust.

Antonio's gaze locks onto mine, and for the first time since my captivity began, true fear skates down my spine. His expression guts me, the raw betrayal there slicing deeper than I could have imagined.

Before I can process it, before I can say a single word to explain, he's moving.

I barely register the way he lifts me from the carpet like I weigh nothing more than a feather, his grip bruising, his movements swift. My breath leaves me in a gasp as he throws me over his shoulder, and I beat his back in protest, but he doesn't falter, doesn't loosen his hold.

He carries me up the stairs, each step vibrating with barely contained fury. The door swings open, and I'm tossed onto the mattress, the impact knocking the air from my lungs.

Antonio stares at me, his fists trembling at his sides, his whole body coiled tight like he's barely holding himself together. His expression is twisted—not just with anger, but something deeper. Something raw.

His storm-gray eyes glisten, and it wrecks me to think that I've hurt him. I thought giving in would make things easier for me.

I was very, very wrong.

"What is this, Aemelia?" His voice is rough, cracked, and edged with something dangerously close to heartbreak. He takes a step back, pressing against the wall as if putting space between us will help him make sense of what he's seeing.

I force my chin up. "What is what?"

"What are you doing with Alexis and Luca?" His jaw tightens, the muscle ticking violently beneath his olive skin.

"You're jealous?" I ask, my voice quieter than I want it to be.

Antonio's nostrils flare. He juts out his chin and it seems as though he wants to laugh, but there's nothing funny in his eyes. "This is serious."

"More serious than being held captive by three dangerous men?" I snap, wrapping my arms around my middle.

He runs his hand over his head and clutches the back of his neck, eyes burning. "We can't keep you safe if our minds are between your legs. Can't you see that?"

I blink and he huffs, frustration rolling off him in waves. "You have to understand. It's for your own good to keep your distance. You're in real danger. It's not a game."

"I know I'm danger, Antonio. I know who you are." I narrow my eyes and grit my teeth, as my heart picks up.

His expression darkens. "I don't mean from us. I mean from your father."

Everything inside me turns to stone.

"My father?" My breath is shallow, my heart hammering against my ribs. "You've heard from him?"

Antonio nods, rubbing a hand down his face before meeting my gaze again. "Before we left the penthouse, he sent a bunch of roses. Tied up with a bullet."

"A bullet?" The room tilts, and I reach blindly for the

mattress to steady myself.

"Your name was carved into the side," Antonio adds grimly.

A tremor runs through me, my stomach twisting painfully. "How do you know it was from him?"

"He signed the card with a C."

A choked noise escapes my throat, and I drop my face into my hands as my entire body begins to shake.

Antonio's footsteps are heavy against the old wooden floor as he moves closer. The mattress dips beneath his weight, his presence a solid, grounding force.

"Aemelia," he murmurs, his voice softer now. His hand slides over my shoulder, tracing a slow path down to my elbow, stroking over and over. The warmth of his touch, the steady repetition—it's meant to soothe, but it only makes my breath hitch harder. "It's okay. We'll keep you safe.

I squeeze my eyes shut. I have to tell him. It's not fair that he believes Carlo has made contact. They're hiding out here to protect me but from the wrong person. "The flowers... they're not from my father."

Antonio stills.

His hand tightens just slightly, his fingers flexing against my skin. "What do you mean?"

Swallowing hard, I force myself to meet his gaze. "In Maryland, I used to work with this guy named Cohen. I was friendly with him, like I am with everyone, but he took it the wrong way. When he asked me out and I turned him down, he became fixated on me."

Antonio's face becomes granite, his jaw locking.

I keep going, needing to get it all out. "He started following me. Leaving gifts outside my front door. Calling my phone, bombarding me with messages. It was overwhelming, but I wasn't worried at first. He was just some guy I knew. I thought it was sad... that he'd get bored."

Antonio's lip curls, but he doesn't speak.

"Then, one day, he saw me with a male friend... and he

flipped out. That's when the threats started. Stuffed bears with their heads ripped off. A box of chocolates with a knife stabbed through the packaging. Blood red roses with a bullet tied to the ribbon, and a card scrawled with the letter C."

Antonio's breathing grows heavier, his fingers curling into my skin.

"I reported him to the police, but they didn't do anything. No proof that the threatening gifts were from him." My voice is hollow, each word scraping its way out of me. "Then, my aunt worsened, and we had to leave. I thought I left it behind. I thought I was free of him." I shake my head, my vision blurring. "But he followed me."

Antonio mutters something vicious in Italian, his entire body rigid with fury.

"Why didn't you tell us?" His voice is sharp now, demanding.

I bark out a laugh, but it's humorless. "Tell the three crazy men who bought me at auction and trapped me in their tower about my stalker?"

He exhales sharply, rubbing a hand over his face before brushing a tear from my cheek with surprising gentleness. "We're not crazy, Aemelia. We just want justice—for Mario, and now for you."

I blink, my pulse roaring in my ears. "What do you mean?"

Antonio leans in, his voice dropping, dark and lethal. "This Cohen. I want you to tell me everything you know about him."

A chill runs down my spine. "Antonio—"

His fingers tighten on my chin, forcing me to hold his gaze. "I promise you; we'll make him go away."

I flinch back. "Go away... or *go away*?"

His lips tilt into something that might be called a smile if it weren't so cold, so full of malice for the man who terrified me. "You don't need to worry about anything, *bella*. Just tell me his name, where he works, any information."

I bite my lip, but he fixes me with a look that brooks no argument. I either do as he says willingly, or he'll find a way. I tell him and he rises to his feet with smooth, calculated ease, his shoulders squared, his expression unreadable.

Then, without another word, he turns and strides toward the door.

"Antonio." My voice trembles slightly, but he doesn't pause.

"Stay here," he orders.

The door clicks shut behind him, and I let out a shaky breath, pressing my fingers to my temples.

I don't know whether to feel relieved or terrified.

CHAPTER 24

ALEXIS

SWEET CHERRY

Antonio descends the stairs with the weight of a man who's spent too long waging war with himself. His fists flex at his sides, his knuckles white with tension. His expression is a battlefield of emotions: rage, grief, and something dangerously close to heartache.

I throw my hands up, palms wide. "*Ma che vuoi?!* You act like I'm the bad guy here. Last time I checked, she wasn't yours."

Antonio exhales sharply, his teeth grinding audibly. "Listen," he growls as he swipes a hand through the air, dismissing my protest like it's nothing. "She just told me something."

Luca, who's been lingering in the kitchen doorway, straightens. "What?"

"She had a stalker back in Maryland. A guy named Cohen. The flowers that were delivered to the penthouse weren't from Carlo. They were from him."

Luca's head tilts slightly, the only sign he's registered this new information. "A stalker?"

"Yeah. She worked with him. He got obsessed. She turned him down, and he lost his fucking mind. She reported him, but the cops didn't do shit."

"And you're sure about the flowers?"

Antonio nods in response to Luca's question. "She nearly came apart when I told her about them. She's fucking terrified of this asshole."

Luca processes for a beat before he nods, already making decisions. "Find out who he is. We'll send Vito to deal with him." Luca exhales through his nose, pressing his lips together before he speaks again. "This changes things. If the flowers weren't from Carlo, it means he's made no contact."

"So Enzo was right," Antonio mutters. "He doesn't care."

Luca's face is unreadable, but his nod is slow and deliberate. "It would seem that way. There's no reason for us to stay here now. We can take Aemelia back to the penthouse."

"For how long?" Antonio asks. "And then what?"

I step forward before something's decided without my input. "Let's be honest. None of us wants to let her go."

Luca's expression flickers, but he doesn't deny it. Antonio stays silent, but his gaze drifts to the stairs, the path leading back to her. The girl we stole—the girl who's making us question everything.

"Her home life is a fucking nightmare," I continue. "And we all know it. What's waiting for her out there? A mother who lets her work her fingers to the bone. A brother who's one hit away from an overdose? A dying aunt. Poverty. Misery. And now some psycho's sending her bullets with her name carved into them." My voice lowers, dark with certainty. "She's not safe anywhere but with us. Nero took her once. If he finds out we released her and she's still untouched, he'll take her again. Or someone else will."

Luca stays quiet, unreadable, but his silence is telling.

Antonio's hands flex like he's imagining wrapping them around someone's throat. Eventually, he speaks. "You're saying we keep her for her own good?"

I roll my shoulders. "I'm saying if she's willing, she could be ours."

"Ours?"

I nod. "I'm not prepared to fight you over her, but none of us has a greater claim than the others. It's share or nothing, and I'd rather she was with all of us than none of us."

Antonio exhales sharply, shaking his head. "Who the fuck shares a woman in our world, Alexis? Most of the men we know have two, three women each."

"Good luck to them," I say. "None of them have a woman like Aemelia. If they did, they wouldn't be out running the streets like a bunch of stray *cani.*" I spit the word—*dogs*—because I need them to understand how serious I am. We could have almost any woman. We've had more than our fair share. But Aemelia? She's the fire inked on my skin, burning through my bones, impossible to ignore. She's wild, hot-tempered, passionate, determined, craving to submit; everything I never thought I wanted—but exactly what I fucking need.

Luca nods, his decision made. Antonio closes his eyes for a second, shutting out the world while he thinks. When he opens them, his hands go to the back of his neck, gripping like he's trying to hold himself together.

"What if she doesn't want us?" he asks, voice raw. "Not really. What if she's pretending because she believes it's the only way she'll survive us?"

I shrug. "We show her what we want. We make her understand."

His laugh is bitter, mocking. "You think it's so easy?"

I step closer, lowering my voice. "Don't put up barriers, Tonio. Not when she's everything you ever wanted, and holding yourself back is killing you."

He barks out another rough laugh, shaking his head.

"What the fuck do you know, little brother."

I smirk. "I'm thirty-two. Mama told me I'm ready to get married."

Luca's brow lifts. "She did?"

"She told me she's given up on you two. Said you're too old."

Both my brothers snort, their lips twitching despite themselves.

"Anyway," I continue, waving my hand. "She's desperate for a grandchild. All we need to do is plant a seed inside Aemelia and she'll come around."

"She's a virgin, and you're talking about knocking her up." Antonio shakes his head, just like our papa used to when I was fooling around.

That's a nice segue into the other issue we still need to discuss.

"Speaking of her cherry…"

Luca straightens, and Antonio's jaw tightens. I don't back down. "Come with me," I bark.

I stride outside to a patch of scrubby weeds and bend at the waist, finding three blades of grass. I pinch off two at the same length, leaving one slightly shorter. Holding them in my fist with only the tips visible, I look between my brothers. "Pick," I say.

Our crew watches us curiously. They don't know what we're deciding, but whatever it is, we make an odd picture. Luca moves first, tugging a blade free. A long one. He nods, accepting the outcome without a word.

Antonio hesitates.

For the first time in my life, Antonio fucking Venturi hesitates.

His fingers hover over my hand, torn. I see it in his eyes—this is bigger than the act itself. It's about what she means to him.

"You want it that much?" I murmur.

He doesn't answer.

I pull the next blade for myself—the short one.

A sharp sting settles in my chest, but I hold it out to him, my jaw tight. "Take her, Antonio. She's yours for tonight."

His breath shudders, his lips parting slightly in stunned disbelief. He looks down at the blade of grass like it's something sacred.

"If she wants me," he whispers.

And I know—without a fucking doubt—that I've done the right thing.

CHAPTER 25

AEMELIA

A NEW WORLD

The evening is closing around me when the door opens, spilling an arc of yellow light into the room, interrupted by the huge, shadowed shape of Antonio. I remain curled on my mattress, arms wrapped around myself, anger and humiliation warring in my chest. I hate the way he hauled me up the stairs like a misbehaving child. Hate that he locked me inside like I'm something fragile and breakable that he has to keep safe. But most of all, I hate the way I feel shamed and exposed.

I don't know why I feel ashamed, but I do. There's a strange sense of loyalty stirring inside me, like Antonio's kisses and the orgasm he gave me so unselfishly mean more than they should. And he caught me with my mouth around his brother's fingers. I flush hot.

He steps into the room, the door clicking behind him. The dim light from the hallway fades, casting him as a shadow, an ominous presence filling the space. He's carrying a bag, which he sets on the floor with deliberate care before leaning back against the door, his broad shoulders making the room feel even smaller.

"I'm sorry," he says softly, his voice lower than I've ever heard it. "For earlier. I'm sorry."

That wasn't what I was expecting him to say at all. "You don't own me, Antonio," I say, my tone guarded, my fingers tightening around the blanket pooling around me.

"I know." He drags a hand through his hair, exhaling roughly. "It was a shock."

The strain in his features, the shadowed lines bracketing his mouth, make something twist in my chest. Even with the weight of his turmoil, he's devastatingly handsome. Too much so.

In Maryland, there were no men like Antonio. No men who commanded space the way he does, who exude raw power with every breath. Maybe that's why I was never interested in the boys back home. Maybe growing up surrounded by men like the Venturis—dangerous, dominant, unyielding—imprinted something deep inside me. Something I can't erase.

And maybe that's why my first memory of desire is of Antonio himself.

Antonio watches me, his eyes dark, searching. "Aemelia…" His voice is hesitant, like he's unsure how to navigate the space between us.

I swallow hard. "So that's why you lost it downstairs?"

The silence stretches between us, thick and charged. I should be angry at him. Maybe I am. But there's something deeper beneath my frustration, something I don't want to name.

"Is that the only reason you're sorry?" I whisper.

Antonio's jaw tightens. His gaze flickers to my mouth, then back to my eyes. "No."

The air shifts, charged and heavy. He takes a step forward, closing the distance between us, his presence consuming. My breath hitches as he reaches out, his knuckles grazing my cheek in a touch so light it barely registers.

"I shouldn't want you," he murmurs, his voice thick, rough. "But I do."

A shiver runs down my spine, my fingers curling into the blanket as if it's the only thing keeping me tethered. "You make it sound like it's a terrible thing."

"Isn't it? You're so young. So sweet. So innocent."

"Old enough," I whisper, turning my face into his palm and kissing the center. His tightly held control surrounds me like a blanket of safety. It's okay for me to be soft because he is so hard. It's a truth I never faced, a need I didn't know I had.

"We shouldn't have kept you."

It's too nice a way to describe holding me hostage, but there is more for me to say.

"You rescued me from the auction... paid a high price and didn't take what you paid for."

His eyes search my face as though he can't believe what I'm saying. "That's a kind way of putting it."

"Maybe, but it's the truth. Those other men—"

I don't get the opportunity to finish because he interrupts me with a growl. "Those other men would have lost their hands and more if they touched you."

A shiver inexplicably runs up my spine. I shouldn't like the idea of Antonio's violence against those who would hurt me, but I do. I never had a man to step in and protect me. I've been the strongest in my family since I reached double digits.

"I shouldn't have..." His eyes drop lower like he's thinking about what he did to me in the shower.

"I wanted you to," I whisper. "I could have told you no."

"You think I'd have listened?"

"Yes," I say simply. It's true. He said, *'Tell me to stop.'* He gave me a way out.

His eye lids drop, and I reach out to touch his face; the rough place where his beard is trying to form, the soft skin of his cheek. This close, I notice the slight bump to his nose, the denseness of his dark brows, and the way his dark lashes frame his pale eyes.

"When you touch me..." His voice is lost to a whisper.

"When you touch me..."

His mouth finds mine like our lips possess a force that will always bring them together. His hands slide to my waist, pulling me flush against him, and I melt into his touch, any resistance leaving my body entirely.

We are heat and desperation tempered with tenderness and longing. His body arcs over mine like the sail of a ship, billowing in resistance to the wind, sheltering me against the dangers in life.

He's dangerous, my mind whispers. Antonio Venturi is one of the most dangerous men in this city, but he's like a highly trained security dog, only a danger to his enemies, not me.

He pulls back, panting. "I shouldn't—"

I cut him off, pressing my finger to his kiss-swollen lips. "I want this. I want you. Please, Antonio."

His expression softens, like he'd give me the world if I asked, and my hands become needy and greedy, grabbing his muscled shoulders and back, the power in him thrilling me to my core. He eases me onto my back, the springs in the old mattress creaking under the weight of him pressed into me. His hands find my wrists and grip them next to my ears as he stares down at me.

"You don't understand what you've done to me, Aemelia. You found your way inside my head. I can't eat, I can't sleep, I can't breathe without thinking about you, without remembering your sweetness on my tongue, hearing the moans you made echoing around my skull. I shouldn't want you this way..."

"I want you," I tell him again, tugging at his sweater, desperate to get to the heat of him, the thickness of his muscles, the smoothness of his skin. Beneath all the black clothes, his body has a soft warmth to it, like the sun couldn't resist kissing him. Dark hair dusts his rounded pecs and trails between the tight muscles of his abs, disappearing into the waistband of his pants. I press my hand to the place where his heart is beating erratically, and he remains still except for his ragged breathing.

"Aemelia." My name has never sounded so treasured on anyone's lips.

"Touch me," I tell him, and he groans like a wounded animal.

His ruthless hands push up my shirt, baring my breasts and cupping them gently, pushing them together while his thumbs brush over my nipples. I arch into his touch as it brings me to life between my legs. His mouth is an inferno that engulfs my nipple as his rough palm cups my soft flesh, kneading it over and over in a desperate rhythm.

I'm lost and, at the same time, found. Adrift, yet anchored. He switches to the other side as my exposed nipple cools and hardens, and my body squirms beneath him.

This is what it's supposed to be like. No fumbling. No questions, just desire, longing, desperation, and craving.

He mouths down between my breasts, breathing me in as he goes, his tongue circling my navel, kisses pressed deep into my warm, soft flesh. "Aemelia," he groans, his fingers hooking into the sides of my panties. I bring my legs together to assist their removal, then wait for him to part me, the anticipation as good as physical touch. Gripping my knees, he opens my legs like a book, staring at my most private place, enraptured.

"You're beautiful," he tells me. "So pretty." His fingers skim my dark curls over and over like he relishes their softness. He slides his rough hands up the outside of my thighs to my hips, digging his thumbs into the place where my body meets my legs, pulling me open just enough to see inside my labia, where I'm pink and wet. Like last time, he doesn't rush, he just rests his mouth against me and breathes until I'm writhing and panting, desperate for more friction.

"Please," I beg, as he kisses my clit, over and over, so

gently it makes the hairs rise on the back of my neck.

"I'm not going to rush this," he says. "I want to take my time… remember every moment."

"Taste me," I whisper. "Make me feel good."

He lets the tip of his tongue circle my clit and I almost levitate. He laps lower, nudging inside a place that only Luca's finger has identified. "Fuck, Aemelia. Fuck. Yes." My sex clenches and he groans, maybe thinking about how tight it will be, wondering if I'll want to go that far.

My need to be filled is a new and thrilling one, the idea of my body opening to accept him is a craving I don't understand. How is it possible to frantically want something you've never had?

I let my legs drop open wider, and his hands reach beneath me, tipping my hips like I'm a bowl to drink from, lapping and lapping at me like I'm nectar. I shudder, reaching for his hair, short and soft beneath my palms. *Please*, I think, but I don't beg him. I don't even know what to say. Fuck me. Break me. Take what no one else deserves to take. Mark me the way you marked that woman fifteen years ago. Make me a woman, too.

His finger trails over my clit, gently parting my labia until he's there, resting against my entrance. "That's it. Just relax, sweet girl. Relax." My pussy flutters with awareness and his breathing turns even more ragged. His eyes meet mine, checking that I'm still with him. I flush hot with understanding. Then he eases inside me.

The stretch makes me arch my back and gasp. "Yes."

Even just his finger feels huge as it twists, making me groan. He withdraws dragging against something just inside me that makes him shudder. My hymen, maybe. That disgusting doctor supposedly could tell I'm still a virgin and thinking about him with his hand up my skirt, nodding, fills me with disgust.

But Antonio's touch has a very different effect.

"Aemelia," he whispers.

"I want it," I say. "I want you."

I rise to reach for his belt, unfastening it with shaky hands. He watches as I drag down his zipper and part the fabric, revealing the thick length of him beneath tight black boxer briefs. I let my knuckles trail over the heat, surprise making me gasp when it moves beneath my fingers. He's only patient for a few seconds before he shoves off the last of his clothes until he's totally naked and I'm flushing at the sight. I didn't know a man could be so beautiful.

My heart rolls over and thuds erratically, as my mouth goes dry at his perfection. I've never seen a man's naked body before, but I know enough to see how potently masculine Antonio is. His cock is thick and long, jutting out between powerful thighs, and the muscles across his hips angle into a sharp V. Higher, his body is packed with muscle which ripples beneath his olive skin. Tattoos mark him and beneath the scars this life has inflicted carve out their story.

He's devastatingly handsome. And terrifying, too.

This is a man who's been fucking since before I was born. A man with more experience than I could ever possess, and I'm innocent. He fists his cock, pumping it up and down, rolling the skin tight against the head. His hungry expression softens as he notices me watching him with fear-wide eyes.

"Is it too much?" he asks. "Am I—"

"No," I say. "I mean, I don't know."

"It will fit, kitten. Don't worry. I'll go slow if you still want—"

"I do."

He smiles and reaches for his wallet which he pulls from his discarded pants, retrieving a foil packet. "This will make it easier, smoother." With one animalistic motion, he tears that packet with his teeth and rolls the condom over his dick with practiced ease.

I touch his chest and abs, letting my fingers play as his body shifts in response. He takes my hand and brings my wrist to his lips, kissing it softly. Then he lowers his body over mine, fitting our hips together, kissing my mouth with long, languid strokes of his tongue. I'm lightheaded and blissed out, so when the blunt, wide head of his cock nestles against me, I'm relaxed, and when he shifts his hips, pushing in just a little, I open my mouth and sigh.

"Okay?"

His serious eyes find mine in the gloom and I nod, arching my neck to kiss the corner of his lips, making him sigh. The pressure is good, but what's better is the way he looks at me like I'm the most precious woman in the world. The pure adoration in his gaze is like a drug that worms its way through my veins and into my heart. He strokes my hair away from my face, cupping my cheeks with his big, calloused hands. He licks the underside of my lip and I tremble, knowing that this is the calm before the storm. "Are you ready, sweet girl?"

How can I be ready for a man like Antonio?

My world is in pieces.

I'm still his prisoner.

He's nearly twice my age, and a mafia assassin.

This could be the most foolish thing I've ever done, but it feels right.

His violent hands cradle me. His savage mouth kisses me tenderly.

"Yes," I breathe.

And then he pushes inside me.

CHAPTER 26

ANTONIO

PLAY WITH ME

Aemelia is my first sweet little virgin, and the feeling of claiming her, of being her only, chases my heart between my ribs.

Her body is so small and lithe beneath mine, her tight pussy almost too much for me to bear. She cries out as I thrust inside her hard enough to break through her hymen, and I feel it tear as she whimpers. I kiss her mouth, stroke her face, and try to soothe away the pain as she stares up at me like she doesn't quite believe what is happening. I don't believe it, either.

I rise onto my knees to look at the place we're joined, and the sight of me buried deep inside her unravels me. My hands shake where they grip her hips, and she trembles beneath me. A streak of blood runs along the condom and I wince at her pain, slowing my movements.

"Are you okay?"

"Antonio," she whispers. "Yes." Her voice is the only thing that can cut through the daze I'm in. I rest my hand over her belly as I slowly withdraw, feeling the invasion of my body into hers through her flesh. I take her hand and press it under mine. "Feel that," I say. "Feel me move inside you."

She closes her eyes, and her lips part as I slowly draw myself in and out.

"How?" she gasps. "You're so…"

"Big, and you're so…"

"Full," she says.

Full. Yes. Full of me.

I slick my thumb over my tongue and press it to her clit, feeling it swell as I tease in slow circles, lost in the tightness of her body around mine. Lost in a moment I could never have predicted. My throat burns with wanting her, even though I have her. She's mine at this moment, but after…

She touches my chest, her fingers drifting down over the scars on my body, the war-wounds this underworld life has tarnished me with. Her brow furrows, like touching them causes her pain, and I lower myself over her so she doesn't have to look at them anymore. "Kitten," I whisper, grazing her lips with mine, rubbing the tip of my nose over hers. "You make me ache."

It's the truth. I was dead inside, and then she came into my life, and all I can think about, all I want, all I need, is her.

Her arms go around my back, drawing me closer. Her legs spread wider to accommodate our closer contact, her feet pressing to my ass, urging my thrusts harder than I thought she could take. I grind into her, and she moans, and I lick her neck, tasting the saltiness of her skin, marking her like an animal.

When she cries out like she's in pain, I stop moving, only to feel the rippling clasp of her pussy around me, and the knowledge that I gave her such pleasure for the first time tears away the last of my restraint. I move inside her, using her body, desperate to drive myself into the oblivion I know is coming.

I gather her in my arms so there's no space between our slick bodies, and when I come, it's with a cry that could wake the dead from their graves.

Luca and Alexis will have heard us both. They'll know it's done.

I've taken something I never should have wanted. Stolen something that should never have been mine. Turned Aemelia Lambretti from an innocent girl into a woman. Marked her with my body and given her my soul.

Her voice is now rich and throaty when she says. "So that's what sex is like. Now I understand why people make such a fuss about it." And I smile against her neck as she touches the short hair at my nape, her pulse still hammering in her throat.

"You're a woman now," I say, bringing her hand to my lips.

"I was a woman before, Antonio. The only difference now is that I'm a woman who brought Antonio Venturi to his knees."

I bark a laugh. As she stares at the ceiling, her face lights up with a wide, pleased smile.

"You did," I tell her. "But it wasn't the sex that did it. From the moment I saw you, I was ruined."

She twists to look at me better, and her dark eyes are soft. "Antonio Venturi. I never would have imagined you were such a romantic."

"I'm Sicilian. We're born with nothing but passion in our veins."

"Passion, yes, but sweetness?"

"I eat a lot of cannoli." I pat my trim belly, and she laughs, stroking my cheek, my brow, my temple. It's been a long time since I let a woman close to me like this, and it feels good in a bone-deep way I don't want to lose.

"Do you like Maryland?" I ask as my mind becomes a runaway train.

"It's nice," she says. "Safer than here."

"The people?"

"We live outside of Baltimore, but there's a big Italian American community there."

"But you miss this city?" The hope in my voice is pathetic and needy.

Her expression turns serious. "I don't know, Antonio. This city... it comes with a sickness that makes it impossible for people like us to escape. All I wanted was to waitress enough to feed my family and look where I've ended up."

"In my arms," I say, my hope turning bitter.

"That's not what I meant."

I know what she means. She's fallen into a hole of her father's making, unable to escape the ripples of the past. "You wouldn't have to worry about that with us," I say.

"Us?" Her eyes search my face.

"How I feel about you, Aemelia. What I want. My brothers feel the same."

She blinks a few times and then closes her eyes. "It's easy for a man to want a woman's body," she says.

I take her face in my hand, gripping hard enough to make her open her eyes. "If we wanted a body, Aemelia, there are others who come with far less complication."

"Luca wants to break me, and Alexis wants to make me beg," she whispers.

"And what do you want, my sweet girl?"

It takes her a long time to answer and when she does, I feel as though my heart will break. "Love," she says softly. "The kind of love that will burn cities to keep me safe. I've spent my whole life fighting my own battles, and I'm tired, Antonio. So damned tired. I don't want to fight anymore."

"Then let us do the fighting for you, sweet girl. Let us be that for you."

She smiles a watery smile, and I hold my breath for her answer, wanting more than anything to keep her and never let her go. "Maybe."

"There's no *maybe*, kitten. You can fight me, scream at me, hate me. I'll still hold you when you cry. You can push me away, but I'll always come back. I'm not a man who walks away from what's his."

I kiss her, deeply and possessively, wanting to make her see how twisted up I am over her and she moans, her fingers tugging my arm and my back. When I pull back to gaze down at her pretty face, she shivers, and I suddenly remember my gift, relieved to have another way of showing her I care. I reach for the bag, finding her staring at my half-hard dick with fascination. I get the feeling she's had no experience of a man's body before mine.

"I got you something," I say, pulling out the robe. She smiles and reaches for it, bringing the soft fabric to her chest and pressing her chin into it.

She smiles shyly. "This is perfect, thank you."

I help her push her arms into the sleeves, but she leaves it untied, her body still bared for my touch, and I gather her into my arms, holding her close, kissing her softly, wanting to make the moments after something she'll remember. Because as much as I want to keep her, I know what the world is like.

The people we love who we wish could be with us forever can be taken from us when we least expect it.

CHAPTER 27

LUCA

WHAT IT MEANS TO BE OURS

Antonio and Aemelia don't appear until midnight is closing in, and Alexis and I are half asleep on the couch. Antonio's pants are half undone, and Aemelia is wrapped in the thick, plush robe he bought her which swallows her small frame. Her cheeks are flushed, her lips swollen, and Antonio... he looks different. More at ease than I've seen him in years. The sharp edges of his face are smoothed by a rare, satisfied smile that's shaved years off him.

"You almost took off the roof," Alexis murmurs sleepily, holding up his thumb in approval.

"No sex talk," Antonio says, shooting him a warning look that's only fifty percent menacing. "You'll embarrass the girl."

"Nothing to be embarrassed about." Alexis rubs his face, swiping away the last traces of sleep before straightening. "Nice robe. Antonio fingered a lot of them before he found the perfect one."

I shake my head at my brother's comment, catching the double meaning, hoping Aemelia doesn't. When I glance at her, she's smiling with a softness to her expression that makes my chest tighten. It's like nothing can touch her after Antonio's performance: a bride on the first glorious day of her honeymoon. If I said I wasn't jealous, I'd be a liar. With all this drama, my only companion has been my right hand, and though experienced, he's lacking in many departments.

"So, what are you doing down here?" I ask, my voice gravelly. If I'd been in Antonio's shoes, I'd be upstairs, making Aemelia's legs shake, taking the roof off again and again. She's lucky it was Antonio for her first time.

"Hunting for snacks."

Ah, she's hungry. I'll forgive him. "We left plenty in the kitchen." I wave in the general direction, and he nods, steering Aemelia with his hand on her lower back, an intimate gesture that speaks volumes. They whisper between themselves, her laugh a soft, happy sound that wraps around me like silk. I shut my eyes for a second, remembering the brush of her lips over mine, the way she'd curled up against me when she slept.

She wanted to kiss me. Maybe she'll want more.

I still want Carlo's head on a stick but maybe this is the way he repays us until then.

I watch Antonio as he helps to plate up a snack, his gaze wide and full of hope. He seems so relaxed that it's hard to reconcile that he's the same man. He watches her like she's a dream he never thought he'd touch. Our mother has been like a stuck record with her views on marriage. *You need a woman in your life, Luca. A woman to make you happy.* But how do you find a woman when your life is dedicated to everything but love?

By buying her and taking her captive? It's not exactly the start of an epic romance, and yet...

Antonio isn't just interested in Aemelia for a place to stick his dick. He's finding a way out of the darkness that consumes us. Redemption. He's falling in love.

Alexis, too, watches her with fascination rather than hunger. We've never had a shortage of female company, but no woman has ever made my brothers look at her like she's something more than a warm body.

Antonio lifts a sweet pastry to Aemelia's lips, and she takes a bite. Her moan is soft, pleased, but it still makes my cock twitch because it's impossible not to remember the sounds that were carried from upstairs earlier.

Patience, I remind myself. My turn isn't coming tonight.

"We should leave here tomorrow," I tell Alexis, leaning in so Aemelia and Antonio won't overhear the rest. "With Carlo uninterested in our threats, there's no risk in taking her back to more comfortable surroundings. Sleeping on a mattress in one room won't show her what life could be like if she decides to stay with us. This kind of life might be what she's used to, but we could give her so much more."

"How about tonight?" Alexis asks, stretching his arms above his head, already eager.

"Tomorrow morning."

He nods, then stands and strolls to the door so he can brief the men outside.

For now, we have to get through another night on the mattresses with Aemelia between us.

***

"We're leaving tomorrow."

Aemelia pauses mid-scrub, her fingers tightening around the dish in her hands. Water drips from her fingertips, sliding down the plate and into the soapy sink. Slowly, she turns, dark eyes searching mine.

"We're going back?"

"To the penthouse," I confirm. "It's time."

She blinks, processes, then presses her lips together. Instead of answering, she resumes washing, her movements slower, more deliberate. I can feel the weight of her unspoken questions hanging between us, thick as smoke.

"You don't need to worry about anything," I say, my voice low and steady. "That man, the stalker, is in your past. And your father? He's still a ghost."

She nods, but she doesn't look at me. Her shoulders remain stiff, her posture guarded.

Antonio moves in behind her, close but not suffocating, his warmth an unspoken reassurance. He rests a broad palm against the small of her back, his touch light yet firm—an anchor.

"Everything's going to be okay," he murmurs.

For a second, she closes her eyes, just breathing. Then, with a slow exhale, she places the final dish on the drying rack and dries her hands on a dishtowel, her movements careful and controlled.

And finally, she turns to us, something softer, almost vulnerable, in the depths of her gaze.

"Okay," she whispers.

Antonio squeezes her waist, a silent promise, while I hold her gaze, giving her the same vow without words.

Tomorrow, we'll return to the world we left behind.

Tomorrow, we'll take her home.

***

When we finally make our way upstairs, the air between us is different. The tension is still there, but it's shifted, heavier with something unspoken.

The bedroom is dimly lit, the soft glow of a bedside lamp casting long shadows against the wall. Aemelia hesitates at the doorway, glancing between the three of us. "What happens when we go back?"

Antonio steps forward first, brushing his scarred knuckles over her cheek. "You'll see what life could be like. What it means to belong to us."

She looks around, exhaling slowly, her expression thoughtful. "And if I don't want to stay?"

Alexis leans against the wall, his grin wolfish. "Then you

walk. But not yet. Not until we've cleared your path."

"But if you like it, maybe you'll never want to leave." Antonio takes her hand gently in his, an indication of how things could be and a clear communication that he wants her to stay.

Her lips part, but she doesn't speak; instead, she steps into the room that still carries the lingering scent of sex to sleep between us.

"Okay," she whispers. It's a single word, but it carries weight, threading through the air like a promise. She's choosing to stay. For now.

"Aemelia," I say as we follow her. "You forgot something."

Her eyes, bright and a little fearful that she's disappointed me in some way, flick between us, searching for answers.

"You forgot to kiss us all goodnight."

She blushes, and her first instinct is to find Antonio in the room, the man she knows most intimately. He takes her face in his hands and bends to kiss her lips like he's sipping from a chalice of the finest wine. Her soft moan takes my breath away, anticipation drumming through me like the thunder of wild horses in my chest.

Alexis is closer than I am, and she hesitates in front of him. He slides his hand around her neck, tangling his fingers in the hair at her nape. He ducks his head so his mouth is close to her ear. "Beg," he murmurs, only just loud enough for me and Antonio to overhear.

Antonio expresses displeasure with a tut, but he knows what our brother likes, and Aemelia will have to understand if this is going to work.

Her jaw flexes as though she's gritting her teeth. Submission doesn't come easy to her, but she will learn, and she will enjoy it. She's spent too long shouldering too much responsibility. It's time for her to hand all of that over to us.

Her dark eyes meet Alexis's dancing hazel irises, searching. "Please," she says softly. "Kiss me."

It's perfect. Alexis exhales, pleasure surging through him. Then he leans in to kiss her, long and lingering, a tease of what's to come. She sways on her feet, letting go of the edges of the robe she is holding together to stabilize herself with her hand on his shoulder. Beneath the robe is a white nightdress that cuts low in the center and high on the thigh.

Beautiful.

When my youngest brother is done with her, he taps her on the ass. "Now, go kiss your boss."

I never liked the title. I didn't choose to be in this position, but tonight, the power it gives me drips through me like an IV infusion. Aemelia's approach is tentative, her eyes wide as she searches my expression. *What does he want? What will he do?* The questions are written clearly on her face. Up to now, our contact has been a mixture of gentle and harsh, my hand on her ass and between her legs but a distant memory to the feel of my arms around her.

"Luca," she says, interrupting my thoughts.

I hold out my hand high enough that she knows what I expect. Holding my gaze, she bends to press her lips to my knuckles—such *a good girl*. The sweetness of her submission makes me close my eyes for just a second. When I open them, she watches me, biting back a smile.

Taking her by the chin, I draw her up so she's balancing on the tips of her toes. Then I deliver a punishing kiss, pressing the sides of her jaw so she has to open up to accept my tongue. Her hands grip my shirt as I invade her mouth, tasting the sweetness of cannoli, remembering that my brothers' kisses are still present on her lips. I plunder her, own her, prepare her for what's coming, and she moans like the perfect good girl that she is.

We'll find another way to get to Carlo. Aemelia isn't part of that plan anymore.

But she's still ours.

Willing captive.

Marked by one of us.

Soon to be claimed by us all.

CHAPTER 28

ALEXIS

THE GIFT OF LOYALTY

It doesn't take long to pack up the house. Andre and Vito carry the bags out to the SUV, Luca spins the keys around his finger, waiting to lock up, and Aemelia stands around looking pretty.

My god. She's beautiful. Like the first sun breaking through the bleakest of winter skies over this sprawling city. Effortless in a knitted dress and long boots, her hair loose and trailing down her back, her face bare of makeup. Aemelia smiles at Antonio, who keeps appearing with cannoli like some kind of deranged grandmother intent on fattening up her grandkid. Watching him try to spoil her is fucking amusing and poignant.

I sip coffee, wanting to be alert. Although the risks in this transfer are minimal, my sleep-clouded brain needs help.

"Let's go," Luca shouts.

"Hang on." I gulp the last of the hot, black liquid and

drop the mug into the sink.

"Rinse it," he barks, so I do, and rest it on the drainer for the next time our asses need to hide out.

We leave the house and hustle Aemelia into the back of the SUV. Antonio drives, Luca takes the passenger seat, and I get to sit next to our princess.

I reach over to take hold of her belt and tuck her in safely. She smells of jasmine, roses and vanilla creme. Delicious.

"I can do that myself," she says.

"Yes, kitten. But I want to do it for you. This is what it means to be ours."

I touch her cheek, then her soft silky hair. When I plant a kiss on her cheek, she smiles. "I get that one for free, huh?"

"Don't get used to it."

Vito and Andre pull away from the curb, and Antonio follows, resting his elbow on the car door. Luca's phone rings, and he talks business in the usual way, saying very little that could be picked up by wiretaps. These days, he's shifted most of our business into gambling and construction, but there are still legacy commitments that it's harder to shut down.

It takes thirty minutes for us to reach the penthouse, and Aemelia spends most of the time looking out the window, and I spend most of my time looking at her. When I take her hand and press it to my mouth, her smile is a little wary.

"Today, we'll eat, drink and be merry."

She nods, biting her bottom lip. "I want you to tell my mama I'm okay."

It's not an unreasonable request that we can fulfill. "We can do that."

"And my aunt."

"What about her?"

"I'd like to see her... under the circumstances."

The woman looked like she was halfway over the threshold of death's door. "Talk to Luca."

She nods, and I squeeze her hand as Antonio signals to pull over in front of our building. The underground parking garage should open automatically, but there's a sign pinned to the gate that reads 'Ongoing Maintenance.'

Antonio swears. "Who ordered this?"

Luca tuts, still on the phone.

"Just pull up outside, and we can park the car later," I say, pointing to a space behind Vito's car. Behind us, Gabe and Matteo park up two vehicles away.

I jump out of the car and round the back to open the door for Aemelia. She slides both perfect legs off the edge of the seat and slips into the space between the door and the vehicle. Luca's still talking animatedly, his free hand gesticulating wildly. Aemelia's eyes drift from mine to the space over my shoulder, and then suddenly, she shoves me so hard that I lose my footing, dropping awkwardly onto the asphalt. I reach for her on my way down, convinced she's trying to make a run for it despite what we said, but then she falls on top of me, and the sound of firecrackers cuts through the air, followed by Antonio swearing and Luca going suddenly silent.

Not firecrackers.

Gunshots.

I grab Aemelia around the waist and roll her body beneath mine, holding her so tightly, her breathing becomes labored. I reach for my gun, pulling it from my back, twisting to fire it in the direction Aemelia was looking. More gunshots tear the air, faster than my racing heart, as Vito and Andre unload their clips. A car engine revs, and tires squeal and it's over in seconds that felt like the worst kind of slow motion.

I stare down at Aemelia, shock hitting like a slap to the cheek. "Are you okay?"

"Yeah." Her voice cracks. "Yeah. I'm fine."

I scramble to my feet and tug her up, still sheltering her with my body. "Inside," I shout, and we run into the secure lobby as our men finally do their fucking jobs and provide cover for us.

The lobby, all bright marble, white sofas, and bronze accents, make a strange sanctuary. I drag Aemelia into the stairwell and up a flight of stairs before seeking out the elevator to take us to the top floor. Once we're inside, Antonio and Luca swear, punching the button for the penthouse, and we all look at Aemelia—the dirt on her dress, her disheveled hair, her scuffed boots—she's alive and only superficially harmed.

"She saved my life." I yank her against me, cupping the top of her head with my palm and kissing her hard on the forehead. "She pushed me down." I don't know if I'd have been hit, but it doesn't matter. Her first thought was to save me before she thought about herself.

The elevator bell dings, the doors slide open, and Antonio covers the sensor with his hand, but none of us move. This girl was our captive, but she just proved her loyalty.

Fuck everything else in this world.

We're never letting her go.

***

The penthouse carries its familiar, clean scent, the space meticulously tidy, the windows stretching to reveal the skyline beyond. I lead Aemelia to the kitchen, settling her onto a stool at the counter with another kiss, and open the cupboard to retrieve the brandy and four glasses. I pour double measures into three and hand Aemelia the single. We all knock it back, the liquid burning as it makes its descent to settle our nerves.

"Come," I tell Aemelia, holding out my hand. I lead her to her room and, at the doorway, say, "Stay here while we talk. I'll come to you when we're done." She nods, and I close the door behind her.

Back in the open plan living area, Antonio exhales sharply, rubbing a hand over his jaw as if trying to ground himself. Luca shakes his head, darkness turning his clear blue eyes to the depth of the ocean.

"A hit?" Luca finally asks, his voice controlled, but there's rage simmering beneath the surface.

"Looked like a warning." Antonio clenches his hands into fists.

"They're dead," I growl, throwing my hands in the air, fingers splayed wide. My heart is still hammering, my blood surging through my veins with a mix of adrenaline and fury. Whoever just tried to take a shot at us—at her—signed their death warrant.

Luca straightens; his decision is made. "We find out who sent them. This goes higher than a few bottom feeders."

Antonio nods, his expression dark. "We have to keep her safe."

"No one will touch her," I grind out. "No one will damage even a fingernail."

No one takes what belongs to us.

Not now. Not ever again.

CHAPTER 29

AEMELIA

THE DEVIL HAS KIND HANDS

My hands are still shaking when Alexis returns to check on me. I'm sitting on the bed, and he crouches in front of me running his hand through my hair, easing out the tangles.

"Aemelia." He brushes his thumb over my cheek, tender as a lamb.

"Why?" I ask. "Were they coming for me?"

"We'll find out, and we'll deal with it. For now…"

He kisses me sweetly, searching, and I reach for him, tangling my fingers in his soft, dark curls, slipping into a place of safety within his arms. He covered me with his body and protected me as I had protected him. No man has ever sheltered me that way.

His touches are practiced and gentler than I imagined it could be with him. Gone is his demanding edge, his need to make me beg. It's like, by pushing him to the ground, I showed him that I'm worthy of his care and his love, and now I have nothing to prove.

"Are you okay?" He cups my throat where my pulse beats a steady rhythm.

"I'm not used to it. The violence, the threat."

His jaw flexes. "And you don't have to get used to it. Everything will be okay."

He draws me to my feet, wrapping his arms around me, cradling me like I'm precious. I slide easily into his embrace, starved of affection, still shaking from the sight of the menacing men pointing their guns toward us and the sharp echo of the gunshots. Alexis sways us, and before I realize what's happening, he's dancing with me slowly in a small circle, with just the low hum of a murmured song in the background.

His broad hands stroke in long, slow swipes down my back, calming and reassuring. I press my face into his warm, solid chest and close my eyes so I can try to forget where I am and why and sink into this feeling of safety and security.

My mama was always filled with words of wisdom which she mostly aimed at my brother, who needed sense knocked into him regularly. Her favorite: the devil doesn't come to you with anger or to inspire fear. He comes to you offering everything you ever wanted and everything you didn't know you needed, with kind hands and a soft smile. He lulls you into believing he wants what's best for you until it's too late.

My throat convulses in a noisy gulp as I try to draw together my splintered thoughts and feelings. Is Alexis the angel or the devil? The men outside wanted to kill us and he became my shield. But with his brothers, he's taken me from everything I know and love and kept me captive.

He looks down at me with tender, wide eyes, as though he's seeing me for the first time.

"Did you dance at your prom?" he asks me.

"I didn't go," I whisper.

He tips my chin, forcing me to meet the fire in his eyes. "Why not?"

"I couldn't afford the dress. There was no one..." I trail off because he doesn't care about my childish experiences.

He's a grown man from a world where life and death flip at the click of fingers.

"That's a shame," he says. "Every girl should dance with a handsome boy at her prom."

"Not every girl has a life like mine."

It's the truth, and I'm not afraid to admit it. Not now. Not after everything that's happened. I feel tired down to the polished white of my bones.

He strokes my hair, the soft skin behind my ear, the length of my throat.

"I can make you feel good, baby doll. Make you forget."

Our eyes meet, and his question is reflected between us. Do I want him to make me forget?

Against his tall, broad, muscular frame, I feel tiny and insubstantial, but not afraid. Not anymore.

I nod and he brushes my bottom lip with his thumb.

He eases me back onto the bed, spreading my legs gently. I'm still wearing my boots that he unzips and slides off one by one. Next, he removes my stockings, peeling them over my skin, pressing kisses to the insides of my calves, my ankles, and the arches of my feet. Then he turns his attention higher, sliding his hands up my thighs, removing my panties inch by slow inch.

With Antonio, I didn't have time to think about this part. We were in the shower, both overwhelmed with emotion that felt too raw. And in the bedroom yesterday, it built on what we'd already done.

This is so much more deliberate, intentioned, and intimate. My heart is slow and quiet while he brings my panties to his face and breathes me in. I flush hot at his hungry expression, and when he places his palms inside my thighs and eases my legs wide, the heat in my cheeks crescendos.

"Look at you." He exhales a ragged breath. Our eyes meet, and emotion swells between us. A memory from the past of him hiding a coin in one of his closed fists and telling me to find it flashes back. He was so heartbreakingly good-looking then. I'd been shy of him, even as a five-year-old, but after a few games, I'd laughed so much, and at the end, he gave me the coin to buy sweets.

And now, Alexis is still as heartbreakingly good-looking but with a harder edge, like time has toughened him up. His smiles are not as unbidden, the laughter in his eyes tinted with a hint of cruelty. Life has worked me over, but it's done the same to these men.

"I want to touch you," he says. It's not a question as such, but the way he looks at me makes it feel as though he's asking for permission.

"Please."

His lion's eyes flash with just a little spark of danger. His index finger finds where I'm wet, and he groans. "Baby," he says. "How did you stay pure for so long? How did no one else come before us?"

There was no one else, I could tell him. No one who matched up to the memories I had of the Venturis and the fantasies I created from them. No men came close.

And now...

His touch is reverent, his eyes a pool of longing and fever.

"You know," he says softly as he slides two fingers inside me, deep and testing, and I arch my spine like a cat. "There will never be a time when I won't kill to keep you safe."

My fingers tighten around fistfuls of the comforter, and he leans over me to kiss my clit, his eyes still devastatingly connected to mine. I grip his hair, desperate to hold him where I'm needy. His tongue slides over my clit in one long rasp, and I almost come, moaning and clutching at him as he smiles against my flesh.

"Please," I say again, knowing how much he likes it, but mostly because I want what he can give me; dark, sinful pleasure that will tear me apart at the seams.

"It's okay," he tells me, sliding a hand over my belly to press down against my sternum. Fire tattoos cover his forearm, a twisted inferno like the one raging between my thighs. "It's okay, sweet girl. There's no rushing what I want to do to you."

He draws back, and I pant up at him, watching as he tears off his shirt with one arm, revealing a torso that's so ripped, it almost doesn't look real. His nimble fingers tug the belt from their loops with a whoosh. His dark jeans are shoved over narrow hips, along with tight gray boxer briefs, until he's standing naked before me, body covered in tattoos of fire, angels, and devils, twisted in something that at first glance seems painful, but on closer inspection is rapture.

He fists his long, thick cock roughly, slicking his palm over the wet tip.

"You see this." His eyes focus between my thighs. "I think I need to open you with my fingers first."

I nod because the size of him is more than a little terrifying. Not so different from Antonio, but my body is a little sore already, and with Antonio, I was more confident he'd go at my pace. Alexis is less restrained, more impetuous. He lays back on the bed beside me, stretching his arms over his head, bringing his musculature into high relief, and my mouth becomes a barren wasteland.

"Take off your dress and bra," he says, "then climb onto me. Sit on my face."

His words are like a spell, and before I can even question his instructions, I'm carrying them out. When I face him, he pats my hip and then hauls me around like I weigh nothing, dropping me over his face and pushing against my spine so my mouth lines up with his cock. I flush hot, realizing the view he must have of my spread cunt, then the tip of his tongue taps the straining point of my clit, and I forget the world.

"Suck me," he tells me, his voice dark and sharp. "Take me into your throat."

And when I do, when I get that first taste of him, musky, warm, and a little tart, he pushes his fingers inside me and twists.

Fuck. I flounder, my bobbing movements faltering, then

restarting like he reset my body and brain in one motion. I'm full. Impossibly full, but then he draws out and shoves back in again, harder and deeper, and this must be what full feels like. Three thick fingers. Pleasure and pain bloom. The soreness left over from Antonio becomes an ache of want.

"Deeper," he tells me, thrusting his hips until the head of his cock enters my throat, and I gag, tears leaking from my eyes. His taste intensifies, and I gulp, making him hiss and groan.

"I think you can take more," he says, pulling out and pushing back in. Wet noises fill the room as he pumps most of his hand in and out, and I flush hot. Four fingers, and I'm stretched beyond what I thought was possible. "Fuck, that's it. You're perfect."

Perfect.

His perfect little captive.

And he's my perfect mafia prince.

I pull away from him, lighting fast, until I'm straddling his hips, facing him. I slide my pussy along the underside of his cock, arching my spine. I'm so wet that I leave a trail of slickness over him, and he watches, his smile lingering at one corner of his mouth.

"You want to ride the bull?" he asks.

"I want to look at you," I say.

"Did you do this with Antonio?" He tips his head and strokes my knee, reassuring me that his question isn't rooted in jealousy but curiosity.

I shake my head.

"Okay." He taps the bed, finding a condom he tossed from his pocket. Tearing it with his teeth, he sheaths himself with practiced ease. He grips my waist with both hands, almost fully spanning. "Climb on."

I wrap my hand around the base of him, my fingers not meeting, in awe of what I'm expecting my body to be able to take. When he's notched at my entrance, taking him inside me seems like an impossible feat. "I can't," I whisper, staring at the way my soft pink pussy looks against his rigid length.

"You can." His hands grip tighter, and his hips rise, and suddenly, he breaches my clenched muscles just an inch. He grits his teeth, sweat beginning to bead at his hairline. "Jesus. You're so fucking tight."

"I don't think the Lord cares," I say, and his eyes meet mine, flashing with dark humor.

"I could call out for Lucifer. Would you like it better?"

I shake my head, tensing my thighs to push down. He grunts as I rise again, pushing down even harder. I've got him halfway in, and I feel like a puppet on a man's fist.

"That's it." He stretches his arms above his head, gripping the comforter in his huge hands. "That's it. You fucking take control. Work me inside."

With all of the control now in my hands, I rest my palms on his taut abs and roll my hips, spreading my body's wetness higher and higher inside me with every thrust.

The deeper he penetrates me, the fuller I feel until it seems like there's nowhere else to go. I slide my hands up his sides, in awe at the way his body expands from a narrow waist to a broad chest. Beneath his tattoo, my palm catches a rough stretch of skin, a scar, I realize, covered by the black ink. A gunshot? A knife wound. Whatever it was, it could have hit vital organs. My heart clenches at what he's faced and how it must have affected him.

He flips me onto my back, looming over me with hungry, desperate eyes. Palming my breast, he pinches the nipple as he thrusts deep, over and over, until he's fully seated, and my eyes are leaking tears. Shouldn't there be a training wheel's dick size for an inexperienced woman like me? Men who are this well-endowed should be reserved for the women who've had practice or huge babies.

"Hey." Alexis ducks his head to press kisses to the corners of my eyes, licking up my tears. He rests against me, unmoving, letting my body adjust to the invasion. His lips ghost over mine, then move with more determination until his tongue is in my mouth, stroking and stroking, swamping my senses so much that I don't even notice he's started moving his hips.

I grip his ass as a flicker of uncertainty cools my veins. If he went too hard, he could really hurt me, so I keep my hands where I can resist him if I needed to, but it turns out Alexis is a true lover, and his body becomes a languid, undulating thing above me, grazing my clit with every slow thrust, teasing my nipples with his full lips until I'm so close to coming I begin to beg.

"Fuck, Alexis, fuck, please... please..."

He smiles down at me as he thrusts harder, pleased by my begging.

"Please. Fuck. I'm going to..." The rest of my words are lost to his mouth as he kisses the orgasm out of me, and I writhe and clench and claw my way through the pulsating bliss he's extracted from me.

Alexis turns feral, grinding into me like a machine, his chest and abs as taut as marble. He ducks close to my ear, his breath coming in fast, hot gusts. "You drive me insane, Aemelia. And I like it. You make me reckless. Make me want to throw the whole world into hell just to keep you warm."

I groan and grasp at him, my nails digging into his flesh, urging him on, and he's not far behind me, thrusting so deep to release that I arch from the bed, the ache a violation that triggers a second orgasm. The words that spill from his lips are a garbled mix of broken Italian curses and endearments that's like music, and I cling onto his back, slick with sweat, soul bared and body wracked.

"Aemelia." He draws me so close I can hardly breathe, but his embrace feels desperate, so I don't resist. "Baby. Fuck."

"I... oh my God."

He exhales a laugh. "Now, who's calling for the almighty."

"I don't think you're going to be able to pull out," I groan, my pussy continuing to pulse in constricting waves. "I think we're stuck together like this forever."

"I think the need to pee might force the issue," he says, and I start to wriggle away from him as he laughs, dragging me back.

"Kitten." He strokes my hair back from my face, staring down at me with what can only be described as fondness. "I love it when you beg me to come."

Inside me, his cock jumps, illustrating his point.

"I think I like begging."

He kisses the tip of my nose. "I think we're made for each other."

My limbs feel heavy, lazy, and too relaxed to move, and Alexis stretches out beside me, one arm folded beneath his head, the other tracing slow, idle circles over my hip. His eyes, heavy-lidded and sated, study me like he's memorizing every inch of my face. Like he's afraid if he blinks, I might disappear.

He catches me watching him and smirks lazily—that wicked mouth. I should know better by now.

"Careful, *dolcezza*," he murmurs, voice still rough from what we just did. "Keep looking at me like that, and you'll be too sore to walk tomorrow."

I let out a breathless laugh, the sound rasping through my still-raw throat. My body aches in all the best ways, but I arch a brow, playing along. "Big words, considering you're the one who just collapsed on top of me two minutes ago, panting like a ninety-year-old."

He makes a sound in the back of his throat—a low, playful growl—then props himself up on his elbow. His knuckles drift lazily over my bare shoulder, then down, tracing the curve of my arm like he can't help himself.

"Collapsed?" he repeats, mock-offended, his lips curving into a grin. "I was letting you catch your breath, baby. Being a gentleman."

I snort softly, but my heart skips a beat when his fingers catch mine, slowly tangling them together. I glance at our joined hands, suddenly feeling too exposed, too raw, but he holds on tighter.

"You're such a liar," I murmur.

He dips his head, brushing his lips over my knuckles, a reverent, almost tender gesture that leaves me stunned and breathless.

"Only when it matters," he counters smoothly, his gaze suddenly too serious, too piercing.

And just like that, he has me again, ruining me again, with nothing but a look.

For a long moment, we just stare at each other, the playful banter falling away, leaving something heavier in its place. Something that makes my chest ache.

But then, he leans in close, his mouth brushing my ear, and his warm breath fans across my skin, making me shiver.

"Besides," he whispers, low and sinful, "you're the one who was screaming my name so loud, I'm pretty sure they heard you in Sicily."

I slap his chest, heat rushing to my face, but he only chuckles, smug and satisfied. Completely unrepentant.

"Asshole," I grumble, trying to squirm away, but he catches my wrist and hauls me back against him, my spine flush with his chest.

"You love it," he murmurs against my neck, his voice a dark, velvety promise.

And God help me, I do.

Because when he holds me like this, so possessive, so sure, I know he could ruin me a thousand times over, and I'd still come back to him.

He touches my cheek, suddenly, more seriously, holding my gaze like he's at war with himself over something. Then he says, "I'm not a good man, Aemelia. But with you, I want to be. I want to deserve you. But even if I never do, it won't matter because I'm keeping you, whether I've earned you or not."

And even though there are many reasons for me to fear his confession, I pull him down to kiss me, wanting to be kept.

CHAPTER 30

LUCA

HIS LAST MISTAKES

The elevator hums softly as I descend into the basement, the smooth motion doing nothing to settle the rage simmering beneath my skin. Antonio stands beside me, his knife already twirling between his fingers with effortless precision. He doesn't need to speak; I already know his thoughts. Whoever took that shot at us outside our own building made a grave mistake.

When the doors slide open, we emerge into the hallway and access the concealed entrance to the basement. As we make our descent the scent of damp concrete, sweat, and old blood fills my nostrils. At the bottom of the stairs, the room is dimly lit, a single bulb flickering above the *uomo di merda* shackled to the chair in the center. Vito and Andre flank him, their faces expressionless, the unwavering stance of men who have done this a hundred times before. The bastard's head is slumped forward, his breathing heavy and uneven. A trickle of sweat drips down his temple, his torn shirt clinging to his chest like a second skin.

I step forward, slow and deliberate, the echo of my shoes against the concrete like the gunshots he was so happy to rain down upon us today.

"You were sloppy," I say, my voice calm, almost conversational. "Taking a shot at us in broad daylight? Missing?" I shake my head in disappointment. "It's almost insulting."

The man lifts his head just enough to glare at me through swollen eyes. I don't recognize him, but that doesn't make him any less of a threat. Blood crusts along his temple, his split lip barely able to form a sneer. "*Va' fan culo.*"

Fuck me? Me? This piece of shit has more than a death wish. He's begging for pain.

Antonio exhales sharply, a dark chuckle slipping from his lips. "You first."

I crouch before the man, resting my arms on my knees, watching him with the patience of a priest before a sinner. "Tell me who sent you."

Silence. His jaw tightens.

Vito shifts behind him, but I hold up a hand. "You know how this goes. You talk, maybe I let you walk out of here with most of your fingers. You don't…" I glance at Antonio, whose grip tightens on the knife. "Well, let's just say my brother is very creative."

The man spits at my feet. "I'm not telling you shit."

Antonio doesn't hesitate. He steps forward, grabbing the man's hand, and drives the knife straight through his palm, pinning it to the wooden arm of the chair. A strangled scream rips from his throat, his body jerking against the restraints. His back arches, muscles straining against the unbearable agony.

"Not the answer we were looking for," Antonio murmurs, twisting the blade just enough to make the bastard's agony double. "But maybe this will help you think." His voice is almost soothing like a father patiently scolding a disobedient child.

I stand, rolling my shoulders, tugging at my shirt cuffs, letting the moment stretch. The slow burn of anticipation coils in my gut. "Let's try again."

His breathing is ragged now, his forehead slick with sweat. He groans, eyes squeezing shut against the pain. When he finally speaks, his voice is a hoarse rasp. "Enzo... It was Enzo."

Antonio and I exchange a glance. My stomach tightens.

"Enzo Lambretti?" I ask, though I already know the answer.

He nods, biting down on another pained cry. "He sent us to kill the girl... take you all out." He sucks in a sharp breath.

Antonio growls, twisting the knife deeper. The man howls in agony, thrashing in the chair, his free hand curling into a useless fist.

I step back, exhaling slowly, letting the rage simmer just beneath my skin. "That's all I needed."

The man sags against the restraints, his body trembling. Relief flickers across his face for a fleeting second before he looks at Antonio's emotionless mask and realizes his mistake.

I turn on my heel, cold with the ease at which the *coglione* Enzo sent to kill Aemelia could have succeeded in ending her life, or ours, and pause. No one takes what is mine. When I speak, my voice is smooth and cold. "Finish him."

Antonio nods, wicked and deadly, as he pulls another blade from his pocket. The last thing I hear as I step into the hallway is the sound of another scream, then silence.

Enzo Lambretti just made his last mistake.

***

By the time I return to the penthouse, the tension in my shoulders is on the brink of snapping. Alexis is the first thing I see as I enter the living room. He's leaning against the counter, arms crossed, looking entirely too satisfied with himself. His shirt is half-buttoned, his hair still damp from a shower, and there's something smug about the way he lifts his chin at me.

"You look like shit," he says, pushing off the wall.

I ignore his attempt at humor and glance toward Aemelia's door. "She okay?"

He nods, expression softening just slightly. "She's fine. Shaken but fine. She's tougher than she looks."

Good. The last thing we need is for her to break. "Enzo's behind the shooting."

Alexis lets out a low whistle, dragging a hand through his hair. "Fucking Lambretti scum. Mario wasn't enough for them?"

I move to the bar and pour myself a drink, watching the amber liquid swirl in the glass. "He wanted to kill Aemelia."

Alexis exhales sharply, rolling his shoulders. "You think she'll be upset to lose him?"

I take a sip, the burn of whiskey settling deep in my chest. "We need to talk to her. Find out everything she knows. About her family, about the past. If we're going to take Enzo out..."

Alexis tilts his head. "You're worried she'll care, and..."

I set the glass down with a quiet clink, my gaze cutting to his. "And."

There's no need to say it out loud. We want her to stay with us and holding her against her will isn't enough. She needs to want to be here, and destroying any family she loves can only drive a wall between us.

Enzo wants to kill her, and we need to find out why.

Then we need to finish him.

I just hope Aemelia will agree because now there are two Lambretti cocksuckers on our hitlist, and there's no saving either of them.

CHAPTER 31

AEMELIA

WHAT HE NEEDS

I'm watching television when Luca enters the room. My door is no longer locked, but when Alexis left, he closed it behind him, and I didn't bother to test if they were truly comfortable with me wandering around the penthouse. Things have changed between us, but I'm not sure how much is real and how much is just a carefully maintained illusion.

Luca's gaze flicks to the screen, where a romance movie plays—a temporary escape from the tension around me. Embarrassment prickles at my skin, and I grab the remote, switching it off as if caught in something forbidden.

Even after hours in the penthouse, Luca is still impeccably dressed, his crisp shirt unwrinkled, his slacks pristine. He carries himself with the kind of effortless power that makes lesser men bow their heads and women forget how to breathe. Without a word, he moves across the room, dragging the chair from the corner and positioning it close to the bed. Then he sits, legs spread, forearms resting on his thighs, his unwavering gaze locked onto me.

His eyes, laser blue and searing, send shivers of awareness down my spine, just as they did the night of the wedding. Spending time in his company, kissing him, and sleeping in his arms has done nothing to lessen the impact of his intensity on my body. If anything, it's made it worse.

"I need to talk to you, Aemelia."

"Okay." My voice comes out smaller than it should, a risk where Luca is concerned. I don't want him to think I've been weakened by his brothers' attention or the gunman outside. Weakness is a magnet for men like Luca. It would make me another thing he could devour.

"Your uncle Enzo was the one who sent the gunman."

My stomach tightens. "How do you know?"

His eyebrows rise slightly as if my question amuses him. I exhale and nod. Of course, he knows. He's Luca Venturi.

"Why now?"

He shrugs one shoulder, a small movement that betrays his irritation. "He wanted to end this. End the shame on his family for good."

The shame. I hang my head.

"Do you love your uncle?"

I hesitate, understanding the gravity of the question. This isn't about my feelings; it's about Luca's intentions. "I don't know him," I whisper. "Not since I was a child. He was never kind to me. He always looked at me like I was something disgusting... the same way my father did."

Luca's jaw tightens, and he tuts, shaking his head. If I didn't know better, I'd think my family's treatment of me when I was younger bothers him. But this is Luca Venturi, the Boss of the Venturi family. His conscience is nothing but ash, his heart a lump of granite.

"You were innocent." Luca closes his intense eyes, his dark lashes framing the sharp line of his cheekbones. Then after a breath, as if the words cost him something, he adds, "You are innocent."

I force a small, bitter smile. "Not anymore."

His eyes flick up, and the fire in them steals the breath from my lungs. There is nothing cold about him now. He is molten, simmering with emotions that are wild and consuming.

"We're going to end Enzo's life for what he did today. Do you understand?"

The cool determination in his tone should chill the blood in my veins, but it doesn't. My uncle sent men with guns. I thought the past was bad enough when he saw my father beat me and did nothing. I could never forgive him for his apathy, worse, his complicity. And now?

"I do," I whisper.

Luca reaches out, his fingers brushing over my cheek before cupping my face. His palm is warm and firm, grounding me. A slow burn starts in my chest, spreading outward as if he's branding me with nothing but his touch.

"My father," I say, barely able to form the words. "Have you found him?"

Luca shakes his head, studying me carefully. "Do you know something? Something you haven't shared?"

"I think he was working with the feds," I admit. It's time to end this—all of it. To prioritize me for the first time before it's too late. "I think that's how he disappeared and why he didn't take us with him. He got a clean start without his cheating wife and Mario's so-called bastard children."

Luca's fingers tighten slightly at the back of my neck. "Why do you think this?"

"My aunt. I don't think she knew for sure, but she always said his disappearance was too clean. He took almost nothing. Left only empty bank accounts and his IDs behind. Wherever he was going, it was as a new man."

Luca nods, but his face is unreadable, his thoughts a storm I can't decipher. His breathing turns choppy, his control slipping for the first time since I met him. The air between us shifts, charged, volatile.

And then suddenly, he moves.

His hands frame my face, his grip firm, unyielding before his mouth crashes against mine. The kiss is fierce, searing, stealing the air from my lungs and replacing it with something wilder. I freeze for only a second before I open to him, letting him take what he wants. His tongue sweeps against mine, demanding, punishing, desperate.

There is no careful seduction, no patience. He kisses me like he's trying to drown in me, to forget something too dark to face. His fingers tangle in my hair, his grip on me possessive, claiming.

I should pull away.

I should fight.

But all my control is lost.

For the first time in my life, I have men who will defend me, protect my life with theirs, and avenge all the wrongs that have happened to me.

Luca growls low in his throat, his hands sliding down my sides, branding me with his touch. He lifts me effortlessly, settling me onto his lap, his fingers gripping my thighs as if he can't stand the distance between us. Heat coils in my stomach, spreading lower, igniting a deep desire inside me.

"Aemelia," he murmurs against my lips, his voice rough.

I swallow hard, my pulse hammering in my ears. "Luca."

His breath shudders at the sound of his name whispered huskily against his cheek. He holds me against him, cupping my head so my face is pressed into the crook of his neck. The past unravels behind me, dissolving into the dark as his warmth engulfs me. I'm back in the Venturi garden, cradled in his arms, inhaling the same clean, sharp scent of his cologne and his skin, safe.

It doesn't make sense that I should feel that way about a man who just promised to stain his hands with my uncle's blood, but not much in my life has ever made sense. I was forced to grow up too soon, a child who became a parent, a girl brutalized by the man who should have defended her. I was a stranger in my own home, out of place in my own life. And yet, here, in the hands of my father's enemies, I feel safer than I ever did in the world I was meant to belong to.

He whispers words in Italian, too fast and low for me to understand, but the cadence is hypnotic. It doesn't feel like words at all but a spell, a confession, a story revealing the secrets of his heart. I close my eyes and let his husky, melodic voice wash over me, losing myself in its dark melody.

"I'd do anything to keep you safe," he says gruffly, his voice rough with emotion like the words cost him something to admit to himself and to me.

His arms tighten around me, powerful and unyielding, as if daring the world to try and take me from him. The steady, controlled Luca Venturi—the man who commands with a look, who kills without hesitation—is shaking. Just barely, almost imperceptibly, but we're too close for me to miss it.

His breath stirs against my hair, warm and uneven. "I've taken lives without a second thought. Moved mountains for my family. Built an empire with blood and fire. But it's been empty, I've been empty, until now."

I swallow hard, my heart slamming against my ribs. "Luca…"

He lifts my chin, forcing me to meet his gaze. His eyes are scorching, filled with raw, terrifyingly real emotions that steal my breath.

"I don't just want to protect you, Aemelia. I want to destroy every fear that's ever haunted you, bury your past so deep that it never dares to touch you again."

A shiver rolls through me—not of fear, but of the kind of devotion that doesn't end in happily ever afters but in blood oaths and sacrifices.

His thumb strokes along my cheek, reverent and possessive. "Tell me you understand."

I nod, my lips parting, but no words come out. I don't need to say it.

He sees it in my eyes.

His confessions make me whimper. Beneath my thigh, his cock stirs thick and hard, and my body primes in response before my mind can catch up. Heat unfurls inside me, slow and insidious, a craving I have no business feeling. I trace the lines at the corners of his eyes, the rough stubble at his jaw flecked with silver along his jaw, the deep scar that cuts into his flesh—marks of a man who's lived, survived, conquered, so much a part of him that I can't imagine his handsome face before time and violence had marked him. He closes his eyes against the gentleness in my fingers as if tenderness is harder for him to accept than a knife in the gut.

When it becomes too much for him, he grasps my wrists, encircling them with one vicious hand, his grip like an iron shackle around my bones.

"I shouldn't want you," he says, his voice gravelly. "You understand that, don't you?"

His fingers tighten, not enough to hurt, but enough to make me feel small, powerless. My pulse pounds. Not in fear. Never in fear with Luca.

"I look at you, and I see a woman who turns my body and mind into an inferno. Your beauty, your strength, your fire, it consumes me. But then I remember carrying you in my arms when you were nothing but a little girl with too big eyes and tiny hands. And now..." He exhales sharply. "Now, all I want is to do what my brothers did—to bury myself in you until I've marked every inch of you, inside and out. To claim you. To own you."

His voice turns hoarse, and something like regret flickers behind his blue fire. "But I'm the Boss of this family. And—"

His voice seems to die at the end, turning into nothing but breath.

"And you should resist?" I finish for him.

His jaw clenches. "I should know better. A thirty-eight-year-old man, losing his fucking head over a twenty-year-old girl."

"Woman," I correct.

His nostrils flare. His grip on my wrists tightens. "At the

wedding, Antonio said that my dick doesn't have to feel guilty for wanting you." He lets out a low, humorless chuckle. "Even then…"

"You wanted me?"

"Yes. Like the first hit of a drug. And you wanted me, too. Every time our eyes met."

"I want you," I whisper. "I want…"

"To forget?" His tone is knowing, like he can see through me, through every broken, needy part of me, to the aching heart at the center who never believed that love could find her.

"Yes…"

"To hand over your power, your will, your sense of self?" He studies me like he's reading the pages of a book only he can understand. "I feel it, Aemelia. How much you hate to be weak, but how much you crave it."

His thumb drags over my lower lip, slow and possessive. He hooks it inside my mouth, pressing against my bottom teeth, forcing my lips apart. Everything with Luca feels like a test, a challenge, a boundary crossed, a line eviscerated.

A battle between resistance and surrender.

I touch his thumb with the tip of my tongue, tasting the salt of his skin, and sense the tensing of his body. Still, he holds me tightly by the wrists, anchoring me to him while he fights a war with himself.

"The things I want," he murmurs, staring transfixed at my mouth. "The things I need… I shouldn't take them from you."

I wrap my lips around his thumb, hollowing my cheeks, and his eyes blaze. I can't voice what I want, but I can show him. His breath hitches, his pupils blowing wide, undone by something so small.

"Sweet Aemelia," he rasps. "So precious. So eager to please. Such a good girl."

A shiver runs through me at his praise, burning through my skin, settling deep in the hollow place inside me that has always ached to be filled. I hate how good it feels—how much I need his praise and compliments. I should have enough backbone to stand on my own, to know my worth without a man's approval. But I was stripped of so much by my father's hatred, left with so little when he abandoned me.

Now, I press myself against Luca Venturi, one of the most feared men in the city, like he's my savior. I take the scraps of his kindness and feast on them. I crave to crumble under the weight of his dominance, to let him tear me apart and piece me back together.

I can't resist the pull of him—the promise of something darker, something deeper, something that feels like belonging.

When he withdraws his thumb, I whimper.

"Please," I whisper, keeping my eyes lowered, my lips parted, ready. Alexis demanded my plea, but Luca didn't need to.

He turns so his face is buried in my hair, his mouth so close to my ear I can feel the dampness of his breath.

"Say it properly."

My pulse pounds. Shame and desire war in my chest, but in the end, only one wins.

"How?"

He touches my ear with his lips, and a shudder wracks my body. "Please, Daddy," he says firmly, and I finally understand.

CHAPTER 32

LUCA

DADDY'S LITTLE PRINCESS

Aemelia trembles in my arms as I whisper the words that will expose my darkest desires, and I wait for her response; for the moment she'll either surrender to me completely or fight against what we both know she craves.

She's been standing on her own for so long, abandoned by the one man who should have protected her. Her father left her in the hands of his enemies, and she's had to survive in a world that has shown her no mercy. But I want her to know she doesn't have to be strong all the time—not with me.

I want her on her knees. I want her to trust me enough to break for me, to let me be the one who takes care of her, cherishes her, and shields her from the rest of the world until the end of my days. Just the feel of her tucked against my chest, her warmth sinking into me, is enough to unravel me.

Every second that ticks by feels like an eternity, the air

between us static with anticipation. The room closes around me, my heart a drum pounding in my ears. Will she say it? Will she give me what I need?

"Please, Daddy," she whispers, her body melting against mine, handing over the last of her resistance as I close my eyes, letting her submission seep inside me, groaning low and deep like a man on the brink of madness.

I was right. From the moment I saw her across the room at my sister's wedding, I could sense we were made for each other. I knew she'd burn my restraint to the ground. She's been the fire in my veins ever since.

Releasing her wrists, I bring each one to my lips, kissing softly over the delicate skin where my grip might have bruised, finding the heart birthmark that started this whole thing.

"*Amuri miu*," I mouth against her skin, over and over, branding her with my words. I cradle her face in my hands and stare into her eyes. "I know what you need," I tell her. "I know how to take away the noise in your head. Submit to me, and everything will be better. I will tear the fabric of the world apart to keep you safe."

She closes her beautiful dark eyes as I kiss her, keeping it slow and chaste, making her ache for more. When she's pliant, whimpering against my lips, I pull back. "Put this hand around my neck and this one on my knee."

She obeys without hesitation.

"Now, open your legs for me, sweet girl. Open your legs for Daddy."

In her pink nightgown, she's every man's dream, but especially mine. Delicate yet willing, her body trembles beneath my hands. Her eyes are wide, watching as I slide my palm up the inside of her thigh, relishing the warmth of her skin. She spreads her legs wider at my urging, jerking when I stroke the tips of my fingers over her panties, the damp heat against my touch igniting all that is feral inside me.

It would be so easy to flip her onto the bed, yank her underwear aside, and take her until I explode, but that's not what I want.

This first time, I want to make memories. I want to teach my sweet baby girl what it takes to sleep in my bed every night... what it means to belong to me.

Because she will. By the time we're done, there will be nothing for her to go back to that will ever be better than what she has here.

The Lambrettis will blame her for Enzo's death, her mother and brother will drain her dry if she lets them, but I won't allow that. She belongs to me.

I drag my fingers higher, pressing against her clit, circling with the lightest touch as she lets her legs drop open further and arches her spine.

"Does that feel good, kitten?" I whisper. "Do you like it when I touch you?"

"Yes," she breathes. "I like it."

I slip beneath the lace of her panties, finding her soaked for me, stroking, teasing, pushing her to the edge before withdrawing, savoring the way her body jerks with need.

"This... what we're doing, it's a game I like to play. Do you understand?"

She nods, her lashes heavy with arousal and submission. I palm her breast and pinch her tight little nipple, hungry to discover every part of her. "If you want me to stop, just tell me... say *fermari* and the game will be over."

Another nod. A promise unspoken. I tuck a lock of hair behind her ear.

"Now, get on your knees, Aemelia. Get on your knees for Daddy. Show me what a good girl you are."

I brace myself for hesitation, for the lingering defiance I saw in her eyes during those first days when I spanked her sweet ass, made her kiss my feet, and touched her without permission. But there is none. This time, she slides to the floor without a trace of hatred or reluctance, her palms resting on the ground, her wide eyes full of trust and need. I touch her cheek with the fingers that smell of her and spread my legs. "Take me out," I command. "See what you've done to me."

Her nimble fingers make quick work of the belt, my button, my zipper, her touch hesitant but eager. She pauses at my boxer briefs, tracing the rigid outline of my straining cock.

"See what you did. See what touching your pretty pussy does to me."

Her tongue swipes over her bottom lip as I reach to palm my dick. It aches in my grip, the skin stretched tight, engorged with blood and heat. At the top, a pearl waits for her tongue.

"Look at what you do to me, sweet girl," I rasp, fisting myself roughly. "You make me so hard, kitten. You make me lose my fucking mind."

As I stroke my cock harshly, she watches. "Give me your hand."

Her dark eyes flick to mine, searching. Then she shakes her head just a little. Oh, Aemelia. How perfect you are, waiting for my order. "Give it to me."

She lifts her right hand from the floor slowly, reluctantly, playing my little game in a way I didn't expect. I take it roughly, pressing her palm to my fabric-covered thigh, sliding it up and up until she's close to my dick. "You want to make me feel good, don't you, princess? Like I'm going to make you feel good."

Taking the tip of her index finger, I coat it with my arousal and rub it over her lip. "Taste me." My dick thickens as she licks her bottom lip. "Now, touch me."

I curl her fingers around my shaft, the first touch of her small, warm hand like a lick over my balls. Showing her how tight to hold me, I move her hand up and down in long, hard strokes, twisting on the way up and down. "No," she whispers, a fragile protest. "I don't want to."

But her hand doesn't stop. And she doesn't say the safe word.

She's mesmerized, her fingers moving over me, and I feel the victory settle deep in my bones.

"Your mouth. Give me your mouth." I cup the back of her neck, tugging her closer. "Open."

She obeys, and I guide her, pressing the thick head of my cock against the flat of her waiting tongue. Like she understands the complex tapestry of my black heart, she remains still, waiting. Her warm breath gusts over the head, and I close my eyes, forcing myself to remain in the moment *before*.

"Such a good girl," I praise, my voice tight with restraint. "Now suck."

The wet heat of her mouth is perfect, a slow, torturous slide that has me groaning. She learns quickly, working me over, and I take a mental picture of this moment, knowing I'll never forget it.

"Eyes on me, Aemelia," I hiss, the clasp of her lips a perfect pressure. Slow, up and down movements draw my belly and balls tight.

"Good," I growl. "So good, kitten. You know just how to make Daddy feel good."

As I tip my head back, relaxing into the slow slide of her mouth, the door to the penthouse slams close, and footsteps thud against the marble.

"Luca?" Antonio's deep voice thunders through the space, cutting into my pleasure.

"In here."

Aemelia stiffens, but I keep my grip firm, holding her in place. "Don't stop," I order. She hesitates for a moment, then continues as Antonio enters the room. When he takes in the sight of Aemelia on her knees between my widespread legs, his confident stride falters, and confusion flickers over his expression. Behind him, Alexis comes to a halt, but he's quicker to regain his composure and quicker to smile.

"What is it?" I ask, my voice calm and controlled. Aemelia continues her work, seemingly unaffected, but I know differently. She'll be wet between her thighs, dripping at the thought of my brothers watching us.

Antonio's posture stiffens like a metal rod is forced through his spinal column. "Who shall I send?" he asks.

I rattle off eight names—our most reliable soldiers and our maternal cousin, who's known only as *il coltello*. Pleasure builds, but I hold myself rigid against the urge to shift my hips, to thrust, to arch my spine and empty deep in Aemelia's throat.

"Tonight?" Alexis asks.

"Now," I say. "They take him to the cellars and keep him there until I'm ready to take my revenge. We send a message that no one comes for our precious girl." I stroke Aemelia's hair, and she hums around my dick. I watch my brothers shift, their cocks already hard, tenting the front of their pants as they focus on Aemelia.

"Give the orders," I say. "Then come back. Our little mafia princess needs all her kings around her."

As they reluctantly leave to handle business, I tip Aemelia's chin, drawing her away. My dick is glossy with her spit and dark with arousal. "You did so well," I tell her. "That can't have been easy, knowing you were being watched."

"I liked it," she whispers, her cheeks pink. "I liked their eyes on me."

Of course, she did. I bend to kiss her, all deep tongue and urgency, and then I pull back, leaving her panting.

"When they come back, do you want them to watch, or more? They can touch you, lick you, fuck you. Whatever you want, we'll give it to you."

She rests her hand on my thigh, her eyes closing like she needs the safety of the dark behind her eyelids to consider my question. She's so pretty that looking at her, taking in her beauty is light forcing its way through cracked walls.

"I want you all," she says, "but how?"

"You don't need to worry about anything, my sweet, innocent girl. Let us take care of you. And any time it gets too much, and you want to stop, all you have to do is say *fermari*, remember, and we'll stop. Okay?"

"Okay."

"Come sit on my knee."

She rises demurely and settles into the space she rested in before, her face buried in my neck. I stroke her arm and link my fingers with hers. She wears no rings, and her ears carry no jewels. This life hasn't been fair to her, taking her wealth, her status, her dignity, delivering little of the kind of love she deserves, but I resolve to make it right.

"Understand something, Aemelia. You belong to me," I say, gripping her jaw fiercely. "Every inch of you, from the tip of your pretty tongue to the soles of your feet. Mine to touch. Mine to worship. Mine to ruin."

Her whimper of agreement is all I need to hear.

Once upon a time, Aemelia Lambretti was a mafia princess. Now I'm going to make her a queen.

CHAPTER 33

AEMELIA

WALK WITH US

I rest in Luca's arms while he holds my hand, his lips brushing over my forehead, whispering words in Italian that sound like a love song. His voice is low and deep, each syllable a promise, a spell that weaves around me, making it impossible to remember a time when I didn't crave his touch. His arousal is evident, pressing against my stomach, but for now, he's content to hold me, to anchor me in this moment.

But I can't forget how easily he coaxed me into taking him in my mouth, how controlled he was as I sucked him, the way he spoke as if I wasn't on my knees, my lips wrapped around him. Knowing his brothers were there, watching him own my mouth, was mortifying and arousing in equal measure. Shame flooded me, but it was fleeting, replaced by something more dangerous—acceptance.

Luca Venturi is the boss of his family, and today, he became the boss of me.

His power takes away all the noise in my head, the fear, the anxiety, and the demands of life, leaving only peaceful silence in its wake.

How long before they return? How long will I have to wait?

Without Luca bending me to his will, my mind spins with questions. What happens when they're done with me? When they've taken me together, when there's nothing left to explore, will they send me home?

The thought makes my stomach turn. I don't want to go home. I don't want to step back into my aunt's suffocating apartment, heavy with the scent of approaching death and despair, where I'm the only one trying to keep everything from collapsing. I'm only twenty, yet I have three dependents. It's too much. It always has been too much.

But the truth is even harder to face.

Wanting to stay with my captors, the men determined to erase half my bloodline should be unforgivable, even if it's the half who despise me. And yet, the Venturis have protected me, cherished me, given me a sense of safety I've never known. How messed up is it that I feel safer in the tank of sharks than I ever did on the shore?

"Do you need some water? Something to eat?" Luca's soft voice pulls me from my thoughts

"Water would be good," I admit, surprised at his consideration. I guess strict mafia bosses can also be thoughtful.

He shifts, gently lowering me onto the bed before tucking himself away. When he leaves the room, I take a moment to rub my hands over my face, breathing deeply. This is real. This is happening.

Am I really going to do this? Be with all of them?

I glance down at my bare legs, my unpainted toenails, and the delicate nightgown clinging to my skin. Why would they want me, just me, when they could have any woman they desired—women who wouldn't need to be shared?

Antonio took my virginity. That was his prize. But since

then, I've surrendered to Alexis, and Luca has claimed my mouth. Any sentiment attached to my first time should be long gone.

Why aren't they married? Why don't they have wives, children, a traditional Sicilian life?

Luca returns, carrying a tall glass of water and a plate. He passes me the glass first, waiting for me to drink, then passes me the plate. Three small Amaretti cookies rest together, delicate and golden.

"You should eat something. Keep your strength up."

The unspoken reason lingers between us. My body is small and weak compared to theirs. I'm one, and they're three. I'm inexperienced, and they have years of sexual history. Three small almond cookies won't be enough to prepare me for when Alexis and Antonio return, but I eat them anyway, not wanting to disappoint Luca or reject his kindness.

He settles into the chair, watching me as I take slow bites.

"How's Rosita," I ask between mouthfuls. "Where did she go on honeymoon?"

"She's fine. The Maldives."

I frown, trying to recall the world map from my geography lessons. "I don't know where that is."

"Islands in the Indian Ocean."

I nod. "Her husband—do you like him?"

Luca arches a dark eyebrow and raises the corner of his mouth into an even darker smile. "Do you think she would have married him if I didn't like him?"

Of course. He's not only a big brother but a mob boss. No man would dare to claim his sister without his approval.

"What's he like?"

"Raphael? He's clever. A lawyer. Strong, from a good family."

Good. A relative term. Does he mean pure-hearted, reputable, or simply an ally in their world?

"They seem very much in love."

He huffs like love is a myth, a fairytale, something only young girls believe can be real. "Rosita is a romantic. Always has been. She used to make me pretend to be her knight in shining armor. I had to keep reminding her I was her brother."

I smile at the memory. I remember that game. She tried to make me pick between her brothers, but even then, I didn't want to choose.

"So, maybe you'll be an uncle soon."

Luca's expression twists for a second but then softens. "It's hard to imagine her as a married woman. She's my little sister, you know. And now she's a Russo and belongs to another man."

I tilt my head. "Women don't belong to men, Luca. We choose to walk next to them, to lie by their sides, to give birth to their children, to tend to their homes, and to suffer when they suffer. If we're lucky, they're worthy of that devotion."

His blue eyes sharpen as I dust the crumbs from my fingers over the plate. The weight of his attention is suffocating in its intensity but welcome still. I remind myself to breathe.

"You don't want to belong to someone, kitten?"

I hesitate, playing with the hem of my nightgown. "I want to belong somewhere," I admit. "I want to know I have a safe place in the world."

Luca's gaze softens, something unreadable flickering in the depths of his eyes. "We can give you that."

I glance up at him, finding his expression as serious as ever, his hands upturned where they rest on his thighs, open like he's ready to accept whatever I have to give. "If you choose to walk with us."

My heart clenches. Those words—my words—echo back at me, wrapping around my ribcage like a promise I never knew I needed to hear.

His smile is quick and devastating, a flash of lightning in a midnight sky. He takes the plate from my hands, setting it aside, then effortlessly lifts me, gathering me in his arms and snuggling me against his body where I feel safest. Where I belong.

"We'll show you what it takes to be ours, princess," he murmurs, his breath warm against my ear. "And then, if you still want to choose to lie by our sides, we'll make it so."

CHAPTER 34

ANTONIO

CLAIMED BY HER FATHER'S ENEMIES

For fifteen minutes, I coordinated our response to Enzo's hit attempt with Alexis, my mind split between strategy and the suffocating need clawing inside me. The rage burning through my veins is a twisted, all-consuming thing—hot and sharp, fueling my hunger for revenge. Enzo's betrayal of Aemelia is unforgivable. A man who would order a hit on his own flesh and blood is less than dirt. He doesn't deserve to take his next breath, and by sunrise, he won't.

But beneath my fury, another desire coils making it difficult to concentrate. The image of Aemelia kneeling for Luca, her lips wrapped around him, her body pliant, the way he stroked her hair while issuing commands like she was nothing but a toy—it rattled something inside me. She didn't flinch when we walked in. She didn't shrink in shame or try to pull away. She remained there, devoted and obedient.

She was a virgin when she came to us, hesitant and unsure, unaware of the depths of pleasure she was capable of feeling. And now? Now she offers herself without hesitation, comfortable in submission, willing to let Luca guide her into his dark proclivities. The thought alone is enough to make my hands tighten into fists.

I've never been a man to share what's mine, but Aemelia—she doesn't belong to just one of us. She's under our protection. She's in our care. She's become something none of us want to let go of. I cannot begrudge Luca a taste of the girl who's burrowed her way under our skin, unraveling us one by one.

"Call us when you have the meat," Alexis says into the burner phone, voice clipped, taking no risks. His words are casual, but we both know Enzo the butcher will soon be reduced to the very thing he's built his trade upon. Tonight, he will know what it's like to be on the receiving end of a blade. But before that, we'll make Aemelia understand exactly what it means to be claimed by her father's enemies.

Alexis leans against the wall, arms crossed, eyes flicking toward the door to Aemelia's room. "You good with this?" he asks, though the heat in his gaze tells me he already knows the answer. . We've shared women before, but never anything serious. Never like this. And never with Luca.

"I don't know what he's going to expect," I admit, rolling my shoulders, trying to loosen the tension coiled within me.

"I guess we just wait and see."

Without hesitation, he strides to the door, as impatient for more of Aemelia as I am. My blood pumps faster, anticipation thrumming through me like a war drum. I follow, stepping inside to find her curled on Luca's lap, eyes closed, his fingers threading through her hair in slow, rhythmic strokes. She looks at peace, completely undone in a way that makes my breath catch. She's wearing the delicate nightgown she had on earlier, the thin fabric hugging her curves, leaving nothing to the imagination.

I wonder if she finished him, if he finished her, or have they been waiting for us?

"Close the door," Luca says in his standard firm tone.

When the door clicks shut, I twist the inside lock, the weight of the moment pressing down on me. All our lives, we've known violence and power; its familiarity is easy to navigate, but this is something different: trust and surrender. My body craves Aemelia, but my heart is stronger, yearning for her gentle caresses, her sweet kisses, desperate to keep her safe.

"Our sweet girl wants to please us, don't you, Aemelia?" Luca murmurs, his fingers trailing along her jaw, tilting her face up to him.

She blinks, eyes heavy with lust, lips swollen, her breathing slow and measured. When she finally meets my gaze, there's no fear, no hesitation. Only something deeper.

"I do," she whispers, and my stomach tightens at her confession.

Alexis smirks, prowling closer, his gaze sweeping over her like he's already imagining all the ways he's going to make her fall apart for him.

"Such a good girl," Luca praises, his hand gliding down her back, soothing and possessive. "Now, go to Antonio and show him how much you missed him."

She rises from his lap slowly, her movements languid, fluid as if she's floating. The girl who came here was coiled tight, vicious with resentment, burning with hatred. This Aemelia is soft and relaxed, ready for anything, and willing to please. When she stands, her clingy nightdress slides over her thighs and dips low between her breasts, teasing me. My heart pounds as she stops inches from me, the heat of her body radiating into mine. My fingers twitch, the possessiveness inside me roaring to life.

I tilt her chin up, forcing her to hold my gaze, breathing her in, her scent of roses and vanilla making my head spin. "Are you sure, Aemelia?" My voice is rough, but I need to ask. I need her to give herself willingly to understand what this means.

She exhales shakily, nodding once, then again, her delicate hands splaying against my chest, her touch searing through the fabric of my shirt.

"Yes," she breathes. "I'm sure."

My restraint snaps.

I claim her mouth in a bruising kiss, pouring every ounce of my hunger, my longing, into her, swallowing her soft moans and tasting her surrender. I lift her easily, gripping her thighs as I carry her toward the bed, ready to show her how much I want her to be mine.

Alexis chuckles darkly from behind her. "Looks like our little kitten is ready to play."

Luca leans back in his chair, watching with the cool detachment of a king surveying his kingdom. But I know better. I see the way his fists clench, the heat simmering behind his ice-blue eyes. He might have had her first tonight, but we're far from finished.

Aemelia trembles in my grasp, her breath coming in soft, uneven pants against my lips. Her hands fist the fabric of my shirt like she needs something to ground her, to tether her to the moment before she's swept away. I slide my hands down the curve of her spine, relishing the way she melts into me, trusting, eager. She was made for this—for us. For me.

Lowering her onto the mattress, I spread her out beneath me, framing her face with my hands as I drink her in. Dark, doe-like eyes peer up at me, pupils blown wide, her lips still swollen from my kiss. She's utterly wrecked already, and I haven't even begun.

"You're so fucking beautiful," I murmur, my thumb tracing the curve of her cheek. "Do you know that?"

She shakes her head slightly, and something deep in my chest tightens.

"Then let me show you. I'll kiss you until you forget you were ever afraid. I'll hold you so close you won't remember where you end, and I begin. And when I'm done, you'll only know one thing—you're mine."

I capture her lips again, this time slower, savoring her taste, teasing her with my tongue until she gasps against me. My hands map her body, memorizing every dip, every delicate curve, the way she arches into my touch, seeking more.

Alexis sits beside us on the bed, his fingers skimming the hem of her nightdress, his voice a dark purr. "Look at you, kitten. You're trembling. Is it anticipation?"

She turns her head slightly, her gaze flickering to him, and my stomach clenches when she exhales. "Yes."

Alexis smirks, trailing his fingers up her thigh, his touch featherlight. "Good answer."

Luca remains where he is, a predator biding his time, watching with cool detachment, but the tension in his frame betrays him. He's waiting. He wants her as much as we do.

I grip her thighs, spreading them slightly as I lower myself, my lips skimming her jaw, her throat. She whimpers, her fingers threading through my hair, tugging, needing more.

Alexis leans down, capturing her lips as I trail my tongue along the hollow of her throat, feeling her pulse race beneath my mouth.

"You're ours now," I growl against her skin, my hand sliding beneath her nightdress, inching it up. "You're my obsession. My sickness. My addiction. I'll never want less of you. Only more. Always more. You understand, don't you, sweet girl?"

She nods, her breath stuttering. "Yes."

Alexis breaks the kiss, tilting her chin toward him. "Say it, kitten."

Her lashes flutter, her voice barely a whisper. "I'm yours."

I groan, pressing my forehead against her shoulder, barely holding myself back. I want to ruin her, to claim her in every way possible until she knows—until she *feels*—that there is no escaping us.

Luca finally moves, prowling closer, his voice deep and authoritative. "Then let's make it official."

Aemelia shudders, her fingers tightening on me, her body caught between submission and hunger.

Tonight, we show her exactly what it means to belong to the Venturis.

CHAPTER 35

AEMELIA

A MAFIA QUEEN

They surround me, touching, kissing, watching. My mind spins with sensations and the feeling of letting go. All my life I've held my chin high, my back straight, ready to shoulder my family's burdens, but with the Venturis close, I feel like I can let everything go.

Their toughness makes me want to be soft; their masculinity draws out my femininity. I want to bend to their will, let their strength envelop me, and experience the relief of not needing to worry about anything other than their hands and mouths on me.

All I want is to be held and protected.

Luca, who was so in charge when we were alone, remains remote, but I can feel his eyes blazing against my skin, feel him watching his brothers begin to take me apart. I want him to tell me what he expects of me. I want to know that I'm pleasing him, even as I please his brothers.

In so little time, he's infiltrated my psyche.

"Take off your panties, Aemelia," he says as Antonio slides his tongue into my mouth, and Alexis pushes down my nightdress and runs his finger around my tight nipple. I push the lace over my hips and pull my legs up so I can get my underwear over my knees. When they're off, Luca hums with approval.

"Open your legs, pretty girl. Display yourself to me."

Heat floods me, flushing my cheeks and making my body tingle. I let my knees fall open, but it's not enough for Luca.

"Use your fingers," he says. "Spread yourself open."

Both Alexis and Antonio have pulled back to look down at me, nightdress revealing everything but my belly, face as warm as the sun, fingers lowering to tease open my labia as Luca had ordered.

The air is cool over my heated, sensitized flesh. I'm wet, and my clit is swollen. I close my lids as three sets of eyes zero in on the place between my thighs.

"Fuck," Luca growls. "Look at that sweet pussy. Look at the way our princess is showing us what's ours." He moves closer, pressing a soft kiss to the inside of my knee, inhaling. I shiver as our eyes meet over the length of my body, and he burns me with the longing in his eyes.

He flicks open the buttons of his shirt methodically. Too slow. I watch as he reveals his strong throat, a sliver of muscular chest, tanned skin, and a dusting of dark hair across his pecs. Lower, his belly is tight, a dark trail leading to the cock he made me suck. My mouth waters as he pushes the fabric from his body, and I take in the majesty of Luca Venturi shirtless.

"Hold her," he tells his brothers, who each take one of my arms in their rough hands and anchor my wrists above my head. Like this, my body is stretched tight, my breasts round and high, my belly concave. Luca pulls the nightgown from beneath me and tosses it to the floor, then spreads me wide with hands on the inside of my thighs.

"What do you want, princess?" he asks, kissing my ankle,

making me shiver.

"Please," I whisper.

Alexis chuckles, but Luca's expression is cool and serious.

"Please, what?"

I bite my bottom lip, unused to the game but desperate to please him. "Please, Daddy. Lick me."

He closes his eyes at my words, and a shudder of pleasure runs through him. Then he dips lower and presses a tender kiss against my clit. "So sweet," he murmurs, kissing again. "So perfect."

Alexis leans closer, his handsome face filling my vision. "You're at our mercy, totally within our control," he says, his eyes dancing. He kisses my mouth, licking under my top lip, savoring me, and Luca does the same between my legs, and then he whispers, "But you have all the power, little kitten."

I shake my head, and he chuckles. "Look at us, worshiping at your body like an altar."

Letting my gaze drift from his, I find Antonio close, his mouth hovering over my nipple, and Luca, his blue eyes blazing as his tongue presses into my hole. I can't move, can't even wriggle; they're holding me so tightly, but Alexis is right. This feels like worship.

They're not taking from me. They're giving. Pleasure, safety, the reverence of their touch. I soak it all in, letting it wind my body higher and higher until I'm quivering and whimpering, and Luca is humming his approval against my flesh. He pushes one thick finger inside me, curling upward, beckoning against my inner walls, and I throw my head back as I'm swept away in a tidal wave of release, lights bursting behind the darkness of my closed eyelids, a keening, desperate sound escaping my lips. Antonio grips my face and kisses my cheeks, whispering. "That's it, Aemelia. Take it. Let go. Let it all go," and I know he sees everything I've been trying to hold together my whole life.

Tears leak from my eyes, and he kisses them away,

stroking my face. "We've got you," he says. "You don't have to worry about anything ever again."

I tremble and Alexis releases my wrist and kisses the soft skin as Luca does the same on the inside of my thigh. I reach for Antonio, drawing his mouth to mine and we kiss, tongues tangling, hands roaming. The hiss of belts tugging through loops and pants hitting the floor provides background noise to our passion, and knees nudge the underside of my thigh as someone climbs between my legs. The cock that's shoved inside me is thick, but I'm slick from my orgasm, and it no longer feels like a strange intrusion to be filled. When whoever is inside me begins to move, I draw back from Antonio to find Alexis and Luca have switched places. Luca is now at my side, his fingers playing with my nipple as Alexis thrusts, his hips undulating, his expression tight and focused.

"Fuck, you feel so good," he says, resting his hand over my belly, his thumb stroking around my too-sensitive clit.

"Climb on top of her," Luca instructs Antonio. "Give her your dick."

While Antonio finished undressing, Luca props me up with two pillows so that when Antonio straddles my upper body, my face is angled to take him. He holds himself, uncertainty widening his eyes, but it drops away when I lick the tip of his dick and wrap my lips around it, sucking gently. I'm not experienced at blow jobs, but Antonio takes charge, sliding his hand under my head and curling his huge, muscular tattooed body over me as he pushes his cock between my lips, over and over. He doesn't work himself in too deep. He's careful, keeping our eyes locked, watching for my responses, staring at me like he can't believe we're together this way. Alexis is thrusting harder now, hitting deeper, and I hum with pleasure, which makes Antonio leak precum over my tongue. "Fuck," they both say at the same time as sensations curl tighter.

Out of the corner of my eyes, I glance at Luca, finding him sitting in a chair, watching, his thick cock in his hand, his pulls slow, tight, and long. Our eyes meet, and he smiles, nodding his approval, and then I get lost in the push and pull and the bone-softening knowledge that Luca is pleased with me.

"I'm close," Antonio hisses.

"Fuck." Alexis's thrusts grow uncoordinated as his dick swells, and then he pulls out, jerking himself over my belly as Antonio freezes over me, shooting his cum over my tongue and down my throat. I swallow, watching him come apart, the salt-sweet taste of his release wiping everything from my mind. He strokes my cheek, slipping from between my lips, his eyes glazed and his movements shaky. When he climbs from me, Alexis is still pumping his cock in his hand, his eyes between my legs, his tattooed arms blazing like the inferno around my heart.

"Very nice," Luca says. "For an innocent girl, you take my brothers well."

"She was made for us," Alexis says, brushing his fingers through the mess he made and stroking them over my clit. I jump at the sensation, which makes him smile. "So sensitive."

I turn to Luca and reach out my hand to him. "Daddy," I whisper.

"Come here."

Antonio and Alexis give me space to slide from the bed and approach Luca. I stand in front of him, my arms hanging limply at my sides, and I gaze down at my body to see what he sees. My belly is marked with Alexis's release, which trickles into the soft curls at the apex of my thighs, and my nipples are red tipped from their mouths and teeth. My lips feel swollen, and my hair must be a mess, but he holds out his hand eagerly. "Come sit in my lap."

Drawing me forward, I settle on his thighs with my legs spread. He runs the back of his hand over my nipple, each knuckle nudging it to a sharper point. "Did you like what they did to you?" he asks, wetting his lips.

"Yes."

My cheeks heat, and he smiles. "But you want more."

"Yes, Daddy."

His hands grip my ass, pulling me forward. "Are you sure?" He slides the head of his cock through my wetness, and I shudder.

I shake my head because I know that's what he wants: a little game where he can flaunt his power and take what he shouldn't.

"Don't worry, princess. It'll only hurt a little."

He notches at my entrance, and I watch as he forces the head of his dick inside me, his thickness spreading me open. Then he shoves hard, tugging me down, and I gasp at the stretch. It does hurt because I'm sore, but he was right. Only a little. A perfect violation.

Resting my hands on his shoulders, I brace myself as he throbs inside me and latches onto my nipple, biting down. When I cry out, he licks me like a cat, soothing the hurt.

"Hold her hands," he says, and Alexis responds, peeling my arms from his brother's shoulders and securing them behind my back with his strong fingers.

Luca moves my body like I'm a doll, a plaything, but he doesn't take his eyes off mine, trapping us together in an unbreakable stare, one that pins me in place more effectively than Alexis' grip. Luca's fingers trace along my jaw, achingly slow, his touch possessive and reverent like he's memorizing the shape of me. The heat in his eyes is sharp, searing through me with unspoken promises of things I can barely dare to fathom.

He tilts my chin higher with a single knuckle, forcing me to expose my throat to him, and a dark smile tugs at his lips, one that's more predator than man. My breathing quickens, shallow and uneven, but I can't look away. I don't want to.

"Like this," he murmurs, his voice a low, dangerous rasp. His thumb brushes over my lower lip, testing its softness, his expression darkening when I tremble beneath his touch. He likes it. My vulnerability. My surrender.

Alexis' fingers flex around my wrists, his grip tightening

ever so slightly as though reminding me of my captivity. His breath skims the shell of my ear, and he chuckles softly, the sound low and wicked, sending a shiver down my spine.

"Look at you," Luca continues, his gaze molten steel as I move in slick strokes, taking his cock as deep as I can. His hand drags down my throat, slow and deliberate, letting me feel every calloused inch of him as he travels lower. "So fragile... so fucking beautiful." His eyes narrow slightly. "Ours."

The possessiveness in that single word makes my knees buckle, but Alexis holds me steady, his chest pressed firmly to my back. Luca notices, of course. He always notices. His eyes glimmer with satisfaction as he watches me sway helplessly between them.

"Hold her tighter," Luca orders, his voice barely above a growl, but there's no mistaking the authority in it. Alexis obeys instantly, his arm a cage around me, keeping me upright.

And then Luca's mouth slants over mine, rough and claiming, no hesitation, no softness. His lips demand—command—as his fingers wrap around my throat, holding me exactly where he wants me. His kiss is all fire and dominance, and I meet it with a helpless moan, starving for more.

My wrists flex against Alexis' grip, but he doesn't loosen his hold. Instead, he tightens his fingers, breathing against my ear with a dark, satisfied chuckle.

"You're not going anywhere, *bella*," Alexis murmurs, his voice thick with sinister amusement, his grip unyielding. "You're exactly where you belong."

Antonio approaches, his gray eyes a storm of hunger and uncertainty, and he strokes my arm, then my breasts, watching my skin pebble with goosebumps.

"Play with her clit," Luca orders, and when Antonio circles there gently, I buck on Luca's cock.

Luca leans in just enough to drag his teeth over my lower lip, his eyes hooded and feral with lust. He brushes his lips against mine again—a cruel ghost of a kiss—before pulling back entirely, leaving me trembling.

He trails a finger along my throat one last time, and his voice comes out low and wrecked. "No more running, Aemelia." His eyes blaze with warning. "Never again."

Then he thrusts up hard, holding me in place, ruthlessly pounding into me until I'm coming again, as fast as a whip crack. "Oh God… oh… fuck… I… I…"

"That's it," he growls, "Yes. Fuck. Yes. Come all over my cock…" Then he jerks inside me, spilling into my pussy, mashing my pelvis against his, my name on his lips like a prayer. "Aemelia, fuck, yes, do it. Take it. Take my fucking cum."

And I do. We're a mess between our bodies, and I'm limp and wrecked, but it's okay. It's more than okay. It's perfect.

Antonio instructs Alexis to release me and lifts me from Luca's lap. He carries me like a sleeping child to my waiting bed, resting my body gently against the crisp white comforter. Antonio lowers me with such care that it makes my throat tighten, and the tenderness in his touch undoes me more than the bruising grip of Luca's hands or the merciless strength in Alexis' hold.

He lingers over me, his breath warm against my temple as he presses my body into the mattress. His palm glides down my arm, his fingers tracing lazy patterns into my skin as though committing me to memory. I exhale shakily, blinking up at him through the haze of my wrecked desire.

"*Rest, bella,*" he murmurs, his voice a low, rasping command, but there's a softness there, a gentleness he doesn't bother to hide. His knuckles graze my cheek, featherlight, and his eyes—storm-dark and heavy-lidded—search mine with almost unbearable intensity.

I should be spent, too weak to respond, but the way he looks at me like I'm some rare, exquisite treasure he never thought he'd hold ignites a whole new ache deep in my chest. My fingers tremble as I reach for him, slipping over his shoulder and his chest.

"Stay," I whisper, barely more than a breath.

Antonio's eyes flicker, raw and vulnerable, before he lowers his head, pressing his forehead to mine. His exhale is heavy, shuddering, and his hand slides around the back of my neck, holding me like a man on the brink of losing himself.

"Aemelia," he rasps, but his voice betrays him. Low and wrecked, heavy with longing he can't suppress. His lips hover near mine, so close I can feel the heat of him, but he doesn't close the distance.

"Please," I breathe.

His throat works around a sound that's almost a groan, but then he gives in. Of course, he gives in. He always will.

His mouth claims mine, slow at first, a brush of lips, delicately testing, but the softness doesn't last. His grip tightens at the base of my neck, anchoring me to him as the kiss deepens. It's not the same punishing hunger Luca had given me, not the teasing desire Alexis always wields. Antonio kisses me like he's breaking. Like he's giving me a piece of himself he'll never get back.

His hands slide down my body, reverent and possessive, and I arch beneath him, desperate for more. But he pulls back suddenly, hovering over me, his breath ragged.

"No more tonight," he rasps, his voice thick. "You need to rest."

I blink up at him, confusion knitting my brow. "But I want—" What do I want? More sex? My body is sore and weak, and my mind a swirling mass of confusion and need.

"No." His voice is hoarse but firm. His lips part on a ragged exhale, and he rests his forehead against mine once more, desperately grounding himself and rolls to his side. "We won't touch you like that again, Aemelia."

But does he just mean now? Or... is this it?

A cold, hollow fear flares in my chest, twisting through my ribs like a cruel hand squeezing the life from my heart. They've taken what they wanted with ruthless hands and hungry mouths. Is this their revenge now? To cast me aside? To send me home, back to the wreckage of a life I was desperate to escape? Or worse—to finish what they started and end me altogether?

No.

I won't believe it.

They're brutal men, ruthless, calculating, and dangerous, but they have hearts. Scarred and bruised, yes, tarnished by blood and vengeance, definitely. But still capable of tenderness, deserving of devotion in their own jagged, broken ways.

I glance at Luca, my eyes searching his handsome, scarred face desperately. He's still seated, watching from his vantage point, but his hands are curled into fists on his thighs, his knuckles white. His expression is hard, almost impassive, but his eyes betray him. Midnight ocean, dark with unspoken emotion, they're locked on me like he's barely holding himself back, like if he moves, he might destroy everything.

My gaze flicks to Alexis, who stands slightly apart, his fingers clamped around the back of his neck, gripping so tightly his bicep flexes. His chest rises and falls heavily, the cords in his throat straining with the effort to contain whatever dark, restless emotion simmers beneath his skin. But his eyes are on Antonio, watching him fight for restraint with an unreadable expression, half resentment, half reverence.

And then I look at Antonio, the man who refused me when I would've given him everything. His broad shoulders are tight with tension, his fists flexing at his sides. His head is bowed slightly, as though he's fighting his own demons, or maybe just battling the urge to come back to me.

I can't take it.

"I don't want to go home, Luca," I whisper, my voice trembling but loud enough for all of them to hear. My eyes find him across the aching space between us, and I reach for him, stretching out a trembling hand that suddenly feels too small, too weak, but desperate to touch him.

"I can't go back there," I plead, my voice barely above a breath. "I want to stay here. With you."

Luca's eyes darken with something primal, something so fiercely protective that it robs the breath from my lungs. His chair scrapes back sharply, and before I can blink, he's on me, closing the distance between us in two powerful strides.

"Ssh, kitten," he murmurs, gathering me into his arms and pulling me against his chest as if I belong there. His voice is a low, soothing growl laced with possessiveness.

"You don't have to go anywhere," he promises as his brothers gather closer. "You're safe now. You're ours."

CHAPTER 36

ANTONIO

A WOMAN SCORNED

The basement reeks of blood and sweat, the acrid scent mixing with the faint traces of damp stone and bleach. Enzo sits before us, wrists bound behind the chair, ankles zip-tied to the legs. He's bruised, bleeding from a split lip, his temple dark with dried blood, but his eyes burn with undiluted rage. Spitting at the ground, he glares up at us like a rabid dog caught in a steel trap.

"You can't do this," he snarls, his voice hoarse from hours of yelling. "I'm a *made man*. You think you can take me like this and not answer for it? Alfonso will retaliate and kill every last Venturi rat."

Luca steps forward, his hands in his pockets, looking down his nose at Enzo with that deadly calm of his, the kind that promises slow, deliberate retribution. "You ordered a hit on Aemelia, Enzo. On your own blood. While she is under our protection. That alone is enough reason to put a bullet in your skull."

"I did what had to be done," he hisses. "She's nothing to me."

Alexis leans against the metal table, spinning a knife between his fingers. "You and your brother rejected her when she was a child. What kind of person does that? You think she's not a Lambretti, but she is. She's your niece, and you tried to kill her."

Enzo's sneer deepens as his gaze flicks to where Aemelia stands, just behind Luca, her arms crossed, her expression unreadable. "I know she's Carlo's spawn. His filthy blood runs through her veins." He laughs, shaking his head. "Everything Carlo touched should be exterminated. That bitch of a wife, her sickly sister, the addict brother—all of them."

Aemelia doesn't flinch. If anything, her chin lifts higher. I glance at her, searching for fear, for hesitation, but she seems bulletproof against his words. I exchange a look with Alexis. Does he know why Enzo is so determined to wipe Carlo's family off the face of the Earth? I can't even imagine having the same impulses about any family of my brothers.

Luca steps in closer, crouching so he's at eye level with Enzo. "Does your boss know about your little vendetta?"

Enzo clenches his jaw, refusing to answer, but I see the flicker in his gaze. Doubt. Guilt. His actions have put him at odds with his boss's interests. He stepped over the line that provided his protection.

Luca sighs as if this entire conversation bores him. "Let's make this easy," he says, nodding to me.

I step forward, gripping the knife Alexis was toying with. Without a word of warning, I slam it through Enzo's hand, pinning him to the wooden arm of the chair. His scream echoes off the concrete walls, but I don't move, don't let go of the blade. I press down, twisting it slightly, watching as pain overtakes his anger.

"Does your boss know?" Luca repeats, his voice is softer now, almost gentle.

Enzo pants as sweat beads on his forehead. His fury is

still there, but the pain has stripped away the bravado. "No," he finally grits out. "This is my decision."

Luca nods, unsurprised. "And Carlo?"

The laughter that spills from Enzo's lips is manic, unhinged. "Carlo's dead," he spits, eyes wild. "I killed him myself."

"You killed your brother?" Luca laughs and shakes his head. "You expect me to believe you killed your own brother?"

"That bastard meant nothing to me."

Luca turns to me and raises his brow. I guess I should be relieved that he thinks fratricide is so unthinkable. I twist the knife, watching thick red blood drip to the floor. Enzo screams, his body arching back, his other arm and legs straining at their bonds.

"Why?" I growl, twisting again.

He doesn't answer and I twist some more, opening a hole between the bones of his hand.

"He seduced my wife," he screams, writhing from the pain. His face is red and slick with sweat, veins bursting across the whites of his eyes.

A silence falls over the room, punctuated only by his ragged breathing. I frown, recalling that Enzo's first wife disappeared around the same time Carlo did. Divorce was the explanation.

Even Alexis stops twirling the second knife he pulled from his jacket.

Enzo grins through the pain, his teeth stained with blood. "He thought he could fuck around with my wife behind my back. After he cried over what your brother did with his. He deserved the way Mario treated him, like a fucking cuck. I slit his throat and dumped his body where no one will ever find it." He leans forward as much as his restraints permit him to grin with defiance.

Aemelia's breath hitches, the first sign of emotion I've seen from her since this started. I glance at her again, finding her rigid with hands clenched into fists. There's no sadness in her eyes, no grief for a father who never cared for her—only cold calculation.

"Why the fuck didn't you tell us?" I spit, thinking about how easily he lied to my face, how much we put Aemelia through because of his deceit, and I want to peel the skin from his flesh, piece by piece.

"Your brother was the start of this. Why the fuck should I give a shit about you." Then Enzo smirks through the pain that's made his eyes wild and his skin slick and gray. "And while we've been sitting here having this conversation, my men have already been sent to finish the job." He turns to Aemelia, his eyes dancing. "Your mother, your aunt, your junkie brother—they'll all be dead before sunrise, and you as soon as they can get to you."

Luca doesn't hesitate. He turns to me, his voice sharp as a blade. "Send a crew. Get them out. Now."

I'm already pulling my phone from my pocket, calling Vito, and issuing orders.

Then I dial Aemelia's mother's number. She picks up on the first ring with an anxious, "Hello."

"You need to take your sister and your son and get out of the apartment right now. Enzo's sending his men to kill you." I hang up before she can ask questions. There's no time to debate. She just has to act. It's the best I can do.

This just became more than a personal vendetta for us. It's a war against Aemelia and her family, Enzo desperately trying to make a brother he's already killed pay with more blood.

When does it end?

I'm tired down to my bones, sick to death of this pain, and misery. All I want to do is wash my hands and take Aemelia to bed. Use my body to make us both forget.

Enzo, despite the knife still embedded in his hand, chuckles darkly. "It's too late, Venturi. They'll be bleeding out before your men even get there."

Luca doesn't respond. Instead, he turns to Aemelia.

"What do you want to do with him?"

Her expression is blank, unreadable. But when she speaks, her voice is steady, absolute. "Kill him."

Enzo scoffs. "You think you have the stomach for this, little girl? You're like your father. A coward who couldn't face up to his own mistakes."

She steps forward then, close enough that he can see the fire in her gaze. "You made your choice," she says, her voice cold as ice. "Now live with the consequences."

Before Alexis can react, she snatches the blade resting loosely in his palm and plunges it into Enzo's chest.

"NO," we all shout in unison, not because we want Enzo to live but because none of us want Aemelia to live with this blood on her hands. I'd shoulder that burden for her. All of us would. But it's done now.

Enzo's eyes are wide as he stares at his niece, leaning over him. "An eye for an eye," she says softly. "You better hope my family is okay, or I'll come looking for yours."

He opens his mouth to speak, but a well of blood spills over his lip with a gurgle of garbled sound. His gasped breathing is wet, forming bubbles in the blood that coats his lips.

I think about all the years we've grieved our brother while the opportunity for retribution was out of our hands. Now, we find out Enzo took Carlo's life for his own vengeance. What a twisted situation. What a waste of anger and pain. All because Mario and Carlo couldn't respect the marriage vows of others.

Aemelia steps back, but she doesn't take her eyes off her uncle. She watches him twitch and gasp and choke, watching him take his last breath and flop forward, limp, as life drains from him.

Alexis shakes his head. "A *made man* dying like a dog in the dark."

"Justice," I say as Aemelia finally turns away to seek comfort in my arms. I'm so proud of her and devastated for her. This life. All it does is take. "And justice in our world is never merciful."

She shakes in my arms, the shock of what she's done registering too late. I cradle her close. "Forget about this," I say. "I'll take your darkness and make it mine. I'll carry it, so you never have to."

"Thank you," she whispers, and it's enough

CHAPTER 37

ALEXIS

FAMILY TIES

I leave Aemelia with Luca and Antonio, trusting them to keep her safe and ensure the mess is cleared up. This war with Enzo is reaching its peak, and while my brothers handle one end of the battlefield, I take four of my best men—Nico, Leo, Rafa, and his brother, Sandro—to handle the other.

The ride to Aemelia's aunt's apartment is tense, the low growl of the engine the only sound as we weave through the city streets. Vito, Andre, Gabe, and Matteo got there ahead of us, and their last update confirmed two of Enzo's men had been captured and another three were being pursued. That's a small comfort. It means we still have the upper hand—barely.

As we pull up outside the building, I survey the rundown complex again with a frown. The place is a dump, bricks crumbling, windows stained with years of city grime—no place for anyone, least of all the mother of the woman we love.

Vito and Andre are waiting by the side entrance, their boots planted firmly against the backs of two restrained men who are on their knees, heads bowed in forced submission. One of the bastards is bleeding from his temple, his face half-swollen, while the other keeps his mouth shut, likely contemplating how much more of his own blood he's willing to lose tonight.

"Where are they?" I ask, stepping out of the vehicle, the night air sharp against my skin.

Vito jerks his chin toward the alleyway. "They can't have gotten far. There's an alley further down. Try there first."

I nod once, imagining Aemelia's sick aunt out in the cold. That motherfucker Enzo trying to kill a woman who's already on her deathbed. If Aemelia hadn't pierced his heart with my knife, I'd have done it with pleasure. Remembering the cool way she handled business makes me smile. She's fire and ice, heart and blood, sweet and vicious, a delicious conundrum. "Secure these two. I'll handle the family."

Vito grins. "Already got a place picked out for them. They won't be a problem."

I wave him off and gesture at Leo and Nico to follow me. The alleyway is dark, the weak glow of a flickering streetlamp barely illuminating the narrow path between buildings. The scent of rotting garbage clings to the damp air, and my stomach turns at the thought of Aemelia's family crouched out here, hiding like prey.

Then I see them.

Carmella Lambretti clutches her sister, her body curled around the frail woman, shielding her from the night's cold. Aemelia's brother, Carlo Junior, pale and gaunt, is crouched beside them, his arms wrapped around himself, shaking with either fear or withdrawal—I don't have the patience to figure out which right now.

I approach slowly, hands visible, voice low but firm. "Signora Lambretti."

Her head snaps up, eyes wild, rimmed with exhaustion.

"Venturi—"

"We're taking you somewhere safe. Come with me."

She tightens her grip on her sister. "Why should I trust you? Where is my daughter?"

I crouch beside her, meeting her eyes. "Because my brother warned you that Enzo sent men to kill you. If we wanted you dead, you wouldn't still be breathing."

Her thin lips part as a shuddering breath escapes. She glances at her son, then at her sister, before nodding. "Okay."

"Good. Let's move."

I help her stand, my hand firm but careful on her arm. Leo lifts the sickly woman, carrying her as gently as possible, while Nico steers Aemelia's brother toward the waiting vehicles. He stumbles but keeps moving. His weakness disgusts me.

As we make our way back to the SUV, Carmella grips my wrist. "Aemelia?"

"She's safe," I assure her. "She's the reason we're here."

That seems to ease some of the tension in her shoulders, but she doesn't speak again.

We urge them into the vehicle, and I'm just about to slide in next to Carmella when a white van creeps to a stop across the street. Its engine ticks once, twice, then goes still. The windows are tinted, making it impossible to see who's inside, but every hair on my body stands on end. A low, instinctual prickle of awareness scrapes down my spine.

Vito and Andre pull up at the curb, ready to follow us back to the penthouse. Vito's half leaning out the window. "You okay, boss?"

"The van," I hiss, voice low and sharp. The air thickens, heavy with the promise of violence.

He glances over, his eyes narrowing into slits. Then they widen. His hand is already slipping inside his jacket, fingers curling around the grip of his Glock.

"It's him," he hisses, his voice dripping with venom.

My grip tightens around the handle of my gun. "You're

sure. The one who bought the roses?"

Vito's already sliding out of the vehicle, his knuckles white on the weapon, the fury in his eyes cold and raw. "That fucking cock-sucking piece of shit."

"Keep talking," I growl, pulling out my phone.

Without missing a beat, Vito straightens, squaring his shoulders, and launches into a bullshit story about how his wife wants him to take her on vacation to Florida and how she's picked a five-star hotel that's going to bleed him dry. His tone is casual, almost bored, his free hand gesticulating, but his other hand stays steady on the gun.

While he talks, I dial Matteo. The moment he picks up, I cut straight to the point.

"The white van. Box it in."

I hang up and slam my hand against the side of the vehicle carrying Aemelia's family.

"Drive. Up two blocks."

Nico doesn't hesitate. The car peels away from the curb, separating them from the imminent storm.

Engines roar as Matteo and Sandro's SUVs screech onto the street. Tires scream against the pavement as they block the van in from both ends, cutting off any escape.

Before the van's engine can so much as sputter, my men swarm it, yanking open the doors and dragging the lone hooded man out.

I move fast, crossing the street in long, furious strides, flanked by Vito and Andre, guns drawn. The pavement thuds beneath my feet, but it's my pulse that thunders louder.

Matteo slams the man face-down onto the asphalt, planting a knee between his shoulder blades. The man lets out a wheezing grunt, his cheek scraping against the rough concrete. Matteo's Glock presses into his skull, waiting for my command.

"Is it him?" I ask Vito, my voice a low growl.

Vito spits on the ground. His eyes are dark with certainty. "Yes."

Matteo's face is a mask of ice, unreadable as he pats the man down. He yanks a wallet from the back pocket of his jeans, rifles through it, and shoves the ID into my hand.

Maryland license. Cohen Barker.

My breath stills for half a beat.

It's him.

Aemelia's stalker. The man who sent her roses and terror. The man who tried to make her feel small, afraid. The man who made her tremble in my brother's arms.

Rage floods my veins, thick and sharp, and before I can think, I drive the toe of my boot into his gut.

He gags and curls in on himself, coughing and sputtering.

"I'm a florist," he whimpers, voice reedy with panic. "I just deliver flowers."

Matteo smashes his face into the asphalt again and presses the gun harder against his temple.

"Shut the fuck up."

I crouch down, close enough that he can smell the blood already on my hands.

"You threatened someone I love," I say, my voice low, lethal. "You made her live in fear for her life."

I lean in until my lips almost brush his ear.

"What kind of man does that to a sweet, innocent girl?"

He whimpers something unintelligible, but Matteo cracks him across the back of the head with the butt of his gun. Cohen fucking Barker goes slack, blinking dazedly.

"Now, you piece of shit," I say, flicking open my thin-bladed knife with a sinister click. I let him see it—the razor edge of the blade gleaming in the streetlights. "I'm going to take yours."

The knife glides like butter through his temple, silent and precise.

For a moment, his eyes go wide with terror, his mouth falling open in a breathless gasp. Then, the light leaves them.

Blood seeps onto the concrete, pooling beneath his twitching body.

I straighten, wiping the blade on his pant leg with cold indifference.

"Put him in the van," I instruct Matteo, my voice steady and emotionless. "Drive it into the river."

Matteo nods once, and with Sandro's help, they haul the corpse into the van like a sack of trash.

Andre pulls up in the black SUV, and I climb into the passenger seat, gun still loose in my hand.

As we pull away, I glance once at the empty white van, a coffin with wheels, knowing it'll be rusting at the bottom of the river by morning.

A fitting grave for a man who thought he could terrorize my woman with roses and bullets.

When we rejoin Aemelia's family, I switch cars to slide into the seat beside Carmella, and we drive back to the Venturi building in silence thick with the weight of the night, the faint scent of blood still clogging my nostrils.

Tonight, we put an end to Enzo's reach.

We snuffed out the man who dared to think he could make our woman afraid.

And when we return, Aemelia will know that whatever life she had before, whatever fears she carried—none of them matter.

She's one of us now.

We'll keep her safe.

CHAPTER 38

LUCA

TYING LOOSE ENDS

The deserted lot is silent except for the distant hum of the city, the kind of place where deals are struck, and bodies are buried. The headlights cast long shadows across the cracked asphalt, illuminating the other convoy as they pull in—a sleek, black car followed by two more, their windows tinted, their engines humming low.

From the second the doors open, the men on both sides move with precision. My soldiers step forward first, meeting Alphonso's halfway, weapons visible but not raised, a show of strength without the promise of immediate bloodshed. It's protocol, a delicate dance of power and caution. I step out of the car and the gravel crunches beneath my polished leather shoes as I walk to meet Alfonso Mesina in the center of the lot.

Mesina rolls his shoulders, his expression impassive but his dark eyes sharp as they fix on me. He's older, near sixty, with silver at his temples and lines carved deep into his face, each one earned through blood and betrayal. He's ruled his empire with an iron fist for decades, and he didn't get here by letting slights go unanswered. My father had a lot of respect for the man but warned me about his temper and his black-and-white thinking.

"Luca." His voice is calm and measured. "I assume you have an explanation for why my man has disappeared into the hands of your family."

I hold his gaze, my own mask of indifference firmly in place. "Enzo broke the rules."

His brow lifts slightly. "And what rules are those?"

"He ordered a hit on my family without consulting you. Without sanction."

Mesina exhales slowly, shaking his head like a disappointed father. "Enzo was a *made man,* and the hit was on a member of *his* family."

"Enzo doesn't care about family. He killed his own brother."

"Carlo?"

"This trouble, it's Lambretti, not Mesina."

The older man studies me for a long moment, his face unreadable. "Who killed him?"

I tilt my head slightly, my lips pressing into a thin line. Silence is my answer.

Mesina nods once as if he expected no less. "And what of his crew?"

"Some are dead. The rest are making their peace with God."

He exhales through his nose, considering his options. He knows I've done what had to be done, but there's still a matter of respect—an insult that needs to be balanced. Blood demands blood, but money? Money can smooth superficial wounds.

I reach into my coat pocket, pulling out a small, folded document. "The Venturi Construction project on the East Side. Five percent of the development profits, untaxed."

Mesina takes the paper, unfolds it, and scans it with the

careful eye of a man who knows every number has meaning. Five percent is generous enough to make him think. It's enough to keep him away from Aemelia. His silence stretches, heavy in the cold night air.

Then, he folds the document and tucks it into his jacket. "Enzo," he says after a beat, "will be remembered as a man who broke *omertà*."

I nod slightly, understanding. A neat lie. A public reason for his execution that will keep Mesina's name clean and prevent unnecessary bloodshed between our families. It's a move that benefits us both.

Mesina clasps his hands behind his back, his eyes flicking to mine once more. "And the girl?"

The temperature drops between us. My body tenses before I can stop it, but he catches the shift, his lips curving in the barest hint of amusement.

"She's not up for discussion," I say, my voice cool and final.

Mesina watches me for a beat longer, then chuckles softly, shaking his head. "Careful, Luca. A man like you… caring about something too much can make you weak."

I step closer, my voice dropping to a sinister whisper. "Or it can make me more dangerous."

The amusement fades from his face, replaced calculation. Then, with a slight nod, he steps back. "Your father was a passionate man."

"We all have our passions," I say. "Some keep their passions to one woman. Some like to keep a *goomar*." I meet his gaze. "It's better for all if we keep women out of this business."

He focuses on the middle distance, showing no reaction to my words, then nods. Aemelia's little secret has come in very useful, a way to put him on the backfoot. "Pleasure, as always, Venturi."

We turn at the same time, walking back to our cars as our men fall into formation behind us. No more words are exchanged, no pleasantries. The deal is done. The balance is restored.

As I slide into the back seat, the door is closed behind me, and Alexis starts the engine. I stare out the window as the city lights blur past, my fingers tightening into a fist.

Mesina thinks Aemelia is a weakness. He has no idea she's the reason I've never felt stronger.

CHAPTER 39

AEMELIA

WHERE IS HOME

My mother sits across from me in the penthouse, her hands clenched in her lap, her eyes darting between my brother, my aunt, and me. Antonio leans against the wall, arms crossed, his expression cool and a little menacing, but to me, his presence is a steady force, an anchor in the storm that's my past and present colliding.

My aunt looks worse than before, thin and frail, her skin nearly translucent under the harsh light of the kitchen. The sickness clings to her; an inevitability no one wants to acknowledge. My mother sits beside her, wringing her hands, looking just as exhausted as she did before I was taken captive. But it's my brother who shatters me.

He's strung out. Again.

His pupils are blown, his skin slick with sweat, fingers twitching in his lap. His clothes hang off him, stained and wrinkled. Shame burns through me, swiftly followed by rage.

"Are you high?" My voice slices through the silence, jagged with disbelief.

CJ flinches, barely meeting my gaze before looking away, but his erratic blinking is enough to confirm.

"Aemelia—" My mama starts, but I'm already on my feet, my pulse roaring in my ears.

"You promised me," I hiss, voice shaking. "You swore you'd get clean. I fought for you. I worked my fingers to the bone so you wouldn't have to—"

"You don't get it!" he snaps, his hands clenching into fists. "We thought you were going to die!"

His words hit like a slap, but I don't let them sink in. I refuse to let him use my suffering as an excuse for his self-destruction. It's been going on for years.

"You can't help yourself," I say, my voice raw and broken.

My mother rises, placing a hand on my brother's shoulder, her eyes pleading. "This is why we need to go back, Aemelia. We need to leave all of this behind. You, me, your brother, we need to go home. Back to Baltimore, away from this life. Before it's too late."

Go back? The thought tightens around my throat like a noose, suffocating. Go back to scraping by exhausted, to watching my mother defend my brother while he slowly destroys himself, to return to a life where I exist only to endure, to survive—not to live?

No. I can't.

But it's more than that. The thought of leaving *them* is unbearable, an ache that burrows deep into my chest. Ice spreads through my veins at the idea of never again falling into Antonio's fathomless gaze, never tasting the food he cooks with quiet devotion, never feeling the steady strength of his arms around me, his touch both a promise and a shield. To walk away from Alexis, from his wicked grins and teasing words, his fierce protectiveness hidden beneath charm, his ability to make me feel weightless when the world bears down on me—it's unthinkable.

And Luca… to leave Luca would be to rip out my own heart. To never hear his rough, reverent voice telling me I'm his *good girl*, never feel the searing fire behind his cool control, never watch his composure crack when he looks at me with something dangerously close to love. I cannot break him, not when I know what it's like to be broken.

I belong here. With them.

No. I won't go.

I glance at Antonio. He's watching me, his storm-gray eyes unreadable. My heart stutters in my chest. If he wants me to stay, he has to say it. He has to claim me. If he doesn't, then maybe my mother is right. Maybe I don't belong here.

I swallow hard, willing him to speak, to give me a reason to stay. "Antonio—"

He pushes off the wall and crosses the room in three slow, deliberate steps. When he reaches me, he cups my face, his hands warm, strong, steady. His touch sends a shiver down my spine, a whisper of comfort amidst the chaos. "If you want to go with your family, we won't stop you," he murmurs, his voice low, intimate. "But we want you to stay with us. We want you to…" He pauses like he's thinking through a new idea that hasn't had time to fully take root. "We want to make you a Venturi."

A tremor runs through me, stealing the air from my lungs.

He's claiming me.

Not as a captive. Not as leverage. As theirs.

"Is this a proposal?" I whisper, my lips parting as his breath mingles with mine.

His grip tightens just a fraction. Possessive. "I'm not your savior, Aemelia. I'm your sinner. Your monster. And I swear on every grave I've ever filled, I'll love you better than any saint ever could. Your family will be our family, *dolcezza*. They'll be protected, always. No more struggling. No more running. They'll have everything they need. And you, Aemelia—"

He dips his head closer, his breath warm against my lips.

"We want you to be ours. You were never meant to belong to one man. You were meant to belong to three. Our hands. Our mouths. Our bodies are yours. We'll love you until our last breaths."

Tears burn behind my eyes, and I exhale shakily. I was raised to believe love came with conditions, that loyalty was only as strong as the weight it carried. But this? This is different. They're offering me a choice. They're offering to take on my burdens… the burden of my family.

My mother shifts, her fingers gripping the edge of the table. "Aemelia…"

I turn to her, my decision clear in the depths of my soul. "I can't go back with you, Mama. My place is here."

Her face crumples, but she doesn't argue. She knows me well enough to recognize that I've made up my mind. Maybe she remembers what it was like to love her own Venturi all those years ago.

My aunt sighs, a resigned smile tugging at her lips. "I knew it. Just like your mother. You can't resist the dark and dangerous ones."

My brother shakes his head, his eyes glinting. "You're really staying with them?"

I nod. "I am."

"But who—"

Antonio cuts him off by standing abruptly.

"No one is paying for you to sit on your ass anymore, Carlo. It's time to step into your shoes and be a man. Rehab is non-negotiable. Any support we offer will only continue if you dedicate yourself to getting clean."

I reach for Antonio's hand, so relieved to have someone on my side that tears spill silently down my cheeks.

His fingers tighten around mine, his grip reassuring. "You're not alone anymore, *mia bella*."

Luca and Alexis enter then, their presence commanding as they take in the scene before them. Luca's sharp gaze flicks between me and my mother before settling on Antonio. "Everything settled?"

Antonio nods once. "She's staying."

Luca's expression softens just a fraction. "She said yes?"

I smile, touching my fingers to my lips, unprepared to find out they'd already discussed what they wanted from me. "I said yes."

"Like it was ever an option for you to leave," Luca says with a rare smile. "I already made up my mind that you're not going anywhere, kitten. Not now. Not ever."

I flush hot at his possessiveness, at the fire in his eyes.

Alexis, ever the charmer, flashes me a wicked grin. "I knew you wouldn't be able to resist us."

"Your mama won't like this," my mother aims at Luca, shaking her head. "She never liked me. Never thought I was good enough for your brother."

"Aemelia isn't you, Signora Lambretti," Luca says firmly. "And our mother will accept our choice."

Antonio pulls me closer, tilting my chin up before pressing his lips to mine in a kiss that feels like a vow. Luca moves in next, his kiss softer, lingering, full of unspoken promises. Alexis is last, his lips teasing mine in a way that makes my head spin.

My family inhales sharply, shocked at the display. But I don't care what they think.

These men are going to make me a part of their family.

I don't have to choose between them or find a way to live without them.

Alexis, Antonio, and Luca Venturi are my knights in shining armor, after all.

***

I lay on the bed drenched in their warmth, my skin still buzzing with the aftermath of their touch. My body feels boneless, weightless, wrecked, and adored all at once. The silk sheets stick faintly to my skin, damp with sweat and remnants of their devotion, but I don't want to move.

Because I'm surrounded by them.

By my men.

By their hands and mouths, their strength and tenderness, their claim that will never let me go.

Luca's weight presses into my side, solid and grounding. His hand drifts idly along my stomach, fingers tracing lazy circles over my skin. Possessive, even in tenderness. His face is buried in the crook of my neck, his breath hot and damp against my skin, and he kisses me there—slow, reverent presses of his lips—like he still can't quite believe he's allowed to touch me like this. "Sweet girl," he whispers slowly, like he's on the edge of falling into dreams.

Antonio rests behind me, spooning me, his broad chest forming a wall of safety against my back. One of his arms is thrown heavily over my waist, an anchor that keeps me right where he wants me. His hand cups my breast lazily, thumb lazing stroking over my tight, sensitive nipple as though he has nothing else in the world to do but touch me. His mouth presses softly against the back of my shoulder, rough stubble rasping over my too-sensitive skin, sending a faint shiver down my spine. The gentle scrape of his teeth sends a shiver of arousal through me. "Why do you smell like strawberry ice-cream?" he murmurs, making me chuckle.

And Alexis is sprawling across my legs, his chin propped on my thigh, grinning like the devil. His hair is still damp from sweat, curling slightly at his temples, and his lips are swollen from too many kisses—my kisses. His fingers skate along the inside of my calf, barely touching, just teasing, even though we're all spent and sated.

"I think you've finally killed me, kitten," he rasps, voice low and drowsy but still full of heat. "I'm a goner. Completely ruined. Dead."

I smile sleepily and lift a hand, brushing his damp hair from his forehead, then let out a shaky breath. I'm not sure if it's from their words or their touch.

Maybe both.

Because I feel it everywhere.

Their devotion. Their love. Their claim.

It hums beneath my skin, soaking into my bones, branding me in ways deeper than any mark ever could.

Alexis shifts, sitting up on his knees, the dips of his muscles sculpted by the shadows and I stare at him, no longer shy to take in the raw perfection of his body or the cock that hangs heavy between his thighs.

"There's something I need to tell you," he says, sliding his hand up my thigh and resting it on my hip possessively.

"What is it?" I ask.

"The problem with Cohen... it's not going to be a problem anymore."

"How?" I ask, my heart picking up speed in my chest.

"You don't need to know the details, kitten. Just know that anyone who thinks they can harm you or take you from us will be dead before they draw their next breath."

Before I have a chance for the information to settle, or to respond, he continues.

"You were made for us, kitten," His voice is like gravel sliding into silk as his fingers grip my hip. "Every inch of you."

I shudder at the certainty in his voice, at the reverence in his touch.

"You're ours," Luca growls, his voice dark and rough as his lips skim the corner of my mouth.

"Ours," Antonio echoes against my throat, his hand tightening on my waist.

And I feel every syllable deep in my chest like an iron promise seeping into my bones, binding me to them.

They've claimed me. My saviors, my protectors, my mafia kings.

CHAPTER 40

ANTONIO

THE MOON'S BLESSING

The night settles over the city like a velvet shroud, wrapping the penthouse in quiet warmth. From the kitchen, I watch Aemelia move beside me, sleeves pushed up, flour dusting her fingertips as she follows my every instruction. Her hands are steady, her focus unwavering. Tonight, she isn't a girl haunted by the blood on her hands. Tonight, she is just Aemelia, learning to make my mother's pasta recipe as if she's always belonged in this kitchen, in this life, with us

Alexis leans against the counter, swirling a glass of whiskey, grinning as he critiques our work. "You're letting her knead it too much. The dough's going to be tough."

"Shut up, Alexis," I murmur, adjusting Aemelia's grip on the dough. She glances up at me, amusement flickering in her dark eyes, and I smirk. "You're doing perfect, *bella*."

She smiles, and it's a real one. Not the forced, careful smiles she used to give us, but something deeper, something that touches the part of me that has only been awake since she came into our lives. Luca sits at the head of the table, his sharp gaze taking everything in. He doesn't interfere. He doesn't need to. He's content, watching Aemelia fold into our world.

Music hums from the speakers, something low and warm, picked by Alexis, who, despite his antics, has a way of setting a mood. The scent of garlic and simmering tomatoes fills the air, wrapping around us like an embrace. For the first time in what feels like forever, there is no threat of violence, no desire for revenge, nothing clouding our thoughts—only the sound of laughter, the clinking of dishes, the quiet symphony of a home being built around a woman who was never meant to stay, but now, we hope will never leave.

She said she wants to be with us. I offered her our name, and she said yes. But it was done in front of her family, when Luca and Alexis were absent. Our beautiful kitten deserves prettier words and a ring she can be proud of. She deserves all the good we can extract from the world to lay at her feet.

When dinner is ready, we take it out onto the balcony. The night stretches above us, a sliver of moon hanging in the sky like a knowing smile. The city sprawls beneath us, lights blinking like fallen stars, and for a moment, it feels like we're the only ones in the world.

Aemelia sits between me and Alexis, with Luca across from her, wine glass balanced in one hand and the other, her left resting on the table. I stare at her naked finger, the final part we need to claim, anticipation building. We eat, we talk, we breathe. It's easy, effortless, and the ache in my chest that I've carried for so long eases with every glance she steals, every time her knee brushes mine beneath the table.

Then Luca's patience seems to falter. His chair scrapes against the tile as he reaches into his pocket, pulling out a small velvet box. He turns it over between his fingers thoughtfully before sliding it across the table to her.

Aemelia stares at it, fingers trembling slightly as she

reaches for it. The box clicks open, revealing three interwoven rings, each set with a single diamond that nestles together to form one whole.

Her breath catches. "Luca..."

He leans forward, forearms braced against the table, his gaze steady, unshakable. "*Amore mio...* I never thought I'd find someone like you. Never thought I deserved it. But you... you're the piece of my heart I never hoped to have. The love I never thought was meant for me." His voice is low, reverent. "I have so much respect for you, Aemelia. For your strength, for your fire. For the way you've taken a life that tried to break you and turned it into something beautiful."

Her eyes glisten under the moonlight, but Luca isn't finished.

"I want you to wear these rings, *cara mia*, because you don't just belong to me. You belong to all of us. And if you'll have us, we'll spend our lives proving that you are, and always will be, ours."

Aemelia parts her lips, breath unsteady, but before she can speak, I take her hand, bringing it to my lips, letting the softness of her skin settle something in me.

"He's right," I murmur. "From the moment you walked back into our lives, I knew you were special. I knew you were meant to be ours. I don't care what the world thinks or what's expected. I don't care if everyone thinks we're crazy for wanting one woman. I only care that you stay. That you let us love you the way you deserve. You'll never want for anything again, Aemelia. Not safety. Not love. Not the sun on your face or peace in your heart. I'll give you everything—even if I have to burn the world down to do it."

Alexis, always one to break the tension, grins as he tucks a stray curl behind her ear, turning her gently. "I mean, how could you say no, princess? Three men to worship you at your feet. Three men to provide everything your heart desires. Offers like that don't come around twice in a lifetime."

She laughs, sounding a little choked, shaking her head, and when she turns back to Luca, her voice is barely a whisper. "You're really asking me to marry all of you?"

Luca nods, and for the first time, I see uncertainty flicker in his expression like he's bracing for something he can't control. "*Sì, amore.* I am. Of course, only one of us will be able to marry you in front of God and our families, but the others will be your husbands in all the ways that count."

Aemelia inhales sharply, staring at the rings, at us, at this life she never imagined for herself. Then she exhales, slow and steady, her shoulders relaxing. "Yes."

The word is barely out of her mouth before Alexis whoops, scooping her into his arms, tugging her to her feet, and embracing her so tightly she becomes breathless with laughter. I'm next, wrapping my arms around her from behind, my lips pressed to her neck, breathing her in. And then Luca, strong and sure, his hand at the back of her head as he kisses her, slow and deep, claiming her in a way that seals this moment forever.

She's surrounded, touched by all of us, kissed between heated whispers and murmured promises.

The city fades. The world narrows. And under the sliver of a moon that watches like a silent witness, Aemelia Venturi commits to finally being irrevocably ours.

CHAPTER 41

AEMELIA

A MOTHER'S JUDGMENT

I'm nervous as we approach the Venturi estate. It looms ahead, an elegant testament to power and legacy, a place filled with happy, carefree childhood memories, now a place where I'll have to prove myself. As the car pulls through the wrought-iron gates, memories crash over me like waves against a cliff: a child's perspective, running through these gardens and halls with Rosita, our laughter echoing through the grand corridors and getting lost amongst the tall trees. It had been a lifetime ago before my world was turned upside down.

I glance at Antonio, who sits beside me, his large, warm hand resting possessively on my thigh. Across from us, Alexis hums along to the music playing softly through the car's speakers, his usual carefree smirk in place. Luca, ever the composed leader, watches me carefully, his piercing blue eyes searching my face for any sign of discomfort.

Andre and Vito drive us, but this time, I'm not filled with

terror, just trepidation.

"I haven't been here in years," I murmur, more to myself than anyone else.

"You're home now," Luca says simply, his hand reaching out to take mine.

Home.

The thought settles deep inside me, an ember of warmth in my chest. It's strange to think that, after everything, I belong here. Not as an outsider, not as a pawn, but as a part of this family.

Or, at least, I will be if Signora Venturi approves.

When the car stops in the circular driveway, I take a steadying breath. The doors open, and I step out into the crisp evening air. Rosita and her husband, freshly returned from their honeymoon, are already waiting on the front steps. Her face breaks into a wide smile, and within seconds, she's pulling me into an expensive-scented but real hug.

"I knew they would rescue you," she whispers against my ear, and I can't help but laugh softly, holding her tight. The years between us slip away until we're just two little girls with foolish romantic dreams of a future as wispy as the fog at dawn.

"You remember that?"

"Of course. You could never choose which one of my brothers to make your knight in shining armor."

I laugh softly, glancing over my shoulder at my three gorgeous, but frankly a little terrifying, men. "Choosing between them was never an option."

She pulls back and winks. "This is Raphael Russo, my husband." She holds out her hand for the handsome groom I remember from her wedding. They have similar features and suit each other so much. I laugh as we kiss each other on each cheek.

"Pleased to meet you, Aemelia," he whispers, remaining close. "It's good to have someone else take over the focus of the family. Less pressure."

I chuckle as he releases me, and Luca quickly rests his

hand on my spine to guide me inside.

Inside, the house is just as I remember—elegant, warm, alive with the quiet hum of tradition. The scent of simmering sauce wafts through the air, and my stomach twists with a familiar longing.

Signora Venturi stands in the center of the grand dining room, her back straight, her sharp blue eyes—Luca's eyes—assessing me the moment I enter. She's always been an imposing figure despite her short stature, but now, as I stand before her as the woman in her sons' lives, the weight of her judgment feels heavier.

"Welcome back, Aemelia," she says, her tone polite but cool.

I dip my head respectfully. "Thank you, Signora Venturi. It's good to be here again."

Her gaze flicks to her sons, watching as Antonio helps me remove my coat, Alexis brushes a loose curl behind my ear, and Luca, her most guarded son, places a steadying hand on the small of my back. Something shifts in her expression, but she says nothing.

Dinner is a quiet affair at first. The table is long, grand, and filled with food that reminds me of my childhood. Antonio, as always, serves my plate before his own, making sure I have everything I need. When a glass of wine is slightly out of reach, Alexis leans over and hands it to me without a word. Luca keeps his hand around my shoulder, his thumb stroking absent patterns over the fabric of my dress.

Their mother watches it all, missing nothing. But it's not until later, when I insist on helping clear the table, that something changes.

"You don't have to do that," she says, watching as I gather plates.

"I want to," I tell her honestly. "I know what it means to take care of a family."

She studies me for a long moment, then nods, stepping aside to let me help. In the kitchen, as we work side by side,

I finally find the courage to say what's been sitting in my heart.

"I love them," I confess, my voice quiet but firm. "I know this situation is... unconventional, but I don't care. They've given me something I never thought I'd have. Safety. Love. A place to belong. And I will give them everything I am. Love. Affection. A family. A place to be happy."

She says nothing, rinsing a dish before placing it on the drying rack.

"I know who they are," I continue. "I'm young but not foolish. This life... I've seen the worst of it and come through. I will stand next to them when things get tough. I'll do my best to guide and support them."

She nods, continuing to scrub a particularly stubborn pan.

"With my mother and aunt back in Maryland and my brother in rehab, I need a family," I continue, my chest tightening. "I want that family to be you. And Rosita. If you'll have me."

Signora Venturi finally turns to face me, and for the first time, her eyes soften. There's still a weight to her gaze, an unspoken warning that she won't tolerate any harm coming to her sons. But there's something else, too.

Acceptance.

She reaches out, brushing a wet hand over my cheek. "You're stronger than I gave you credit for."

I smile and blink back the sudden rush of emotion. "I had to be."

"Us women, we have to be strong. In secret, without showing it, we bear the weight of our families, steer our men to make good decisions, and guide our children even when they seem to lose their way. It's our burden but also our blessing." She rubs her hands on her apron. "I've waited for a long time for my sons to find a woman worthy of their love. I'd given up hope for Luca and Antonio."

"Why?"

She shrugs. "Anyone who spends too much time alone becomes hard to live with. Their hearts were cold, their minds rigid. I couldn't imagine who would find a way to reach them. Alexis is younger, but he has too much restless energy and too much fire in his veins. I worried that no one would ever be able to pin him down."

She cups my face in her work-roughened hands. "You must be very special to have planted love in such barren and unpredictable soil."

I blush, feeling overwhelmed at her words, unused to being called special by anyone.

"Special," I say. "But also lucky."

Her eyes finally light with the genuine warmth I used to see when I was a child, and she'd pinch my cheeks and feed me extra sweets when my mama wasn't looking.

"I love them," I say. "For all the good and the bad, the difficult and the easy. I love them."

She pats my shoulder and nods. "Me, too, Aemelia. Me, too."

That night as we relax on the terrace beneath the stars, surrounded by family, I feel something settle inside me.

I'm home.

I'm loved.

And I'm exactly where I belong.

EPILOGUE

LUCA

UNDONE BY LOVE

The church is half-filled with guests, more on our side than Aemelia's, but that's to be expected. Her father's family isn't welcome, and her mother's is small. Most of her friends from Maryland couldn't make it, except for a select few we offered to fly out for the weekend.

On our side is a mix of beloved family—Rosita and Raphael with baby Mario asleep in her arms, Mama looking happy and proud, cousins, friends, our crew and their wives and children, and further back, our allies, the men who control this underworld most of the time.

I glance past them because their presence isn't about sentiment, it's about power, about ensuring that alliances remain intact. The only way to secure a safe future for Aemelia and our family is to keep the right people on our side. There's no walking away from this life, so we have to play the game.

By my side, Antonio and Alexis stand, dressed in

matching tuxedos, hair styled, eyes bright, waiting with the same tension I feel coiled inside me.

I don't like it when Aemelia is out of our sight. That's one of the benefits of sharing a woman—three husbands can protect her far better than one.

We're an anomaly in this world. Men like us don't share. They hoard, they claim, they devour. But with us, it has always been different. Sharing Aemelia has brought me a peace I never thought possible. While it took time for our mother to understand, Aemelia's desire to fill our home with children has softened her heart. She just wants to see us happy, and it's impossible for anyone to deny that we are.

"She's late," Alexis hisses, raking a hand through his curls, ruining their styled perfection. He looks more like himself now, a little disheveled, a little reckless.

"It's a bride's prerogative," I remind him.

Carmella Lambretti sits in the front with her sister beside her. Christina is even thinner than when we last saw her, but she's hanging on, determined to witness her niece's wedding. Who knows what will happen after? She has already outlived every doctor's prediction.

I adjust my cuffs, my fingers grazing the links Mario gave me so many years ago. He should have been here today. He was always the one who believed in love, the artist, the poet, the dreamer.

Before grief can weigh me down, music begins to play. Aemelia's brother, CJ, appears in the doorway. And beside him, our bride.

She's the picture of elegance, enveloped in cream lace that clings to her curves before spilling out into a fluted skirt. Tight sleeves drape over her hands, modest yet breathtaking. Over her head rests her mother's veil, a final tether to the past she's leaving behind. As the congregation turns to watch, she slides her hand into her brother's arm, her posture regal, her steps measured.

The world slows, each step she takes carving away the years of violence and blood that led us here. The weight of my past, the sins I have worn like armor, seem to splinter as she draws closer. These hands—stained with blood, calloused and unworthy—have taken life without hesitation, but today, they will only hold hers, gentle and reverent. I have known power and commanded fear, but today, for the first time, I'm undone by something greater.

Her.

Nothing has ever unraveled me like the soft, steady way she looks at me now. Like I'm worthy of her love. She was never meant to be mine—never meant to belong to any of us—but fate, who's been as cruel as she's been generous, wove our paths together in the kind of story that shouldn't have a happy ending. And yet, here she is, walking toward us, the only men who have ever been willing to burn the world to keep her safe. My chest tightens, my heart a raw, aching thing in my ribs. I never believed I'd find love and still don't fully believe I deserve her.

"You ready?" Antonio asks, interrupting my thoughts.

"I was born ready," I mutter, which earns a chuckle from both my brothers. I'm thirty-nine, and the wait for the perfect woman has been long. Now that she's ours, I vow to make all the years we're given together count. No more waiting for life to start.

"Unlike other mafia brides, at least this one has backup husbands," Alexis chuckles darkly.

"I'm not planning to die any time soon," I mutter, but he isn't wrong. There is strength in numbers, and with three of us by her side, she and our children will never be alone.

My gaze locks on Aemelia, tracing the slow sway of her hips and the proud lift of her chin. She has always carried herself with a quiet grace, but now, she walks like a queen.

Aemelia Venturi. It has a much better ring to it than Lambretti. I can't say I'm sorry to see Carlo's name go.

When she reaches the altar, she waits for her brother to lift her veil. Since his time in rehab, his hands have been steady, his eyes clear. There's no going back for him. He understands what will happen to him if he does.

Aemelia's eyes shine, her skin glows, and her full lips curve into a soft, eager smile. We've all been waiting for this day, but Aemelia especially. It's important to her that everyone sees that she's not just our captive anymore. She's our love, and now our wife.

I reach out for her hand, drawing her gently toward me. Once, I had to stoop to hold her hand. Not anymore. She meets my gaze, her own intensity like an open palm against my chest.

"You kept us waiting," I whisper, and she gives me a cheeky smile.

"Was I worth the wait?"

I brush my thumb over the back of her hand. "I waited thirty-nine years for you, Aemelia. What's a few more minutes?"

Her blush is sweet, her surprised expression enough to warm my heart. Antonio and Alexis gather closer as the priest begins the service.

His words wash over me like a dream because all I can think about is our life beginning today. From the moment Mario was murdered, our lives were knocked off course—grief, anger, and vengeance consumed us, driving away any hope of happiness. But now, we're putting that chapter to rest.

When the priest instructs us to repeat after him, my throat tightens. Aemelia's voice is soft but steady, unwavering as she commits herself to me, to us. The emptiness I have carried for so long is filled by her promises. I turn to my brothers, seeing the same devotion in their eyes.

The service ends, and I'm told to kiss my bride. My hands tremble as I cup her face, drawing her close. The first brush of our lips as husband and wife is unlike any kiss before—it's the beginning of something new, something sacred. The first words inked in a book.

Once upon a time...

...a girl was rescued by three brothers to live happily ever after.

It's a shortened version of the truth. The path was rocky,

but we got there.

And we'll love her, and she'll love us.

Aemelia is breathless when I finally release her to the shouts and cheers of our friends, loved ones, and tentative allies. I take her hand and pass her to Antonio, who wraps his arms around her and kisses her like a man starving for her touch. More whoops and cheers erupt, though the priest has already withdrawn—displeased perhaps but content with the generous donation we made to the church.

Money is power, after all.

Alexis is last and, of course, always the showman, dipping her low with his usual flair, pressing a kiss to her lips like something out of a black-and-white film. When he pulls her upright, she's flushed and radiant, glowing with happiness. So perfect that my throat burns with unshed emotion.

I swallow it down. No one will ever see this mob boss cry.

Except maybe Aemelia, later, when we're alone, and I show her how much it means that she has chosen to walk beside us, to lay by our sides, to be ours in every way that matters.

***

The ballroom is as breathtaking as it was for Rosita's wedding, with chandeliers casting golden light over the polished marble floor, flowers tumbling over crystal vases, and candles flickering romantically. Except, rather than my sister gliding around the dance floor in the arms of her husband, it's Aemelia dancing with Alexis, her hair spilled loose and lightly curled down her back, the sleeves of her dress removed to reveal thin straps that show off her radiant olive skin.

Her face is alight with happiness, her body moving seductively, and Alexis is enraptured as he guides her, taking his turn for a first dance. The band plays a soft, romantic melody meant to slow the heart and heighten the moment. Alexis twirls her, dipping her low before drawing her back against his chest, his lips grazing her temple in a gesture that's both possessive and reverent. She laughs, like the soft chime of silver, her eyes glimmering in the golden glow.

I sip from a tumbler of aged whiskey, letting the burn settle deep in my chest as I watch my wife move between my brothers, my heart clenched in something primal and reverent. Aemelia Venturi. She's no longer our captive. She's no longer a pawn. She is our queen, our most treasured possession, mine to protect until my dying breath.

"She's beautiful," Mama murmurs beside me, placing a weathered hand on my forearm. I glance at her, noting the soft smile on her lips and the approval in her deep-set eyes. I place my hand over hers, engulfing it.

"She is," I agree, my voice thick with pride.

"And she's yours," she adds, squeezing my arm gently. "This responsibility you've taken is not just a game, Luca. She's your family now. Our family. She carries the Venturi name. She will birth the Venturi legacy."

I catch sight of Mama's wedding band, which is still wedged tightly onto her finger. Her marriage was the catalyst for our existence, and now, our marriage will bring more children to the bloodline—the never-ending cycle of life. "I know, Mama. She's safe with us."

"It is not just about safety," she says, her gaze sharp, knowing. "A woman like that needs more than protection. She needs devotion. She needs a home. You have given her your name, but now you must give her a life. A future."

A future. I sip my drink, letting the weight of her words settle over me. My world has revolved around vengeance, blood, and duty for so long. But now, I have something beyond that. Aemelia is my future, our future. She is the reason I will wake up every morning with a purpose beyond the family business.

"You're taking her away?" she asks, though she already knows the answer.

"Tonight. We leave for the Maldives after the reception. I want her to have the honeymoon she deserves."

My mother smiles approvingly, lifting her glass to her lips. "Good. A woman should know luxury. She should know what it means to be adored."

Adored. The word perfectly fits with how I feel about Aemelia.

I turn my attention back to my wife just in time to see Antonio take her from Alexis, his hand settling on the small of her back as he leads her into a slower dance. He presses his forehead to hers, whispering something that makes her blush and smile, her fingers curling into the lapel of his tuxedo.

A flicker of possessiveness rolls through me, but it is quickly replaced by satisfaction. We're not like other men in our world. We don't fight over our woman. We share, we protect, and we love. Together.

The night continues in a blur of laughter, wine, and celebration. Aemelia never leaves my sight, moving between me and my brothers and greeting our guests with the grace of a queen. When the time comes to cut the cake, she looks up at me with eyes so full of light that I think I could drown in them.

"You ready to leave after this?" I murmur against her ear as we make the final rounds of the evening.

She nods, her fingers tightening around mine. "Yes. Take me away from here, Luca."

Minutes later, we slip out, escorted by our men through the back entrance of the grand estate. A sleek black car waits for us, its driver already at attention. Antonio and Alexis climb in behind us, their hands resting protectively on Aemelia's knees as she leans into me, exhaustion and excitement warring in her eyes.

The drive to the private airstrip is silent, filled only with the quiet hum of the engine and the sound of our kisses as we pass Aemelia between us, hungry for our wife. Our private jet is waiting when we arrive, and the crew is already prepared for takeoff.

Aemelia's breath catches as she steps onto the plane, taking in the plush leather seats, the dim golden lighting, and the bottles of champagne chilling in a crystal bucket. "This is… incredible."

Alexis grins, pulling her onto his lap as he pours a glass. "Only the best for our wife."

Antonio sits across from them, his gaze softening as he watches her. "We want you to have everything you never had before, Aemelia."

I sit beside her, tilting her chin toward me so she has no choice but to meet my gaze. "From now on, you'll never want for anything again, *mi amore*. The world is yours."

She swallows hard, her fingers tightening around my wrist. "I already have everything I need. I have you."

I grip her jaw in my hand, staring into the eyes of the woman who's found her way into my heart. "You were never meant for this life., but you were meant for us. You'll wear our name before the world, Aemelia Venturi. And in private, you'll wear nothing but our marks."

Her smile illuminates the universe.

The engines roar to life, and as the plane ascends into the night, carrying us toward the sun-soaked paradise of the Maldives, I know with certainty that the war we have fought, the blood we have spilled, was all worth it because it has led to this.

To her.

To us.

Forever.

ABOUT THE AUTHOR

International bestselling author Stephanie Brother writes high heat love stories with a hint of the forbidden. Since 2015, she's been bringing to life handsome, flawed heroes who know how to treat their women. If you enjoy stories involving multiple lovers, including twins, triplets, stepbrothers, and their friends, you're in the right place. When it comes to books and men, Stephanie truly believes it's the more, the merrier.

She spends most of her day typing, drinking coffee, and interacting with readers.

Her books have been translated into German, French, and Spanish, and she has hit the Amazon bestseller list in seven countries.

Printed in Dunstable, United Kingdom